Nora Roberts is the *New York Times* bestselling author of more than one hundred and ninety novels. A born storyteller, she creates a blend of warmth, humour and poignancy that speaks directly to her readers and has earned her almost every award for excellence in her field. The youngest of five children, Nora Roberts lives in western Maryland. She has two sons.

Visit her website at www.noraroberts.com.

Nora Roberts

The Magic of Home

SILHOUETTE®

Silhouette and Colophon are registered trademarks of
Harlequin Books S.A., used under licence.

Published in Great Britain 2011.
Silhouette Books, an imprint of Harlequin (UK) Limited,
Eton House, 18-24 Paradise Road, Richmond, Surrey TW9 1SR

THE MAGIC OF HOME © Harlequin Enterprises II B.V./S.à.r.l. 2011

The publisher acknowledges the copyright holder of the individual works
as follows:

Home for Christmas © Nora Roberts 1986
Search for Love © Nora Roberts 1991

ISBN: 978 0 263 89034 1

026-1011

Harlequin (UK) policy is to use papers that are natural, renewable
and recyclable products and made from wood grown in sustainable
forests. The logging and manufacturing processes conform to the legal
environmental regulations of the country of origin.

Printed in the UK
by CPI Mackays, Chatham, ME5 8TD

CONTENTS

Nora Roberts's
Holiday Recipes

POP'S PANCAKES

A longtime tradition in my family is Christmas breakfast. My parents' home was always crowded and noisy, and everyone lent a hand—watching the light on the waffle iron, holding their plates out for more. We were allowed to fry the bacon or flip the pancakes on the griddle. But nobody—nobody—made the pancake batter except my pop. There were two huge bowls of it to feed the horde before we got down to exchanging gifts and ripping coloured paper to shreds. Because there were so many of us, we often ate in shifts, crowding around the dining room table and spilling over to the breakfast bar. Wherever I sit, the first bite takes me back to childhood.

6 eggs, beaten
1 can evaporated milk
¼ cup butter or margarine, melted
1½ cups regular milk (1 cup for waffles)
3 cups flour
6 tbsp baking powder

Combine ingredients in the order listed. Mix well. Let stand for 10 minutes to rise. For pancakes, spoon batter onto hot griddle. Be patient—don't flip until bubbles appear.

Enjoy!

PLAIN OR PAINTED HOLIDAY COOKIES

Baking helps put me in the mood for the holidays. There's nothing like a little flour on your hands to start "Jingle Bells" ringing in your head. The tradition in my house goes this way: first put on an album of Christmas music. It isn't possible to work over a hot oven without the proper setting. Gather your ingredients:

¾ cup shortening
1 cup sugar
2 eggs
1 tsp vanilla extract
2½ cups flour
1 tsp baking powder
1 tsp salt
Optional: evaporated milk, food colouring, small paintbrush, coloured sugar or sprinkles

If you have kids, this is the time to step back and let them do some of the work. It makes it fun, and the mess is almost worth it. Let one of them mix the shortening and sugar together. Let another one crack the eggs into the bowl. Then you can help by picking out the pieces of eggshell. Add the vanilla extract and mix thoroughly. Blend in flour, baking powder and salt. Cover and chill for at least an hour.

Preheat your oven to 400°F. Now comes the time when the kids fight over who rolls out the dough. See that it's rolled about an 1/8" thick on a floured board. If you don't have cookie cutters in cute little Christmas shapes, you should. We generally stick to the tried-and-true angels, Santas and trees.

When you cut the cookies, make sure to dip the cutter into flour now and then or you'll end up with a jammed-up Santa. Place cookies on an ungreased cookie sheet. Now you can either sprinkle them with plain or coloured sugar and be done with them, or if you're feeling adventurous you can use that little paintbrush. Divide small amounts of evaporated milk into several cups, along with a little food colouring in each. Then go ahead and paint. Remember, it doesn't matter if Santa's blue or the Christmas tree is red. And just add a little water as the mixture thickens.

Bake for six or seven minutes. Break off a couple of times to sing a round of "Deck the Halls." You'll feel better. You should have about four dozen cookies, but then, if you have children, forget it. When your husband comes home and asks what's for dinner, shove a cookie in his mouth!

OLD-FASHIONED BREAD PUDDING

I do a lot of complicated baking at this time of year— time-consuming treats that keep me in the kitchen for hours. I really don't mind, but there's something to be said for simplicity. One of my men's favourites is an old family recipe handed down through the Scottish branch of my family, through my father to me. It's wonderfully simple and old-fashioned, something that can literally be tossed together when you discover unexpected holiday visitors are coming to call. Best of all, since it's made in one dish, there's little to clean up. I should warn you, most of the measurements are estimates. Experiment. It's that kind of dish.

6 to 8 slices bread, torn into pieces
3 to 4 eggs, lightly beaten
¼ cup margarine, melted
¼ to ⅓ cup sugar
3 to 3½ cups milk
About ¼ cup raisins (it's up to you)
Cinnamon to taste (I like a lot myself, maybe 3 tbsp or so. I really don't measure—I go by how it looks.)

Preheat oven to 400°F. Mix all ingredients, gently but thoroughly, in a casserole dish. Pop it into the oven for 1 hour. Can be eaten warm or cold.

Home for Christmas

Chapter One

So much can change in ten years. He was prepared for it. All during the flight from London and the long, winding drive north from Boston to Quiet Valley, New Hampshire, population 326—or it had been ten years before when Jason Law had last been there—he'd thought of how different things would be. A decade, even for a forgotten little town in New England was bound to bring changes. There would have been deaths and births. Houses and shops would have changed hands. Some of them might not be there at all.

Not for the first time since Jason had decided to

visit his hometown did he feel foolish. After all, it was very likely he wouldn't even be recognized. He'd left a thin, defiant twenty-year-old in a scruffy pair of jeans. He was coming back a man who'd learned how to replace defiance with arrogance and succeed. His frame was still lean, but it fitted nicely into clothes tailored on Savile Row and Seventh Avenue. Ten years had changed him from a desperate boy determined to make his mark to an outwardly complacent man who had. What ten years hadn't changed, was what was inside. He was still looking for roots, for his place. That was why he was heading back to Quiet Valley.

The road still twisted and turned through the woods, up the mountains and down again, as it had when he'd headed in the opposite direction on a Greyhound. Snow covered the ground, smooth here, bumpy there where it was heaped over rocks. In the sunlight trees shimmered with it. Had he missed it? He'd spent one winter in snow up to his waist in the Andes. He'd spent another sweltering in Africa. The years ran together, but oddly enough, Jason could remember every place he'd spent Christmas over the last ten years, though he'd never celebrated the holiday. The road narrowed and swept into a wide curve. He could see the mountains, covered with pines and dusted with white. Yes, he'd missed it.

Sun bounced off the mounds of snow. He adjusted his dark glasses and slowed down, then on impulse, stopped. When he stepped from the car his breath came in streams of smoke. His skin tingled with the cold but he didn't button his coat or reach in his pockets for his gloves. He needed to feel it. Breathing in the thin, icy air was like breathing in thousands of tiny needles. Jason walked the few feet to the top of the ridge and looked down on Quiet Valley.

He'd been born there, raised there. He'd learned of grief there—and he'd fallen in love. Even from the distance he could see her house—her parents' house, Jason reminded himself and felt the old, familiar surge of fury. She'd be living somewhere else now, with her husband, with her children.

When he discovered that his hands were balled into fists he carefully relaxed them. Channeling emotion was a skill he'd turned into an art over the past decade. If he could do it in his work, reporting on famine, war, and suffering, he could do it for himself. His feelings for Faith had been a boy's feelings. He was a man now, and she, like Quiet Valley, was only part of his childhood. He'd traveled more than five thousand miles just to prove it. Turning away, he got back in the car and started down the mountain.

From the distance, Quiet Valley had looked like a Currier and Ives painting, all white and snug between mountain and forest. As he drew closer, it became less idyllic and more approachable. The tired paint showed here and there on some of the outlying houses. Fences bowed under snow. He saw a few new houses in what had once been open fields. Change. He reminded himself he'd expected it.

Smoke puffed out of chimneys. Dogs and children raced in the snow. A check of his watch showed him it was half past three. School was out, and he'd been traveling for fifteen hours. The smart thing to do was to see if the Valley Inn was still in operation and get a room. A smile played around his mouth as he wondered if old Mr. Beantree still ran the place. He couldn't count the times Beantree had told him he'd never amount to anything but trouble. He had a Pulitzer and an Overseas Press Award to prove differently.

Houses were grouped closer together now, and he recognized them. The Bedford place, Tim Hawkin's house, the Widow Marchant's. He slowed again as he passed the widow's tidy blue clapboard. She hadn't changed the color, he noticed and felt foolishly pleased. And the old spruce in the front yard was already covered with bright-red ribbons. She'd been kind to him. Jason hadn't forgotten how she had fixed hot chocolate and listened to him for hours when he'd told her of the travels he wanted to make, the places he dreamed of seeing. She'd been in her seventies when he'd left, but of tough New England stock. He thought he might still find her in her kitchen patiently fueling the wood stove and listening to her Rachmaninoff.

The streets of the town were clear and tidy. New Englanders were a practical lot, and Jason thought, as sturdy as the bedrock they'd planted themselves on. The town had not changed as he'd anticipated. Railings Hardware still sat on the corner off Main and the post office still occupied a brick building no bigger than a garage. The same red garland was strung from lamppost to lamppost as it had been all through his youth during each holiday season. Children were building a snowman in front of the Litner place. But whose children? Jason wondered. He scanned the red mufflers and bright boots knowing any of them might be Faith's. The fury came back and he looked away.

The sign on the Valley Inn had been repainted, but nothing else about the three-story square stone building was different. The walkway had been scraped clean and smoke billowed out of both chimneys. He found himself driving beyond it. There was something else to do first, something he'd already known he would have to do. He could have turned at the corner, driven a block and seen the house where he grew up. But he didn't.

Near the end of Main would be a tidy white house, bigger than most of the others with two big bay windows and a wide front porch. Tom Monroe had brought his bride there. A reporter of Jason's caliber knew how to ferret out such information. Perhaps Faith had put up the lace curtains she'd always wanted at the windows. Tom would have bought her the pretty china tea sets she'd longed for. He'd have given her exactly what she'd wanted. Jason would have given her a suitcase and a motel room in countless cities. She'd made her choice.

After ten years he discovered it was no easier to accept. Still, he forced himself to be calm as he pulled up to the curb. He and Faith had been friends once, lovers briefly. He'd had other lovers since, and she had a husband. But he could still remember her as she'd looked at eighteen, lovely, soft, eager. She had wanted to go with him, but he wouldn't let her. She had promised to wait, but she hadn't. He took a deep breath as he climbed from the car.

The house was lovely. In the big bay window that faced the street was a Christmas tree, cluttered and green in the daylight. At night it would glitter like magic. He could be sure of it because Faith had always believed so strongly in magic.

Standing on the sidewalk he found himself dealing with fear. He'd covered wars and interviewed terrorists but he'd never felt the stomach-churning fear that he did now, standing on a narrow snow-brushed sidewalk facing a pristine white house with holly bushes by the door. He could turn around, he reminded himself. Drive back to the inn or simply out of town again. There was no need to see her again. She was out of his life. Then he saw the lace curtains at the window and the old resentment stirred, every bit as strong as fear.

As he started down the walk a girl raced around the side of the house just ahead of a well-aimed snowball. She dived, rolled and evaded. In an instant, she was up again and hurling one of her own.

"Bull's-eye, Jimmy Harding!" With a whoop, she turned to run and barreled into Jason. "Sorry." With snow covering her from head to foot, she looked up and grinned. Jason felt the world spin backward.

She was the image of her mother. The sable hair peeked out of her cap and fell untidily to her shoulders. The small, triangular face was dominated by big blue eyes that seemed to hold jokes all of their own. But it was the smile, the one that said, isn't this fun? that caught him by the throat. Shaken, he stepped back while the girl dusted herself off and studied him.

"I've never seen you before."

He slipped his hands into his pockets. But I've seen you, he thought. "No. Do you live here?"

"Yeah, but the shop's around the side." A snowball

landed with a plop at her feet. She lifted a brow in a sophisticated manner. "That's Jimmy," she said in the tone of a woman barely tolerating a suitor. "His aim's lousy. The shop's around the side," she repeated as she bent to ball more snow. "Just walk right in."

She raced off holding a ball in each hand. Jason figured Jimmy was in for a surprise.

Faith's daughter. He hadn't asked her name and nearly called her back. It didn't matter, he told himself. He'd only be in town a few days before he took the next assignment. Just passing through, he thought. Just cleaning the slate.

He backtracked to walk around the side of the house. Though he couldn't imagine what sort of shop Tom could have, he thought it might be best to see him first. He almost relished it.

The little workshop he'd half expected turned out to be a miniature of a Victorian cottage. The sleigh out in front held two life-size dolls dressed in top hats and bonnets, cloaks and top boots. Above the door was a fancy hand-painted sign that read Doll House. To the accompaniment of bells, Jason pushed the door open.

"I'll be right with you."

Hearing her voice again was like stepping back and finding no solid ground. But he'd deal with it, Jason told himself. He'd deal with it because he had to. Slipping off his glasses, he tucked them into his pocket and looked around.

Child-size furniture was set around the room in the manner of a cozy parlor. Dolls of every shape and size and style occupied chairs, stools, shelves and cabinets. In front of an elf-size fireplace where flames shimmered, sat a grandmother of a doll in lace cap and apron. The illusion was so strong Jason almost expected her to begin rocking.

"I'm sorry to keep you waiting." With a china doll in one hand and a bridal veil in the other, Faith walked through the doorway. "I was right in the middle of…" The veil floated out of her hand as she stopped. It waltzed to the floor with no sound at all. Color rushed away from her face, making the deep-blue eyes nearly violet in contrast. In reaction, or defense, she gripped the doll to her breast. "Jason."

Chapter Two

Framed in the doorway with the thin winter light creeping through the tiny windows she was lovelier than his memory of her. He'd hoped it would be different. He'd hoped his fantasies of her would be exaggerated as so many fantasies are. But she was here, flesh and blood, and so beautiful she took his breath away. Perhaps because of it, his smile was cynical and his voice cool.

"Hello, Faith."

She couldn't move, forward or back. He trapped her now as he had so many years before. He didn't know it then, she couldn't let him know it now.

Emotion, locked and kept secret for so long struggled against will and was held back. "How are you?" she managed to ask, her hands like a vise around the doll.

"Fine." He walked toward her. God, how it pleased him to see the nerves jumping in her eyes. God, how it tormented him to learn she smelled the same. Soft, young, innocent. "You look wonderful." He said it carelessly, like a yawn.

"You were the last person I expected to see walk through the door." One she'd learned to stop looking for. Determined to control herself, Faith loosened her grip on the doll. "How long are you in town?"

"Just a few days. I had the urge."

She laughed and hoped it didn't sound hysterical. "You always did. We read a lot about you. You've been able to see all the places you always wanted to see."

"And more."

She turned away, giving herself a moment to close her eyes and pull her emotions together. "They ran it on the front page when you won the Pulitzer. Mr. Beantree strutted around as though he'd been your mentor. 'Fine boy, Jason Law,' he said. 'Always knew he'd amount to something.'"

"I saw your daughter."

That was the biggest fear, the biggest hope, the dream she'd put to rest years ago. She bent casually to pick up the veil. "Clara?"

"Just outside. She was about to mow down some boy named Jimmy."

"Yes, that's Clara." The smile came quickly and just as stunningly as it had on the child. "She's a vicious competitor," she added and wanted to say like her father, but didn't dare.

There was so much to say, so much that couldn't be said. If he had had one wish at that moment it would have been to reach out and touch her. Just to touch her once and remember the way it had been.

"I see you have your lace curtains."

Regret washed over her. She'd have settled for bare windows, blank walls. "Yes, I have my lace curtains and you your adventures."

"And this place." He turned to look around again. "When did all this start?"

She could deal with it, she promised herself, this

hatefully casual small talk. "I opened it nearly eight years ago now."

He picked a rag doll from a bassinet. "So you sell dolls. A hobby?"

Something else came into her eyes now. Strength. "No, it's my business. I sell them, repair them, even make them."

"Business?" He set the doll down and the smile he gave her had nothing to do with humor. "It's hard for me to picture Tom approving of his wife setting up a business."

"Is it?" It hurt, but she set the china doll on a counter and began to arrange the veil on its head. "You always were perceptive, Jason, but you've been away a long time." She looked over her shoulder and her eyes weren't nervous or even strong. They were simply cold. "A very long time. Tom and I were divorced eight years ago. The last time I heard he was living in Los Angeles. You see, he didn't care for small towns either. Or small-town girls."

He couldn't name the things that stirred in him so he pushed them aside. Bitterness was simpler. "Apparently you picked badly, Faith."

She laughed again but the veil crumpled in her hand. "Apparently I did."

"You didn't wait." It was out before he could stop it. He hated himself for it, and her.

"You were gone." She turned back slowly and folded her hands.

"I told you I'd come back. I told you I'd send for you as soon as I could."

"You never called, or wrote. For three months I—"

"Three months?" Furious, he grabbed her arms. "After everything we'd talked about, everything we'd hoped for, three months was all you could give me?"

She would have given him a lifetime, but there hadn't been a choice. Struggling to keep her voice calm, she looked into his eyes. They were the same—intense, impatient. "I didn't know where you were. You wouldn't even give me that." She pulled away from him because the need was as great as it had always been. "I was eighteen and you were gone."

"And Tom was here."

She set her jaw. "And Tom was here. It's been ten years, Jason, you never once wrote. Why now?"

"I've asked myself the same thing," he murmured and left her standing alone.

Her dreams had always been too fanciful. As a child Faith had envisioned white chargers and glass slippers. Reality was something to be faced daily in a family where money was scarce and pride was not, but dreams weren't just for nighttime.

She'd fallen in love with Jason when she'd been eight and he ten and he'd bravely vanquished three boys who'd tossed her into the snow. It had taken three of them. Faith could still look back on that with a sense of satisfaction. But it had been Jason fiercely coming to her rescue and sending her opponents scattering that she remembered best. He'd been thin, and his coat had been too large and mended at the elbows. She remembered his eyes, deep, deep brown under brows drawn close in annoyance as he'd looked down at her. Snow had coated his pale-blond hair and reddened his face. She'd looked into his eyes and fallen in love. He'd muttered at her, hauled her up and scolded her for getting in trouble.

Then he'd stalked off with his ungloved hands thrust into the pockets of his too-big coat.

Through childhood and into adolescence she'd never looked at another boy. Of course she'd pretended to from time to time hoping it might make Jason Law notice her.

Then when she'd been sixteen and her mother had sewn her a dress for the spring dance at the town hall, he'd noticed. So had several other boys, and Faith had flirted outrageously, with one goal in mind:

Jason Law. Sulky and defiant he'd watched her dance with one boy after another. She'd made sure of it. Just as she'd made sure she looked directly at him before she'd stepped outside to take the air. He'd followed her, just as she'd hoped. She'd pretended to be sophisticated. He'd been rude. And he'd walked her home under a fat full moon.

There'd been other walks after that—spring, summer, fall, winter. They were in love as only the young can be, carelessly, heedlessly, innocently. She told him of her longings for a house and children, for lace curtains and china cups. He told her of his passion to travel, to see everything, and write it down. She knew he'd felt trapped in the small town, hampered by a father who gave him no love and little hope. He knew she dreamed of quiet rooms with flowers in crystal vases. But they were drawn together and tangled all the dreams into one.

Then one night in the summer when the air was sweet with wild grass they stopped being children and their love stopped being innocent.

"Mom, you're dreaming again."

"What?" Up to her elbows in soapy water, Faith turned. Her daughter stood at the doorway to the kitchen, snugly wrapped in a flannel gown that came up to her chin. With her hair freshly brushed and her face scrubbed clean, she looked like an angel. Faith knew better. "I guess I was. You've finished your homework?"

"Yeah. It's dumb having homework when school's nearly out."

"Don't remind me."

"You're grumpy," Clara declared and eyed the cookie jar. "You should go for one of your walks."

"Just one," Faith said, easily outguessing her daughter. "And don't forget to brush your teeth." She waited while Clara rooted through the jar. "Did you see a man this afternoon? A tall man with blond hair?"

"Uh-huh." Mouth full, Clara turned back to her mother. "He was walking up to the house. I sent him to the shop."

"Did he—say anything to you?"

"Not really. He looked at me kind of funny at first, like he'd seen me before. Do you know him?"

While her heart began a slow, dull thud, Faith dried her hands. "Yes. He used to live here a long time ago."

"Oh. Jimmy liked his car." She wondered if she could talk herself into another cookie.

"I think I will take that walk, Clara, but I want you in bed."

Recognizing the tone, she knew the cookie would have to wait. "Can I count the presents under the tree again?"

"You've counted them ten times."

"Maybe there's a new one."

Laughing, Faith gathered her up. "Not a chance." Then she grinned and carried Clara into the living room. "But it won't hurt to count them one more time."

The air was brittle when she stepped outside and it smelled of snow. There was no reason to lock the doors in a town where she knew everyone. Bundling her coat closer, she glanced back at the second-story window where her daughter slept. Clara was the reason why the house wasn't cold, why her life wasn't empty when both things could easily have been true.

She'd left the tree burning and the lights around the door sent out festive color. Four days until Christmas, she thought, and the wonder of it came home again. From where she stood, the town looked as pretty as a postcard with the strings of lights, the tree with its star in the town square, the street lamps burning. She could smell smoke from the chimneys and the bursting scent of pine.

Some might find it too settled, others would find it dull. But Faith had made it a home for herself and her daughter. She'd altered her life to suit her, and it fitted her well.

No regrets, she promised with one last glance at her daughter's window. No regrets at all.

The wind picked up a bit as she walked. There'd

be snow for Christmas. She could feel it. She'd look forward to that, not back any longer.

"Still fond of walking?"

Chapter Three

Had she known he'd find her? Perhaps she had. Perhaps she'd needed him to. "Some things don't change," she said simply as Jason fell into step beside her.

"I've found that out in one afternoon." He thought of the town that had stayed so much the same. And of his feelings for the woman beside him. "Where's your daughter?"

"She's sleeping."

He was calmer than he'd been that afternoon, and determined to stay that way. "I didn't ask you if you had other children."

"No." He heard the wistfulness in her voice, just a sigh of it. "There's only Clara."

"How did you pick the name?"

She smiled. It was so like him to ask questions no one else would think of. "From the Nutcracker. I wanted her to be able to dream." As she had. Dropping her hands in her pockets she told herself they were simply two old friends walking through a quiet town. "Are you staying at the inn?"

"Yeah." Amused, Jason rubbed a hand over his chin. "Beantree took my bags up himself."

"Local boy makes good." She turned to look at him. It was easier somehow walking like this. Odd, she realized, she'd seen the boy when she'd looked at him the first time. Now she saw the man. His hair had darkened a bit but was still very blond. It was no longer unkempt, but cut in a carelessly attractive style that had it falling over his brow. His face was still thin, hollow at the cheeks in the way that had always fascinated her. And his mouth was still full, but there was a hardness around it that hadn't been there once. "You did make good, didn't you? You made everything you wanted happen."

"Most everything." When his eyes met hers she

felt all the old longings come back. "What about you, Faith?"

She shook her head, watching the sky as she walked. "I never wanted as much as you, Jason."

"Are you happy?"

"If a person isn't, it's their own fault."

"That's too simple."

"I haven't seen the things you've seen. I haven't had to deal with what you've had to deal with. I am simple, Jason. That was the problem, wasn't it?"

"No." He turned her to face him and slid his hands up to her face. He wore no gloves, and his fingers warmed against her skin. "God, you haven't changed." As she stood very still he combed his fingers up through her hair, then down to where the tips brushed her shoulders. "I've thought about the way you look in the moonlight countless times. It was just like this."

"I've changed, Jason." But her voice was breathless. "So have you."

"Some things don't," he reminded her and gave in to the need.

When his mouth touched hers, he knew that he'd come home. Everything he remembered, everything he thought he'd lost was his again. She was soft and smelled of springtime even when snow dusted the ground around them. Her mouth was willing, even as it had been the first time he'd tasted it. He couldn't explain, even to himself, that every other woman he'd held had been nothing but a shadow of his memory of her. Now she was real, wrapped in his arms and giving him everything he'd forgotten he could have.

Just once, she promised herself as she melted against him. Just once more. How could she have known her life had such a void in it? She'd tried to close the door on the part of her life that included Jason, though she'd known it wasn't possible. She'd tried to tell herself it was only youthful passion and girlish fancy but she'd known that was a lie. There'd been no other men, only memories of one, and wishes, half-forgotten dreams.

She was holding no memory now but Jason, as real and urgent as he'd always been. Everything about him was so familiar, the taste of his lips on hers, the feel of his hair as her fingers raked through it, the scent of man, rough and rugged, that he'd always carried with him even as a boy. He murmured her name and drew her closer, as if the years were trying to separate them again.

She wrapped her arms around him, as willing, as eager, and as in love as she'd been the last time he'd held her. The wind whipped around their ankles, puffing up clouds of snow while the moonlight held them close.

But it wasn't yesterday, she reminded herself as she stepped back. It wasn't tomorrow. It was today, and today had to be faced. She wasn't a child any longer without responsibilities and a love so big it overshadowed anything else. She was a woman with a child to raise and a home to make. He was a gypsy. He'd never pretended to be anything else.

"It's over for us, Jason." But she held his hand a moment longer. "It's been over for a long time."

"No." He caught her before she could turn away. "It isn't. I told myself it was, and that I'd come back and prove it. You've been eating at me half my life, Faith. It's never going to be over."

"You left me." The tears she promised herself she wouldn't shed spilled over. "You broke my heart. It's barely had time to mend, Jason. You won't break it again."

"You know I had to leave. If you'd waited—"

"It doesn't matter now." With a shake of her head she backed away. She would never be able to explain to him why it hadn't been possible to wait. "It doesn't matter because in a few days you'll be gone again. I won't let you whirl in and out of my life and leave my emotions in chaos. We both made our choices, Jason."

"Damn it, I missed you."

She closed her eyes. When she opened them again they were dry. "I had to stop missing you. Please leave me alone, Jason. If I thought we could be friends—"

"We always were."

"Always is gone." Nonetheless she held out both hands and took his. "Oh, Jason, you were my best friend, but I can't welcome you home because you scare the hell out of me."

"Faith." He curled his fingers around hers. "We need more time, to talk."

Looking at him she let out a long breath. "You know where to find me, Jason. You always did."

"Let me walk you home."

"No." Calmer, she smiled. "Not this time."

★ ★ ★

From the window of his room, Jason could see most of Main Street. He could, if he chose, watch the flow of business in Porterfield's Five and Dime or the collection of people who walked through and loitered in the town square. Too often he found the direction of his gaze wandering to the white house near the end of the street. Because he'd been restless, Jason had been up and at the window when Faith had walked outside with Clara to see her off to school with a group of other children. He'd seen her crouch down to adjust the collar of her daughter's coat. And he'd seen her stand, hatless, her back to him, as she'd watched the children drag themselves off for a day of books. She'd stood there a long time with the wind pulling and tugging at her hair, and he'd waited for her to turn, to look at the inn, to acknowledge somehow that she knew he was there. But she'd walked around the side of the house to her shop without looking back.

Now, hours later, he was at the window again, still restless. From the number of people he could see walk back to the Doll House, her business was thriving. She was working, busy, while he was standing unshaven at a window with his portable typewriter sitting silent on the desk beside him.

He'd planned to work on his novel for a few days—the novel he'd promised himself he'd write. It was just one more promise he'd never been able to keep because of the demands of travel and reporting. He'd expected to be able to work here, in the quiet, settled town of his youth away from the demands of journalism and the fast pace he'd set for himself. He'd expected a lot of things. What he hadn't expected was to find himself just as wildly in love with Faith as he'd been at twenty.

Jason turned away from the window and stared at his typewriter. The papers were there, notes bulging in manila envelopes, the half-finished manuscript pages. He could sit down and make himself work through the day into the night. He had the discipline for it. But in his life there was more than a book that was half finished. He was just coming to realize it.

By the time he'd shaved and dressed, it was past noon. He thought briefly about walking across the street to Mindy's to see if she still served the best homemade soup in town. But he didn't feel like chatty counter talk. Deliberately he turned south, away from Faith. He wouldn't make a fool of himself by chasing after her.

As he walked, he passed a half a dozen people he knew. He was greeted with thumps on the back, handshakes and avid curiosity. He'd strolled down the Left Bank, up Carnaby Street and along the narrow streets of Venice. After a decade of absence he found the walk down Main Street just as fascinating. There was a barber pole that swirled up and around and back into itself. A life-size cardboard Santa stood outside a dress shop gesturing passersby inside.

Spotting a display of poinsettias, Jason slipped into the store and bought the biggest one he could carry. The saleswoman had been in his graduating class and detained him for ten minutes before he could escape. He'd expected questions, but he hadn't guessed that he'd become the town celebrity. Amused, he made his way down the street as he had countless times before. When he reached the Widow Marchant's, he didn't bother with the front door. Following an old habit, he went around the back and knocked on the storm door. It still rattled. It was a small thing that pleased him enormously.

When the widow opened the door, and her little bird's eyes peered through the bright-red leaves of the flowers, he found himself grinning like a ten-year-old.

"It's about time," she said as she let him in. "Wipe your feet."

"Yes, ma'am." Jason scrubbed his boots against the rough mat before he set down the poinsettia on her kitchen table.

No more than five feet tall, the widow stood with her hands on her hips. She was bent a bit with age and her face was a melody of lines and wrinkles. The bib apron she wore was covered with flour. Jason smelled cookies in the oven and heard the majestic sound of classical music from the living-room speakers. The widow nodded at the flowers.

"You always went for the big statement." When she turned to look him up and down, Jason found himself automatically standing tall. "Put on a few pounds I see, but more wouldn't hurt. Come, give me a kiss."

He bent to peck her cheek dutifully, then found

himself gathering her close. She felt frail; he hadn't realized it by looking at her, but she still smelled of all the good things he remembered—soap and powder and warm sugar.

"You don't seem surprised to see me," he murmured as he straightened up.

"I knew you were here." She turned to fuss at the oven because her eyes had filled. "I knew before the ink dried where you signed the registration at the inn. Sit down and take off your coat. I have to get these cookies out."

He sat quietly while she worked and absorbed the feeling of home. It was here he'd always been able to come as a child and feel safe. While he watched, she began to heat chocolate in a dented little pan on the stove.

"How long you staying?"

"I don't know. I'm supposed to be in Hong Kong in a couple of weeks."

"Hong Kong." The widow pursed her lips as she arranged cookies on a plate. "You've been to all your places, Jason. Were they as exciting as you thought?"

"Some were." He stretched out his legs. He'd

forgotten what it was to relax, body, soul and mind. "Some weren't."

"Now you've come home." She walked over to put the cookies on the table. "Why?"

He could be evasive with anyone else. He could even lie to himself. But with her there could only be the truth. "Faith."

"It always was." Back at the stove, she stirred the chocolate. He'd been a troubled boy, now he was a troubled man. "You heard she married Tom."

And with her, he didn't have to hide the bitterness. "Six months after I left I called. I'd landed a job with *Today's News*. They were sending me to a hole in the wall in Chicago, but it was something. I called Faith, but I got her mother. She was very kind, even sympathetic when she told me that Faith was married, had been married for three months and was going to have a baby. I hung up, I got drunk. In the morning I went to Chicago." He plucked a cookie from the plate and shrugged. "Life goes on, right?"

"It does, whether it tows us along with it or rolls right over us. And now that you know she's divorced?"

"We promised each other something. She married someone else."

She made a sound like steam escaping from a kettle. "You're a man now from the looks of you, not a bull-headed boy. Faith Kirkpatrick—"

"Faith Monroe," he reminded her.

"All right then." Patiently, she poured heated chocolate into mugs. After she set them on the table, she seated herself with a quiet wheeze. "Faith is a strong, beautiful woman inside and out. She's raising that little girl all alone and doing a good job of it. She's started a business and she's making it work. Alone. I know something about being alone."

"If she'd waited—"

"Well, she didn't. Whatever thoughts I have about her reasons I'm keeping to myself."

"Why did she divorce Tom?"

The old woman sat back, resting her elbows on the worn arms of her chair. "He left her and the baby when Clara was six months old."

His fingers tightened around the handle of the mug. "What do you mean, he left her?"

"You should know the meaning. You did so yourself." She picked up her chocolate and held it in both hands. "I mean he packed his bags and left. She had the house—and the bills. He cleaned out the bank account and headed west."

"But he has a daughter."

"He hasn't laid eyes on the girl since she was in diapers. Faith pulled herself out. She had the child to think of after all if not herself. Her parents stood behind her. They're good people. She took a loan and started the doll business. We're proud to have her here."

He stared out the window to where the boughs of an old sycamore spread, dripping with snow and ice. "So I left, she married Tom, then he left. Seems Faith has a habit of picking the wrong men."

"Think so?"

He'd forgotten how dry her voice could be and nearly smiled. "Clara looks like Faith."

"Hmm. She favors her mother." The widow smiled into her mug. "I've always been able to see her father in her. Your chocolate's getting cold, Jason."

Absently, he sipped. With the taste came floods of memories. "I hadn't expected to feel at home here again. It's funny. I don't think I felt at home when I lived here, but now…"

"You haven't been by your old place yet?"

"No."

"There's a nice couple in there now. They put a porch on the back."

It meant nothing to him. "It was never home." He set the chocolate down and took her hand. "This was. I never knew any mother but you."

Her hand, thin, dry as paper, gripped his. "Your father was a hard man, harder maybe because he lost your mother so young."

"I only felt relief when he died. I can't even be sorry for it. Maybe that's why I left when I did. With him gone, the house gone, it seemed the time was right."

"Maybe it was, for you. Maybe the time's right to come back again. You weren't a good boy, Jason. But you weren't so bad either. Give yourself some of that time you were always so desperate to beat ten years ago."

"And Faith?"

She sat back again. "As I recall, you never did much courting. Seems to me the girl chased after you with her eyes wide open. A man who's been all the places you been oughta know how to court a woman. Probably picked up some of those fancy languages."

He picked up a cookie and bit into it. "A phrase or two."

"Never knew a woman who wouldn't flutter a bit with some fancy language."

Leaning over he kissed both her hands. "I missed you."

"I knew you'd come back. At my age, you know how to wait. Go find your girl."

"I think I might." Rising, he slipped into his coat. "I'll come back and visit again."

"See that you do." She waited until he opened the door. "Jason—button your coat." She didn't pull out her handkerchief until she heard the door close behind him.

Chapter Four

The sun was high and bright when he stepped outside. Across the street a snowman was rapidly losing weight. He found the streets as he'd found them yesterday on his drive in—full of children fresh out of school. He felt the surge of freedom himself. As he headed north, he saw a girl break away from a group of children and come toward him. Even bundled in hat and scarf he recognized Clara.

"'Scuse me. Did you use to live here?"

"That's right." He wanted to tuck her hair into her cap but stopped himself.

"My mother said you did. Today in school, the teacher said you went away and got famous."

He couldn't stop the grin. "Well, I went away."

"And you won a prize. Like Marcie's brother won a trophy for bowling."

He thought of his Pulitzer and managed, barely, not to laugh. "Something like that."

To Clara he looked like a regular person, not someone who bounded around the world on adventures. Her eyes narrowed. "Did you really go to all those places like they said?"

"That depends on what they said." In tacit agreement they began to walk together. "I've been to some places."

"Like Tokyo? That's the capital of Japan, we learned that in school."

"Like Tokyo."

"Did you eat raw fish?"

"Now and again."

"That's really disgusting." But she seemed pleased all the same. She bent and scooped up snow without breaking rhythm. "Do they squish grapes with their feet in France?"

"I can't say I ever saw it for myself, but I've heard tell."

"I sure wouldn't drink it after that. Did you ever ride a camel?"

He watched her bullet the snowball into the base of a tree. "As a matter of fact, I did."

"What was it like?"

"Uncomfortable."

It was a description she readily accepted because she'd already figured it out for herself. "The teacher read one of your stories today. The one about this tomb they found in China. Did you see the statues?"

"Yes, I did."

"Was it like *Raiders?*"

"Like what?"

"You know, the movie with Indiana Jones."

It took him a minute, then he laughed. Without thinking he tipped her cap over her eyes. "I guess it was, a little."

"You write good."

"Thank you."

They were standing on the sidewalk in front of her house. Jason glanced up, surprised. He hadn't realized they'd come so far and found himself regretting he hadn't slowed his pace a bit. "We have to do this report on Africa." Clara wrinkled her nose. "It has to be five whole pages long. Miss Jenkins wants it in right after Christmas vacation."

"How long have you had the assignment?" It hadn't been that long since his school days.

Clara drew a circle in the snow at the edge of her lawn. "Couple of weeks."

No, he realized with some pleasure, it hadn't been so very long. "I guess you've started on it."

"Well, sort of." Then she turned that quick, beautiful smile on him. "You've been to Africa, haven't you?"

"A couple of times."

"I guess you know all kinds of things about climate and culture and stuff like that."

He grinned down at her. "Enough."

"Maybe you should stay for dinner tonight." Without giving him a chance to answer, she took his hand and led him around to the shop.

When they walked in, Faith was boxing a doll. Her hair was pinned up in the back and she wore a baggy sweatshirt over jeans. She was laughing at something her customer had said. "Lorna, you know you wouldn't have it any other way."

"Bah, humbug." The woman put a hand on her enormous stomach and sighed. "I really wanted this baby to make an appearance before Christmas."

"You still have four days."

"Hi, Mom!"

Faith turned to smile at her daughter. As she spotted Jason the spool of ribbon in her hand spun in a red stream to the floor. "Clara, you didn't wipe your feet," she managed to say, but kept her eyes on Jason.

"Jason! Jason Law." The woman rushed over and grabbed him by both arms. "It's Lorna—Lorna McBee."

He looked down into the pretty round face of his longtime neighbor. "Hello, Lorna." His gaze drifted down, then back up. "Congratulations."

With a hand on her stomach she laughed. "Thanks, but it's my third."

He thought of the scrawny, bad-tempered girl next door. "Three? You work fast."

"So does Bill. You remember Bill Easterday, don't you?"

"You married Bill?" He remembered a boy who had hung out in the town square looking for trouble. A few times Jason had helped him find it.

"I reformed him." When she smiled, he believed it. "He runs the bank." His expression had her giggling. "I'm serious, stop in sometime. Well, I've got to be moving along. This box has to go into a locked closet before my oldest girl sees it. Thanks, Faith, it's just lovely."

"I hope she likes it."

To keep her hands busy, Faith began to rewind the spool of ribbon. A puff of cold air came in, then was cut off as Lorna breezed out.

"Was that the bride doll?" Clara wanted to know.

"Yes, it was."

"Too fussy. Can I go over to Marcie's?"

"What about homework?"

"I don't have any except that dumb Africa report. He's going to help me." Jason met her smile with a lifted brow. "Aren't you?"

Jason would have dared any man within a hundred miles to resist that look. "Yes, I am."

"Clara, you can't—"

"It's okay 'cause I asked him to dinner." She

beamed, almost sure her mother would be trapped by the good manners she was always talking about. "There's no school now for ten whole days so I can do the report after dinner, can't I?"

Jason decided it wouldn't hurt to apply a little pressure from his side. "I spent six weeks in Africa once. Clara might just get an A."

"She could use it," Faith muttered. They stood together, looking at her. Her heart already belonged to both of them. "I guess I'd better start dinner."

Clara was already racing across the yard next door before Faith pulled the door of the Doll House shut and turned the sign around to read Closed.

"I'm sorry if she was a nuisance, Jason. She has a habit of badgering people with questions."

"I like her," he said simply and watched Faith fumble with the latch.

"That's nice of you, but you don't have to feel obliged to help her with this report."

"I said I would. I keep my word, Faith." He touched a pin in her hair. "Sooner or later."

She had to look at him then. It was impossible not to. "You're welcome to dinner, of course." Her fingers worried the buttons of her coat as she spoke. "I was just going to fry chicken."

"I'll give you a hand."

"No, that's not—"

He cut her off when he closed his fingers over hers. "I never used to make you nervous."

With an effort, she steadied herself. "No, you didn't." He'd be gone again in a few days, she reminded herself. Out of her life. Maybe she should take whatever time she was given. "All right then, you can help."

He took her arm as they crossed the lawn. Though he felt her initial resistance, he ignored it. "I went to see Widow Marchant. I had cookies right from the oven."

Faith relaxed as she pushed open the door of her own kitchen. "She has every word you've ever written."

The kitchen was twice the size of the one he'd just left and there were signs of a child in the pictures hanging on the front of the refrigerator and a pair of fuzzy slippers kicked into a corner. Moving with habit, Faith switched on the burner under the kettle before she slipped out of her coat. She hung it on a peg by the door, then turned to take his. His hands closed over hers.

"You didn't tell me Tom left you."

She'd known it wouldn't take him long to hear it, or long to question. "It's not something I think about on a daily basis. Coffee?"

She draped his coat over a hook and turned to find him blocking her way. "What happened, Faith?"

"We made a mistake." She said it calmly, even coolly. It was a tone he'd never heard from her before.

"But there was Clara."

"Don't." Fury came into her eyes quickly and simmered there. "Leave it alone, Jason, I mean it. Clara's my business. My marriage and divorce are my business. You can't expect to come back now and have all the answers."

They stood a moment, facing each other in silence. When the kettle let out a whistle, she seemed to breathe again. "If you want to help, you can peel some potatoes. They're in the pantry over there."

She worked systematically, he thought angrily, as she poured oil to heat in a skillet and coated chicken. Her temper was nothing new to him. He'd felt the brunt of it before, sometimes deflecting it, sometimes meeting it head-on. He also knew how to soothe it. He began talking, almost to himself at first, about some of the places he'd been. When he told her about waking with a snake curled next to his head while he'd been camping in South America she laughed.

"I didn't find it too funny at the time. I was out of the tent in five seconds flat, buck naked. My photographer got a very interesting roll of pictures. I had to pay him fifty to get the negatives."

"I'm sure they were worth more. You didn't mention the snake in your series on San Salvador."

"No." Interested, he put down his paring knife. "You read it?"

She arranged chicken in the hot oil. "Of course. I've read all your stories."

He took the potatoes to the sink to wash them. "All of them?"

She smiled at the tone but kept her back to him. "Don't let your ego loose, Jason. It was always your biggest problem. I'd estimate that ninety percent of the people in Quiet Valley have read all your stories. You might say we all feel we have a stake in you." She adjusted the flame. "After all, no one else around here's had dinner at the White House."

"The soup was thin."

Chuckling, she put a pan of water on the stove and dumped in the potatoes. "I guess you just have to take the good with the bad—so to speak. I saw a picture of you a couple of years ago." She adjusted a pin in her hair and her voice was bland. "I think it was taken in New York, at some glitzy charity function. You had a half-naked woman on your arm."

He rocked back on his heels. "Did I?"

"Well, she wasn't actually half-naked," Faith temporized. "I suppose it just seemed that way because she had so much more hair than dress. Blond—very blond if my memory serves me. And let's say—top-heavy."

He ran his tongue around his teeth. "You meet a lot of interesting people in my business."

"Obviously." With the efficiency born of habit she turned chicken. Oil hissed. "I'm sure you find it very stimulating."

"Not as stimulating as this conversation."

"If you can't stand the heat," she murmured.

"Yeah. It's getting dark. Shouldn't Clara be home?"

"She's right next door. She knows to be home by five-thirty."

He went to the window anyway and glanced at the house next door. Faith studied his profile. It was stronger now, tougher. She supposed he was too, had had to be. How much was left of the boy she'd loved so desperately? Maybe it was something neither of them could be sure of.

"I thought of you a lot, Faith." Though his back was to her she could almost feel the words brush over her skin. "But especially at this time of year. I could usually block you out when I had work to do, deadlines to meet, but at Christmas you wouldn't let go. I remember every one we spent together, the way you'd drag me through the shops. Those few years with you made up for all the times as a kid I woke up to nothing."

The old sympathy welled up. "Your father couldn't face the holidays, Jason. He just couldn't handle it without your mother."

"I understand that better now. After losing you."

He turned back. She wasn't looking at him now but bent industriously over the stove. "You've been spending Christmas alone, too."

"No, I have Clara."

She tensed as he walked to her. "No one to fill the stockings with you, or share secrets about what's under the tree."

"I manage. You have to alter life to suit yourself."

"Yeah." He took her chin in his hand. "I'm beginning to believe it."

The door slammed open. Wet and beaming, Clara stood dripping on the mat. "We made angels in the snow."

Faith raised a brow. "So I see. Well, you've got fifteen minutes to get out of those wet things and set the table."

She struggled out of her coat. "Can I turn on the tree?"

"Go ahead."

"Come on." Clara held out a hand for Jason. "It's the best one on the block."

Emotions humming, Faith watched them walk out together.

Chapter Five

They were still humming when the meal was over. She knew her daughter was a friendly, sometimes outrageously open child, but Clara had taken to Jason like a long lost friend. She chattered away at him as though she'd known him for years.

It's so obvious, Faith thought as she watched Clara stack dishes. Neither of them noticed. What would she do if they did? She didn't believe in lies, yet she'd been forced to live one.

The other two paid little attention to her as they settled down with Clara's books. In the easy, flowing style he'd been born with, Jason began to tell her stories about Africa—the desert, the mountains, the thick green jungle that teemed with its own life and its own dangers.

As their heads bent together over a picture in Clara's book Faith felt a flood of panic. "I'm going to go next door," she said on impulse. "I have a lot of work backed up."

"Mm–hmm." With that, Jason dismissed her. A laugh bubbled in her throat until it ached. Grabbing her coat, Faith escaped.

They were more than toys to her. They were certainly more than a business. To Faith the dolls who filled her shop were the symbol of youth, of innocence, of believing in miracles. She'd wanted to open the shop soon after Clara had been born, but Tom had been adamantly set against it. Because she'd felt indebted, she'd let it pass, as she'd let so many other things pass. Then when she'd found herself alone, with a child to support, it had seemed the natural thing.

She worked long hours there, to ease the void that even the love for her daughter couldn't fill.

In her workroom behind the store were shelves filled with pieces and parts of dolls. There were china heads, plastic legs and torsos. In another section lay the ones she called the sick and injured. Dolls with broken arms or battered bodies were brought to her for repair. Though she enjoyed selling and found a great creative thrill in making her own dolls, nothing satisfied her quite so much as taking a broken toy that was loved and making it whole again. She turned on the light and her radio and set to work.

It soothed her. As time passed, her nerves drained away. With crochet hook and rubber bands, with glue and painstaking care she replaced broken limbs. With a bit of paint and patience she brought smiles back to faceless dolls. Some were given new clothes or a fresh hairstyle, while others only needed a needle and thread plied by clever fingers.

By the time she picked up a battered rag doll she was humming.

"Are you going to fix that?"

Startled, she nearly stabbed herself with the needle. Jason stood in the doorway, hands in pockets, watching her. "Yes, that's what I do. Where's Clara?"

"She nearly fell asleep in her book. I put her to bed."

She started to rise. "Oh, well I—"

"She's asleep, Faith, with some green ball of hair she called Bernardo."

Determined to relax, Faith sat down again. "Yes, that's her favorite. Clara isn't much on ordinary dolls."

"Not like her mother?" Interested, he began to prowl the workroom. "I always thought when a toy broke or wore out it got tossed away."

"Too often. I've always thought that showed a tremendous lack of appreciation for something that's given you pleasure."

He picked up a soft plastic head, bald and smooth, that grinned at him. "Maybe you're right, but I don't see what can be done about that pile of rags in your hand."

"Quite a lot."

"Still believe in magic, Faith?"

She glanced up and for the first time her smile was completely open, her eyes warm. "Yes, of course I do. Especially at Christmastime."

Unable to help himself he reached down to run a

hand over her cheek. "I said before that I'd missed you. I don't think I realized how much."

She felt the need shimmer and the longing plead inside her. Denying both, she concentrated on the doll. "I appreciate you helping Clara, Jason. I don't want to keep you."

"Does it bother you to have someone watch you work?"

"No." She began to replace stuffing. "Sometimes a concerned mother will stay here while I doctor a patient."

He leaned a hip against the counter. "I imagined a lot of things when I was coming back. I never imagined this."

"What?"

"That I'd be standing here watching you stuff life back into a rag. You may not have noticed, but it doesn't even have a face."

"It will. How did the report go?"

"She needs to do the final draft."

Faith glanced up from her work. Her eyes were wide with the joke. "Clara?"

"She had the same reaction." Then he smiled

as he leaned back. The room smelled of her. He wondered if she knew. "She's a bright kid, Faith."

"Sometimes uncomfortably so."

"You're lucky."

"I know." With quick skillful movements, she pushed the stuffing into place.

"Kids love you no matter what, don't they?"

"No." She looked at him again. "You have to earn it." With needle and thread she began to secure the seams.

"You know, she was out on her feet, but she insisted on stopping at the tree to count the presents. She tells me she had this feeling there's going to be one more."

"I'm afraid she's doomed to disappointment. Her list looked like an army requisition. I had to draw the line." Putting down the thread, she picked up her paintbrush. "My parents already spoil her."

"They still live in town?"

"Mmm-hmm." She'd already gotten a sense of the doll's personality as she'd worked with it. Now, she began to paint it on. "They mumble about Florida from time to time, but I don't know if they'll ever go. It's Clara. They just adore her. You might go by and see them, Jason. You know my mother was always fond of you."

He examined a slinky red dress no bigger than his palm. "Your father wasn't."

She grinned at that. "He just didn't quite trust you." She sent him a quick, saucy smile. "What father would have?"

"He had good reason." As he walked toward her, he saw the doll she held. "I'll be damned." Charmed, he took it, holding it under the light. What had been a misshapen pile of rags was now a plump, sassy doll. Exaggerated lashes spiked out from wide eyes. Curls had been sewn back into place so that they fell teasingly over the brow. It was soft, friendly and pretty as a picture. Even a full grown man could recognize what would make a small girl smile.

She felt a ridiculous sense of accomplishment at seeing him smile at her work. "You approve?"

"I'm impressed. How much do you sell something like this for?"

"This one's not for sale." Faith set it in a large box at the back of the room. "There are about a dozen little girls in town whose families can't afford much of a Christmas. There are boys too, of course, but Jake over at the five-and-dime and I worked a deal a few years back. On Christmas Eve, a box is left on the doorstep. The girls get a doll, the boys a truck or a ball or whatever."

He should have known. It was so typical of her, so much what she was. "Santa lives."

She turned to smile at him. "He does in Quiet Valley."

It was the smile that did it. It was so open, so familiar. Jason closed the distance between them before either of them realized it.

"What about you? Do you get what you want for Christmas?"

"I have everything I need."

"Everything?" His hands cupped her face. "Aren't you the one who used to dream? Who always believed in wishes?"

"I've grown up. Jason, you should go now."

"I don't believe that. I don't believe you've stopped dreaming, Faith. Just being with you makes me start again."

"Jason." She pressed her hands to his chest, knowing she had to stop what could never be finished.

"You know we can't always have what we want. You'll leave in a few days. You can walk away and go on to a hundred other things, a hundred other places."

"What does that have to do with right now? It's always right now, Faith." He drew his hands through her hair so that pins scattered. Rich warm sable tumbled over his fingers. He'd always loved the feel of it, the smell of it. "You're the only one," he murmured. "You've always been the only one."

She closed her eyes before he could draw her close. "You'll go. I have to stay here. Once before I stood and watched you walk away. I don't think I can bear it if I let you in again. Can't you understand?"

"I don't know. I know I understand I want you so much more now than I ever did. I'm not sure you can keep me out, Faith." But he backed away, for both of them. "Not for long anyway. You said before I didn't have a right to all the answers. Maybe that's true. But I need one."

It was a reprieve, it was space to think. She let out a long breath and nodded. "All right. But you promise that you'll go now if I answer?"

"I'll go. Did you love him?"

She couldn't lie. It wasn't in her. So her eyes were direct and pride kept her chin high. "I never loved anyone but you."

It came into his eyes—triumph, fury. He reached for her but she pulled away. "You said you'd go, Jason. I trusted your word."

She had him trapped. She had him aching. "You should've trusted it ten years ago." He swung from the workroom and into the frigid night.

Chapter Six

Quiet Valley bustled with Christmas energy. From a jerry-rigged loudspeaker on top of the hardware store roof carols rang out. An enterprising young man from a neighboring farm got a permit and gave buggy rides up and down Main Street. Kids, keyed up with lack of school and anticipation, shouted and raced on every corner. The skies had clouded over, but the snow held off.

Jason sat at the counter in the diner and sipped coffee while he listened to town gossip. Word was the Hennessys' oldest had the chicken pox and would be scratching himself through the holidays.

Carlotta's was selling Christmas trees at half price and the hardware store had a sale on ten-speeds.

Ten years before Jason would have found the conversations mundane. Now he sat content, sipping his coffee and listening. Maybe this was what had been missing from the novel he'd been trying to write for so long. He'd been around the world, but everything had always been so fast paced, so urgent. There had been times when his life as well as his story had been on the line. You didn't think about it when it was happening. You couldn't. But now, sitting in the warm diner with the scent of coffee and frying bacon he could look back.

He'd taken assignments, a great many of them dangerous, because he hadn't given a damn. He'd already lost the part of himself he'd valued. It was true that over the years he'd built something back, inch by gritty inch, but he'd never found the whole—because he'd left it here, where he'd grown up. Now he just had to figure out what the hell to do with it.

"Guess they serve almost anybody in here."

Jason glanced up idly then grinned. "Paul. Paul

Tydings." His hand was gripped by two enormous ones.

"Damn it, Jas, you're as good-looking and skinny as ever."

Jason took a long look at his oldest friend. Paul's hair was thick and curly around a full, ruddy face offset now by a bushy moustache. His bull-like frame had assured him a starting place on the offensive line. Over the years, it had thickened into what was politely termed a successful build. "Well," Jason decided. "You're as good-looking."

With a roar of laughter, Paul slapped him on the back. "I never expected to see you back here."

"Nor I you. I thought you were in Boston."

"Was. Made myself some money, got married."

"No kidding? How long?"

"Seven years come spring. Five kids."

Jason choked on his coffee. "Five?"

"Three and a set of twins. Anyway, I brought my wife back for a visit six years ago and she fell in love. Had a jewelry store in Manchester, so I opened one here, too. I guess I've got you to thank for a lot of it."

"Me? Why?"

"You were always filling my head with ideas. Then you took off. It made me think I should try my hand at seeing a few places. In about a year I was working in this jewelry store in Boston and in walks the prettiest little thing I ever laid eyes on. I was so flustered I never imprinted her credit card. She came back the next day with the blank receipt and saved my job. Then she saved my life and married me. Never even would have met her if it hadn't been for you talking about all the places there were to see." Paul nodded as his coffee was served. "Guess you've seen Faith."

"Yeah, I've seen her."

"Throw a lot of business her way being as three of my kids are girls and all of 'em are brats." He grinned and added two packages of sugar to his coffee. "She's as pretty as she was when she was six-teen and dancing in the town hall. Settling in this time, Jason?"

With a half laugh he pushed his cooling coffee aside. "Maybe."

"Come by the house and meet the family, will you? We're just south of town, the two-story stone place."

"I saw it driving in."

"Then don't go out again without coming in. A man doesn't have many friends who go back to red wagons with him, Jason. You know—" he glanced at his watch "—seems to me Faith breaks for lunch about now. I've got to get back." With a last slap on the back, Paul left him at the counter.

Thoughtfully, Jason sipped at his coffee. He'd been away ten years, a long time by any standard, yet everyone in town he ran into saw him and Faith as a couple. It seemed it was easy to blink away a decade. Easy for everyone, he added, but for himself and Faith. Maybe he could brush away the years, the time lost, but how could he ignore her marriage and her child?

He still wanted her. That hadn't changed. He still hurt. That hadn't eased. But how did she feel? She'd told him the night before that she'd never loved another man. Did that mean she still loved him? Jason dropped a bill on the counter and rose. There was only one way to find out. He'd ask her.

The Doll House was crowded with children. Noisy children. When Jason walked in shouts and laughter bounced off the walls. Helium-filled balloons hugged the ceiling and cookie crumbs littered the floor. In the doorway of the workroom was a tall cardboard castle. Just in front of a shiny white curtain stood a puppet of Santa Claus and a green-suited elf. With a lot of chatter and exaggerated effort, they loaded a glittering golden sleigh with colorful boxes. Twice the elf fell on his face while lifting a box and sent the children into peals of laughter. After a great deal of confusion, all the presents were loaded. With a belly-bursting *Ho-ho-ho!* Santa climbed into the sleigh. Bells jingling, it rocked its way through the curtain.

To the clatter of applause, a series of puppets crossed the stage for bows. Jason saw Mrs. Claus, two elves and a reindeer with a telltale red nose before Santa took the stage with a ringing *Merry Christmas!* He didn't even realize he was leaning back against the door and grinning when Faith popped around the castle for a bow of her own.

But she saw him. Feeling foolish, she took another bow as the children clambered up. With the ease of a veteran kindergarten teacher, she maneuvered them toward the punch and cookies.

"Very impressive," Jason murmured in her ear. "I'm sorry I missed most of the show."

"It's not much." She combed her fingers through her hair. "I've been doing it for years now without much variation." She glanced over at the group of children. "It doesn't seem to matter."

"I'd say it does." He took her hand and brought it to his lips while a group of girls giggled. "Very much."

"Mrs. Monroe." A little boy with carrot-red hair and a face full of freckles tugged on her slacks. "When's Santa coming?"

Faith crouched down and smoothed at his hair. "You know, Bobby, I heard he was awfully busy this year."

His bottom lip poked out. "But he always comes."

"Well, I'm sure he'll find a way to get the presents here. I'm going to go in the back in a minute and see."

"But I have to talk to him."

The pout nearly did her in. "If he doesn't make it, you can give me a letter for him. I'll make sure he gets it."

"Problem?" Jason murmured when she straightened up again.

"Jake always plays Santa after the puppet show. We give out a few little things, it's nothing really, but the kids depend on it."

"Jake can't make it this year?"

"He caught the chicken pox from the Hennessy boy."

"I see." He hadn't celebrated Christmas in years, not since…since he'd left Faith. "I'll do it," he told her and surprised himself.

"You?"

Something in her expression made him determined to be the best St. Nick since the original. "Yeah, me. Where's the suit?"

"It's in the little room off the back, but—"

"I hope you remembered the pillows," he said before he sauntered away.

She didn't think he'd pull it off. In fact, five minutes after he walked away, Faith was sure he'd changed his mind altogether and continued out the back door. No one, including the group of kids with mouths full of cookies was more enchanted than she when Santa walked in the front door with a bag over his shoulder.

He had the chance for one booming *Merry Christmas* before he was surrounded. Too stunned to move, she watched the children bounce and jump and tug.

"Santa needs a chair." Jason sent her a long intense look that had her swallowing before her feet could move. Dashing into the back room, she brought out a high-backed chair and set it in the center of the room.

"Now you have to line up," she began, scooting children around. "Everyone gets a turn." Grabbing a bowl of candy canes, she set them on a table beside the chair. One by one, the children climbed up on Jason's knee. Faith needn't have worried. She'd had to school Jake to make the right responses, and most importantly, not to promise and risk disappointing. After the third child had climbed down, Faith relaxed. Jason was wonderful.

And having the time of his life. He'd done it just to help her out, perhaps even to impress her, but he got a great deal more. He'd never had a child sit on his lap and look at him with complete faith and love. He listened to their wishes, their confessions and complaints. Each one was allowed to reach in the sack he carried and pull out one gift.

He was hugged, kissed with sticky mouths and poked. One enterprising boy had a good grip on his beard before Jason managed to distract him. Happy, they began to file out of the shop with their parents or in groups.

"You were great." Faith turned her sign around after the last child had left to give herself a chance to catch her breath.

"Want to sit on my lap?"

Laughing, she walked to him. "I mean it, Jason, you were. I can't tell you how much I appreciate it."

"Then show me." He pulled her down onto his lap where she sank into pillows. She laughed again and kissed his nose.

"I've always been crazy about men in red suits. I wish Clara could have been here."

"Why wasn't she?"

With a little sigh, Faith let herself relax against him. "She's too old for all this now—so she tells me. She went shopping with Marcie."

"Nine's too old?"

She didn't speak for a minute, then moved her shoulders. "Kids grow up fast." She turned her head so she could look at him. "You made a lot of them happy today."

"I'd like to make you happy." Reaching up, he stroked her hair. "There was a time when I could."

"Do you ever wish we could go back?" Content, she let herself be cradled in his arms. "When we were teenagers, everything seemed so simple. Then you close your eyes for a minute and you're an adult. Oh, Jason, I wanted you to carry me away, to a castle, to a mountaintop. I was so full of romance."

He continued to stroke her hair as they sat, surrounded by dolls and the echo of children's laughter. "I didn't have enough of it, did I?"

"You had your feet on the ground, I had my head in the clouds."

"And now?"

"Now, I have a daughter to raise. It's terrifying sometimes to realize you're responsible for another life. Did you…?" She hesitated, knowing the ground was dangerous. "Did you ever want kids?"

"I haven't thought about it. Sometimes I have

to go into places where it's tough enough being responsible for your own life."

She'd thought of that—had nightmares about it. "It still excites you."

He thought of some of the things he'd seen, the cruelty, the misery. "It stopped exciting me a long time ago. But I'm good at what I do."

"I suppose I always knew you would be. Jason." She shifted again so that her eyes were level with his. "I am glad you came back."

His fingers tightened when she rested her cheek against his. "You had to wait until I was stuffed like a walrus to tell me that."

With a laugh, she wrapped her arms around his neck. "It seems to be the safest time."

"Don't bet your life on it." He pressed his lips to hers and felt hers tremble. "What's so funny?"

Choking back the laugh, she drew away. "Oh nothing, nothing at all. I've always dreamed of being kissed by a man in a beard wearing a red hat and bells. I've got to clean up this mess."

When she rose, he hauled himself up. "The timing has to click sooner or later." She said nothing as she gathered up bits of colored paper. Jason picked up his sack and glanced inside. "There's one more box in here."

"It's for Luke Hennessy. Chicken pox."

He looked at the box, then back at her. Her hair curtained her face as she pulled a sticky candy cane from the carpet. "Where does he live?"

Still holding the candy, she stood up. Some might say he looked foolish, padded from chest to hips, wrapped in red and with his face half concealed by a curly white beard. Faith thought he'd never looked more wonderful. She walked to him to pull the beard down to his chin. Her arms went around him, her mouth found his.

Her kiss was warm as it always was, full of hope and simple goodness. Desire raced through him and settled into sweet contentment. "Thank you." She kissed him again in friendship. "He lives on the corner of Elm and Sweetbriar."

He waited a moment until he was steady. "Can I get a cup of coffee when I get back?"

"Yeah." She adjusted his beard again. "I'll be next door."

Chapter Seven

He had to admit, it had given him a kick to walk through town. Kids flocked after him. Adults called out and waved. He was offered uncountable cookies. The biggest satisfaction had been the awe on the young Hennessy boy's face. That had topped the wide-eyed shock of his mother when she'd opened the door to S. Claus.

Jason took his time walking back, strolling through the square. It was strange, he discovered, how easy it was to take on the personality of a set of clothes. He felt…well, benevolent. If anyone he'd ever worked with had seen him now, they'd have fallen into the snow in a dead faint. Jason Law had a reputation for being impatient, brutally frank and quick-tempered. He hadn't won the Pulitzer for benevolence. Yet somehow, at the moment, he felt more satisfaction in the polyester beard and dime store bells than he did with all the awards he'd ever earned.

He was ho-hoing his way along when Clara stepped out of the five-and-dime. She and the little brunette at her side went off in peals of giggles.

"But you're—"

One narrow-eyed stare from Jason did the trick. Cutting herself off, Clara cleared her throat and offered her hand. "How do you do, Santa?"

"I do very well, Clara."

"That's not Jake," Marcie informed Clara. She stepped closer to try to recognize the face behind the puffs of white.

Enjoying himself, Jason sent her a wink. "Hello, Marcie."

The brunette's eyes widened. "How'd he know my name?" she whispered to her friend.

Clara covered another giggle with her hand. "Santa knows everything, don't you, Santa?"

"I have my sources."

"There isn't any Santa really." But Marcie's grown-up sophistication was wavering.

Jason leaned over and flicked at the fluffy ball on top of her cap. "There is in Quiet Valley," he told her and nearly believed it himself. He saw Marcie stop looking beyond the beard and accept the magic. Deciding against pressing his luck, he continued on down the street.

It wasn't easy for a fat man in a red suit to slip into a door inconspicuously, but Jason had had some experience. Once he was in the back room of Faith's shop, he shed the Santa clothes. He wanted to do it again. As Jason slipped into his own slim slacks, he realized he hadn't had so much fun in years. Part of it had been the look in Faith's eyes, the way she'd warmed to him, if only briefly. Part had been the simple act of giving pleasure. How long had it been since he'd done something without an angle? On an assignment there was constant bargaining. You give me this, I'll give you that. He'd had to toughen himself against sympathy, against compassion to find the truth and report it. If his style had a hard edge, it was because he'd always gone for the story that demanded it. It had helped him forget.

Now that he'd come home it was impossible not to remember.

What kind of man was he really? He wasn't sure anymore, but he knew there was one woman who could make or break him. Leaving the suit in the closet, he went to find her.

She had been waiting for him. She was ready to admit she'd been waiting for him for ten years. Throughout the rest of the afternoon, Faith had made her own decisions. She'd made a success of her life. Though the search hadn't always been easy, she'd found contentment. Confidence had come with the years and she knew she could go on alone. It was time to stop being afraid of what her life would be like when Jason left again and to accept the gift she'd been offered. He was here, now, and she loved him.

When he came into the house he found her curled in a chair by the tree, her cheek resting on the arm. She waited until he came to her. "Sometimes at night I sit like this. Clara's asleep upstairs and the house is quiet. I can think about little things, enormous things, just as I did as a child. The lights all blend together and the tree smells like heaven. You can go anywhere, sitting just like this."

He picked her up, felt her yield, then settled in the chair with her on his lap. "I remember sitting like this with you at Christmastime in your parents' house. Your father grumbled."

She snuggled close. There was no padding now, just the long lean body she knew so well. "My mother dragged him into the kitchen so we could be alone for a little while. She knew you didn't have a tree at home."

"Or anything else."

"I never asked where you live now, Jason, whether you found a place that makes you happy."

"I move around a lot. I have a base in New York."

"A base?"

"An apartment."

"It doesn't sound like a home," she murmured. "Do you put a tree in the window at Christmas?"

"I guess I have once or twice, when I've been around."

It broke her heart, but she said nothing. "My mother always said you had wanderlust. Some people are born with it."

"I had to prove myself, Faith."

"To whom?"

"To myself." He rested his cheek on top of her head. "Damn it, to you."

She breathed in the scent of pine while the lights danced on the tree. They'd sat like this before, so long ago. The memories were nearly as sweet as the reality. "I never needed you to prove anything to me, Jason."

"Maybe that's one of the reasons I had to. You were too good for me."

"That's ridiculous." She would have shifted, but he held her still.

"You were, and still are." He too stared at the tree. The tinsel shimmered in the lights like the magic he'd always wanted to give her. "Maybe that's why I had to leave when I did—maybe it's why I came back. You're all the good things, Faith. Just being with you brings out the best parts of me. God knows, there aren't many."

"You were always too hard on yourself. I don't like it." This time she did shift so that her hands were on his shoulders and her eyes were directly on his. "I fell in love with you. There were reasons for it. You were kind though you pretended not to be. You wanted to be considered tough and a trouble-maker because you felt safer that way."

He smiled and ran a finger down her cheek. "I was a troublemaker."

"Maybe I liked that, too. You didn't just accept things, you weren't afraid to question."

"I nearly got kicked out of school twice because I questioned."

The old anger stirred. Had no one understood him but herself? Had no one else been able to see what had been racing and straining inside him? "You were smarter than anyone else. You've proved that if you needed to."

"You spent a lot of time defending me, didn't you?"

"I believed in you. I loved you."

He reached for her face in an old gesture that melted her heart. "And now?"

She had too much to say and not enough ways to say it. "Do you remember that night in June, after my Senior Prom? We drove out of town. The moon was full and the air was so sweet with summer."

"You wore a blue dress that made your eyes look

like sapphires. You were so beautiful I was afraid to touch you."

"So I seduced you."

She looked so pleased with herself he laughed. "You did not."

"I certainly did. You would never have made love with me." She touched her lips to his. "Do I have to seduce you again?"

"Faith—"

"Clara's having dinner next door at Marcie's. She's going to spend the night. Come to bed with me, Jason."

Her quiet voice raced along his skin. The touch of her hand to his cheek seared like fire. But tangled with his need for her was a love that had never grown old. "You know I want you, Faith, but we're not children now."

"We're not children." She turned her face to press her lips into his palm. "And I want you. No promises, no questions. Love me the way you did on that one beautiful night we had together." Rising, she held out her hand. "I want something for the next ten years."

With their hands linked they walked up the stairs.

He pushed away all thought of the other man she'd chosen, of the other life she'd lived. He, too, would block out ten years of loss and take what was offered.

Night came early in the winter so the light was dim. In silence she lit candles so that the room glowed gold and shifted with shadows. When she turned back to him she was smiling, with all the confidence and knowledge of a woman in her eyes. Saying nothing, she came to him, lifted her mouth and offered everything.

Her fingers were steady as she reached for the buttons of his shirt. His trembled as he reached for hers. Murmuring, she waited for the brush of his hands against her skin, then sighed from the sheer glory of it. They undressed each other slowly, not tentatively, but with the quiet understanding that every moment, every instant would be treasured.

When he saw her, as slim, as lovely, as unexplainably innocent as she'd been the first time, his head spun with needs, with doubts, with desires. But she stepped to him, pressed her body against his and dissolved all choices. She was stronger than she'd been. He could feel it, not in muscle but in spirit.

Perhaps she had changed, but the longings that were racing through him were the same as they'd been in the boy on the brink of manhood. As heedlessly as the children they'd once been, they tumbled onto the bed.

They didn't relive the experience. It was as fresh, as wildly thrilling as the first time. But they were man and woman now, more demanding, hungrier. She drew him closer, running her hands over him with an urgency just discovered, with a turbulence just released. She'd waited so long, so very long and wouldn't wait a moment longer.

But he took her hand and brought it to his lips. He quieted her tumbling breath with his mouth.

"I hardly knew what to do with you the first time." Gently he nuzzled at her throat until she moaned in frenzied anticipation. Raising his head, he smiled at her. "Now I do."

Then he took her places she'd never been. Higher, still higher he drew her, then just as suddenly plunged her deep where the air was thick and dark. Trapped in the whirlwind, she clung. She'd wanted to give, but he left her helpless. Tender, soft, easy, his fingers caressed until her body shuddered. He drank in her sigh with lips abruptly urgent, ruthlessly demanding, then patiently soothed her again. Sensations rocketed inside her, leaving no room for thought, for reason or even for memories.

When they came together it was everything for both of them. Time didn't slip back but trapped them and held them close in the here and now.

He kept his arms tightly around her and they were quiet. With her eyes closed, she absorbed the unity. She loved, and for the moment there was nothing else. For him both ecstasy and contentment were troubled with questions. She was so warm, so free with her emotions. She loved him. He needed no words to know it and never had. But the loyalty he'd always understood as an intrinsic part of her had been broken. How could he rest without knowing why?

"I have to know why we lost ten years, Faith." When she said nothing, he turned her head toward him. Her eyes glistened in the shifting light but the tears didn't fall. "Now more than ever I have to know."

"No questions, Jason. Not tonight."

"I've waited long enough. We've waited long enough."

On a long breath, she sat up. Bringing her knees to her chest, she wrapped her arms around them. Her hair cascaded down her back. He couldn't resist taking a handful. She'd been his once, completely. No one else had ever touched her as he had. He knew he had to accept her marriage, and that her child belonged to another man, but he needed to understand first why she had turned to someone else so soon after he'd gone away.

"Give me something, Faith. Anything."

"We loved each other, Jason, but we wanted different things." She turned her head to look at him. "We still want different things." She took his hand and brought it to her cheek. "If you had let me I would have gone anywhere with you. I would have left my home, my family and never looked back. You needed to go alone."

"I didn't have anything for you," he began. She stopped him with a look.

"You never gave me a choice."

He reached for her once more. "If I gave you one now?"

She closed her eyes and let her forehead rest on his. "Now I have a child, and she has a home I can't take away from her. What I want doesn't come first." She drew back far enough to look at him. "What you want can't come first. Before somehow I never thought you'd really go. This time I know you will. Let's just take what we have, give each other this one Christmas. Please."

She closed her mouth over his and stopped all questions.

Chapter Eight

Christmas Eve was magic. Faith had always believed it. When she awoke with Jason beside her, it was more than magic. For a while, she simply lay there, watching him sleep. She'd imagined it before, as a girl, as a woman, but now she didn't need the dreams. He was here beside her, warm, quiet, and outside an early morning snow was falling. Careful not to wake him, Faith slipped out of bed.

When he rolled over, he smelled her—the springtime scent her hair had left on the pillowcase. For a few minutes, he lay still and let it seep into his system. Content, he lay back and looked at the room he hadn't been able to see in the dark.

The walls were papered, ivory, with little sprigs of violets. At the windows were fussy priscillas. There was an antique rosewood bureau cluttered with colored bottles and boxes. On a vanity was an old-fashioned silver-handled brush and comb. He watched the snow fall and smelled the potpourri on the stand beside the bed. The room was so like her—charming, fresh, and very, very feminine. A man could relax there even knowing he might find stockings draped over a chair or a blouse mixed with his shirts. He could relax there. And he wasn't letting her go again.

He smelled the coffee before he was halfway down the stairs. She had Christmas music on the stereo and bacon frying. He hadn't known it would feel so good just to walk into a kitchen and find your woman cooking for you.

"So you're up." She was wrapped from head to foot in a bright flannel robe. Desire dragged quietly at his stomach muscles. "There's coffee."

"I could smell it." He went to her. "I could smell you the moment I woke."

She rested her head on his shoulder, trying not to think that this was the way it might have been—if only. "You look as though you could have slept for hours. It's a good thing you didn't or the bacon would be cold."

"If you'd stayed in bed a few more minutes, we might have—"

"Mom! Mom! It's snowing!" Clara burst through the door and danced around the kitchen. "We're going to go caroling tonight in the hay wagon and there's snow all over the place." She stopped in front of Jason and grinned. "Hi."

"Hi yourself."

"Mom and I are going to build a snowman. She says Christmas snowmen are the best. You can help."

She hadn't known just what reaction Clara would have to finding Jason at the breakfast table. With a shake of her head, Faith began to beat eggs. She should have known Clara would be willing to accept anyone she'd decided to like. "You have to have some breakfast."

Clara fingered the plastic Santa on her lapel, tugging on the string so that the nose lit up. It never failed to please her. "I had cereal at Marcie's."

"Did you thank her mother for having you?"

"Yeah." She stopped a minute. "I think I did. Anyway we're going to build two of them and have a wedding and everything. Marcie wanted the wedding," she added to Jason.

"Clara would prefer a war."

"I figured we could have that after. Maybe I should have some hot chocolate first." She eyed the cookie jar and calculated her chances. Slim at best.

"I'll fix it. And you can have a cookie after the snowman," Faith told her without bothering to turn. "Hang your things by the door."

Scrambling out of her coat, she chattered at Jason. "You're not going back to Africa, are you? I don't think Africa would be much fun at Christmas. Marcie's mother said you'd probably be going to some other neat place."

"I'm supposed to go to Hong Kong in a few weeks." He glanced at Faith. She didn't turn. "But I'll be around for Christmas."

"Do you have a tree in your room?"

"No."

She gave him a wide-eyed look. "Well, where do you put your presents? It's not Christmas without a tree, is it, Mom?"

Faith thought of the years Jason had grown up without one. She remembered how hard he'd tried to pretend it didn't matter. "A tree's only so that we can show other people it's Christmas."

Unconvinced, Clara plopped into a chair. "Well, maybe."

"She used to say the same thing to me," Jason told Clara. "In any case, I don't think Mr. Beantree would like it if I left pine needles all over the floor."

"We've got a tree, so you can have dinner with us," Clara declared. "Mom makes this big turkey and Grandma and Grandpa come over. Grandma brings pies and we eat till we're sick."

"Sounds great." Amused, he looked over as Faith scooped eggs onto a plate. "I had Christmas dinner with your grandparents a couple of times."

"Yeah?" Interested, Clara studied him. "I guess I heard somewhere that you used to be Mom's boy-friend. How come you didn't get married?"

"Here's your hot chocolate, Clara." Faith set it down. "You'd better hurry, Marcie's waiting."

"Are you coming out?"

"Soon." Grateful that her daughter was easily distracted, she set the platter of bacon and eggs on the table. Ignoring the half-amused lift of brow from Jason, she took her seat.

"We need carrots and scarves and stuff."

"I'll take care of it."

With a grin Clara gulped down chocolate. "And hats?"

"And hats."

A snowball hit the kitchen window. Clara was up like a shot. "There she is. Gotta go. Come soon, Mom, you make the best."

"Soon as I'm dressed. Don't forget your top button."

Clara hesitated at the back door. "I've got a little plastic tree in my room. You can have it if you want."

Moved, he only stared at her. Just like her mother, he thought, and fell in love a second time. "Thanks."

"'Sokay. Bye."

"She's quite a kid," Jason commented as the door slammed behind her.

"I like her."

"I'll give her a hand with the snowman."

"You don't have to, Jason."

"I want to, then I've got some things to take care of." He checked his watch. It was only Christmas Eve for so long. When a man was being offered a second chance, it wasn't wise to waste time. "Can I get an invitation for tonight?"

Faith smiled but simply pushed the food around on her plate. "You've never needed one."

"Don't cook, I'll bring something."

"It's okay, I—"

"Don't cook," he repeated, rising. He bent to kiss her, then lingered over it. "I'll be back."

He took his coat from the hook where it had hung beside Clara's. When he was gone, Faith looked down at the toast she'd crumbled in her hand. Hong Kong. At least this time she knew where he was going.

The snow people in the side yard grinned at him as he struggled past. Boxes balanced, Jason knocked on the back door with the toe of his boot. The snow hadn't let up a whit.

"Jason." Speechless, Faith stepped back as he tee-tered inside.

"Where's Clara?"

"Clara?" Still staring, she pushed back her hair. "She's upstairs getting ready for the hayride."

"Good. Take the top box."

"Jason, what in the world have you got here?"

"Just take the top box unless you want pizza all over the floor."

"All right, but…" As the enormous box in his arms shifted, she laughed. "Jason, what have you done?"

"Wait a minute."

Holding the pizza, she watched him drag the box into the living room. "Jason, what is that thing?"

"It's a present." He started to set it under the tree then discovered there wasn't enough room. With a bit of rearranging, he managed to lean the box against the wall beside the tree. He was grinning when he turned to her. If he'd ever felt better in his life, he couldn't remember it. "Merry Christmas."

"Same to you. Jason, what is that box?"

"Damn, it's cold out there." Though he rubbed

his hands together now, he hadn't even noticed the biting wind. "Got any coffee?"

"Jason."

"It's for Clara." He discovered that feeling a bit foolish didn't dim the warmth.

"You didn't have to get her a present," Faith began, but her curiosity got the better of her. "What is it?"

"This?" Jason patted the six-foot box. "Oh, it's nothing."

"If you don't tell me you don't get any coffee." She smiled. "And I keep the pizza."

"Spoilsport. It's a toboggan." He took Faith's arm to lead her out of the room. "She happened to mention when we were building the snowman that some kid had this toboggan and it went down Red Hill like a spitfire."

"Spitfire," Faith murmured.

"And snow like this is just made for going down Red Hill like a spitfire, so..."

"Sucker," Faith accused and kissed him hard.

"Put that pizza down and call me that again."

She laughed and kept it between them.

"Wow!"

Faith raised a brow at the noise from the living room. "I think she saw the box."

At full speed, Clara barreled into the kitchen. "Did you see? I knew there'd be one more, I just knew. It's as tall as you are," she told Jason. "Did you see?" She grabbed his hand to drag him back. "It has my name on it."

"Imagine that." Jason picked her up and kissed both cheeks. "Merry Christmas."

"I can't wait." She threw her arms around his neck and squeezed. "I just can't wait."

Watching them, Faith felt her emotions tangle and knot until her bones ached with it. What should she do? What could she do? When Jason turned with Clara, the lights from the tree fell like wishes over their faces.

"Faith?" He didn't need words to recognize distress, pain, turmoil. "What is it?"

Her hands were digging into the cardboard of the box. "Nothing. I'm going to dish out this pizza before it's cold."

"Pizza?" Delighted, Clara bounced down. "Can I have two pieces? It's Christmas."

"Monkey," Faith scolded gently, tousling her hair. "Set the table."

"What is it, Faith?" Jason took her arm before she could follow her daughter into the kitchen. "Something's wrong."

"No." She had to control herself. She'd managed everything for so long. "You overwhelmed me." With a smile she touched his face. "It's happened before. Come on, let's eat."

Because she seemed to need to keep her thoughts to herself, he let it go and followed her into the kitchen where Clara was already peeking into the cardboard box. He'd never seen a child plow through food with such unrestrained glee. He'd never known Christmas Eve could be special simply because there was someone beside him.

Clara swallowed the last of her second piece. "Maybe if I opened one present tonight there'd be less confusion in the morning."

Faith seemed to consider. "I like confusion," she decided and Jason realized the conversation was an old tradition.

"Maybe if I opened just one present tonight, I

could get right to sleep. Then you wouldn't have to wait so long to creep around and fill the stockings."

"Hmm." Faith pushed aside her empty plate and enjoyed the wine Jason had brought. "I like creeping around late at night."

"If I opened—"

"Not a chance."

"If I—"

"Nope."

"But Christmas is just hours and hours away."

"Awful, isn't it?" Faith smiled at her. "And you're going caroling in ten minutes, so you'd better get your coat."

Clara walked over to tug on her boots. "Maybe when I get back, there'll be just one present that you'll figure isn't really important enough to wait until morning."

"All the presents under the tree are absolutely vital." Faith rose to help her on with her coat. "And so are the following instructions. Stay with the group. Keep your mittens on, I want you to keep all your fingers. Don't lose your hat. Remember that Mr. and Mrs. Easterday are in charge."

"Mom." Clara shifted her feet and sighed. "You treat me like a baby."

"You are my baby." Faith gave her a smacking kiss. "So there."

"Jeez, I'll be ten years old in February. That's practically tomorrow."

"And you'll still be my baby in February. Have a good time."

Clara sighed, long-suffering and misunderstood. "Okay."

"Okay," Faith mimicked. "Say good-night."

Clara peeked around her mother. "Are you going to stay until I get back?"

"Yeah."

Satisfied, she grinned and pulled open the door. "Bye."

"Monster," Faith declared and began to stack plates.

"She's terrific." Standing, Jason helped clear the clutter. "Little for her age, I guess. I didn't realize she was almost ten. It's hard to—" He stopped as Faith clattered dishes in the sink. "She'll be ten in February."

"Umm. I can't believe it myself. Sometimes it

seems like yesterday, and then again..." She trailed off, abruptly breathless. With studied care, she began to fill the sink with soapy water. "I'll just be a minute here if you'd like to take your wine into the living room."

"In February." Jason took her arm. When he turned her, he saw the blood drain from her face. His fingers tightened, bruising without either of them noticing. "Ten years in February. We made love that June. God, I don't know how many times that night. I never touched you again, we never had the chance to be alone like that again before I left, just a few weeks later. You must have married Tom in September."

Her throat was dry as bone. She couldn't even swallow, but stared at him.

"She's mine," he whispered and it vibrated through the room. "Clara's mine."

She opened her mouth to speak, but there seemed to be nothing she could say. Lips trembling, eyes drenched, she nodded.

"God!" He had her by both arms, nearly lifting her off her feet before he backed her into the counter. The fury in his eyes would have made her cringe if she hadn't been willing to accept it. "How could you? Damn you, she's ours and you never told me. You married another man and had our baby. Did you lie to him, too? Did you make him think she was his so you could have your cozy house and lace curtains?"

"Jason, please—"

"I had a right." He thrust her away before he could give into the violence that pushed him on. "I had a right to her. Ten years. You stole that from me."

"No! No it wasn't like that. Jason, please! You have to listen!"

"The hell with you." He said it calmly, so calmly she stepped back as though she'd been slapped. The anger she could argue with, even reason with. Quiet rage left her helpless.

"Please, let me try to explain."

"There's nothing you can say that could make up for it. Nothing." He yanked his coat from the wall and stormed out.

"You're a damn fool, Jason Law." The Widow Marchant sat in her kitchen rocker and scowled.

"She lied to me. She's been lying for years."

"Hogwash." She fiddled with the tinsel on the little tree on the stand by the window. Cheerful strains from the Nutcracker floated in from the living room. "She did what she had to do, nothing more, nothing less."

He prowled around the room. He still wasn't sure why he'd come there instead of heading for Clancy's Bar. He'd walked in the snow for an hour, maybe more, then found himself standing on the widow's doorstep. "You knew, didn't you? You knew I was Clara's father."

"I had my ideas." The rocker squeaked gently as she moved. "She had the look of you."

That brought a peculiar thrill, one he didn't know what to do with. "She's the image of Faith."

"True enough if you don't look hard. The eyebrows are you, and the mouth. The sweet Lord knows the temperament is. Jason, if you'd known you were to be a father ten years back, what would you have done?"

"I'd have come back for her." He turned, dragging a hand through his hair. "I'd have panicked," he said more calmly. "But I'd have come back."

"I always thought so. But it—well, it's Faith's story to tell. You'd best go on back and hear it."

"It doesn't matter."

"Can't stand a martyr," she muttered.

He started to snap, then sighed instead. "It hurts. It really hurts."

"That's life for you," she said not unsympathetically. "Want to lose them both again?"

"No. God, no. But I don't know how much I can forgive."

The old woman raised both brows. "Fair enough. Give Faith the same courtesy."

Before he could speak again, the kitchen door burst open. In the doorway stood Faith, covered with snow, face washed with tears. Ignoring the wet she brought in with her, she ran to Jason. "Clara," she managed to stammer.

When he took her arms he felt the shudders. Terror flowed from her into him. "What's happened?"

"She's missing."

Chapter Nine

"They're going to find her." Jason held her arm as they both stumbled through the snow to her car. "They probably have already."

"One of the kids said he thought she and Marcie went behind this farmhouse to look at the horses in the barn. But when they went back, they weren't there. It's dark." Faith fumbled with her keys.

"Let me drive."

She gave him no argument as she climbed in the passenger side. "Lorna and Bill called the sheriff from the farmhouse. Half the town's out there looking for them. But there's so much snow, and they're just little girls. Jason—"

He took her face in his hands, firmly. "We're going to find them."

"Yes." She wiped away tears with the heels of her hands. "Let's hurry."

He couldn't risk more than thirty miles an hour. They crept down the snow-covered road, searching the landscape for any sign. The hills and fields lay pristine and undisturbed. To Faith they looked unrelenting. But while fear still overwhelmed her, she'd conquered the tears.

Ten miles out of town the fields were lit up like noonday. Groups of cars crisscrossed the road and men and women tramped through the snow calling. Jason had barely stopped when Faith was out and running toward the sheriff.

"We haven't found them yet, Faith, but we will. They won't have gone far."

"You've searched the barn and the outbuildings?"

The sheriff nodded at Jason. "Every inch."

"How about in the other direction?"

"I'm going to send some men that way."

"We'll go now."

The snow was blinding as he weaved through the other cars. He slackened his speed even more and started to pray. He'd been on a search party once in the Rockies. He hadn't forgotten what a few hours in the wind and snow could do.

"I should have made her wear another sweater." Faith gripped her hands together in her lap as she strained to see out the window. In her hurry she'd forgotten her gloves but didn't notice her numb fingers. "She hates it so when I fuss and I didn't want to spoil the evening for her. Christmas is so special for Clara. She's been so excited." Her voice broke as a ripple of fear became a wave. "I should have made her wear another sweater. She'll be— *Stop!*"

The car fishtailed as he hit the brakes. It took every ounce of control for him to deal with the swerve. Faith pushed open the door and stumbled out. "Over there, it's—"

"It's a dog." He had her by the arms before she could run across the empty field. "It's a dog, Faith."

"Oh, God." Beyond control, she collapsed against him. "She's just a little girl. Where could she be? Oh, Jason, where is she? I should have gone with her. If I'd been there she—"

"Stop it!"

"She's cold and she must be frightened."

"And she needs you." He gave her a quick shake. "She needs you."

Struggling for control, she pressed a hand to her mouth. "Yes. Yes, I'm all right. Let's go. Let's go a little further."

"You wait in the car. I'm going to walk across this field for a bit and see if I spot something."

"I'll go with you."

"I can move faster alone. I'll only be a few minutes." He started to urge her toward the car when a flash of red caught his eye. "Over there."

He gripped her arm as he tried to see through the snow. Just at the edge of the field, he saw it again.

"It's Clara." Faith was already struggling away. "She has a red coat." Snow kicked up around her as she ran. It fell cold and wet to mix with the tears that blinded her vision. With all the breath she had she called out. Arms spread wide, she caught both girls to her. "Oh God, Clara, I've been so scared. Here, here now, you're frozen, both of you. We'll get to the car. Everything's going to be fine. Everything's all right now."

"Is my mom mad?" Shivering, Marcie wept against her shoulder.

"No, no, she's just worried. Everyone is."

"Up you go." Jason hauled Clara up in his arms. For one brief minute he gave himself the luxury of nuzzling his daughter. Looking back, he saw Faith gathering up Marcie. "Can you manage?"

She smiled, holding the still weeping girl close. "No problem."

"Then let's go home."

"We didn't mean to get lost." Clara's tears ran down his collar.

"Of course you didn't."

"We just went to look at the horses and we got all turned around. We couldn't find anybody. I wasn't scared." Her breath hitched as she pressed against him. "Just Marcie."

His child. He felt his own vision blur as he wrapped his arms tighter around her. "You're both safe now."

"Mom was crying."

"She's okay, too." He stopped at the car. "Can you handle them both on your lap in the front? They'll be warmer."

"Absolutely." After Faith had settled in with Marcie, Jason handed her Clara. For one long moment, their gazes held over her head.

"We couldn't find the lights of the house with all the snow," Clara murmured as she held on to her mother. "Then we couldn't find the road for the longest time. It was so cold. I didn't lose my hat."

"I know, baby. Here, get your wet mittens off. You, too, Marcie. Jason has the heater turned all the way up. You'll be cooked before you know it." She ran kisses over two cold faces and fought the need to break down. "What Christmas carols did you sing?"

"'Jingle Bells,'" Marcie said with a sniffle.

"Ah, one of my favorites."

"And 'Joy to the World,'" Clara put in. The heater was pumping warm air over her hands and face. "You like that one better."

"So I do but I can't remember just how it starts. How does it start, Marcie?" She smiled at Clara and snuggled her closer.

In a thin, piping voice still wavery with tears Marcie started to sing. She was nearly through the first verse when they came to the rest of the search party.

"It's my dad!" Bouncing on Faith's lap, Marcie started to wave. "He doesn't look mad."

With a half laugh, Faith kissed the top of her head. "Merry Christmas, Marcie."

"Merry Christmas, Mrs. Monroe. See you to-morrow, Clara." Marcie barely had time to open the door before she was scooped up.

"What a night." There were waves and cheers as the car weaved through the crowd.

"It's Christmas Eve," Clara reminded her mother. The world was safe and warm again. "Maybe I should open that one big present tonight."

"Not a chance," Jason told her and tugged at her hair.

Faith turned Clara in her arms and squeezed tight.

"Don't cry, Mom."

"I have to, for just a minute." True to her word, her eyes were dry when they arrived home. An ex-hausted Clara dozed on Jason's shoulder as he carried her inside. "I'll take her up, Jason."

"We'll take her up."

She let her arms fall back to her sides and nodded. They pulled off boots and socks and sweaters and wrapped Clara in warm flannel. She murmured a bit and tried to stay awake but the adventures of the evening took their toll. "It's Christmas Eve," she mumbled. "I'm going to get up real early in the morning."

"As early as you like," Faith told her as she pressed a kiss to her cheek.

"Can I have cookies for breakfast?"

"Half a dozen," Faith agreed recklessly. She smiled and was asleep before Faith pulled the blankets around her.

"I was afraid…" She let her hand linger on her daughter's cheek. "I was afraid I'd never see her like this again. Safe, warm. Jason, I don't know how to thank you for just being there. If I'd been alone—" She broke off and shook her head.

"I think we should go downstairs, Faith."

The tone made her press her lips together. She'd be ready, she promised herself, to handle the accusations, the bitterness, the resentment. "I think I'd like a drink," she said as they walked downstairs. "Some brandy. It looks like the fire's gone out."

"I'll take care of it. You get the brandy. There are some things I have to say."

"All right." She left him to go to the little cabinet in the dining room. When she came back, the fire was just catching. He straightened from it and took a snifter.

"Do you want to sit down?"

"No, I can't." She sipped, but it would have taken more than brandy to steady her nerves. "Whatever you have to say, Jason, you should say it."

Chapter Ten

She stood looking at him, her back straight, her eyes burning with emotion, her hands clasping the snifter tightly. Part of him wanted to go to her, gather her close and just hold on. He'd found a child and nearly lost her in the same night. Did anything else matter? But inside was a void that had to be filled. Questions, demands, accusations had to be answered. There had to be an accounting before there could be understanding, and understanding before there could be forgiveness. But where did he start?

He walked to the tree. There was a star on top

that shed silver light over all the other colors. "I'm not sure I know what to say. It isn't every day a man turns around and finds himself with a half-grown daughter. I feel cheated out of watching her learn to walk, hearing her talk, Faith. Nothing you can do or say can ever give that back to me, can it?"

"No."

He turned to see her holding the brandy at waist level. Her face was very pale and calm. Whatever emotions she was feeling she managed to restrain. Yes, this was a different Faith than the one he'd left. The girl would never have been able to exert the self-control the woman did. "No excuses, Faith?"

"I guess I thought I had them, then tonight when I thought I'd lost her…" Her voice trailed off and she shook her head. "No excuses, Jason."

"She thinks Tom's her father."

"No!" Her eyes weren't calm now but brilliant. "Do you think I'd let her believe her father had deserted her, that he didn't care enough even to write? What she knows is basically the truth. I never lied to her."

"What is the truth?"

She took a steadying breath. When she looked at

him her face was still pale but her voice was calm
again. "That I loved her father, and he loved me,
but he had to go away before he even knew about
her and he wasn't able to come back."

"He would have."

Something rushed into her eyes but she turned
away. "I told her that, too."

"Why?" The fury came back and he fought
against it. "I have to know why you did what you
did. I lost all those years."

"You?" Her temper was less easily controlled
than her grief. Years of holding back bubbled inside
her and burst out. "*You* lost?" she repeated as she
whirled around. "You were gone and I was eighteen
years old, pregnant and alone."

Guilt flared. He hadn't expected it. "I wouldn't
have left if you'd told me."

"I didn't know." She put the brandy down and
pushed back her hair with both hands. "It was just
a week after you'd gone that I found out I was
carrying our baby. I was thrilled." With a laugh, she
wrapped her arms around her chest. For a moment
she looked heartbreakingly young and innocent. "I
was so happy. I waited every day, every night for

you to call so I could tell you." Her eyes sobered. The smile faded. "But you never called, Jason."

"I needed time to set things up—a steady job, a place I could ask you to live in."

"You never understood it didn't matter where I lived, as long as it was with you." She shook her head before he could speak. "It doesn't matter now. That part's over. A week passed, then two, then a month. I got ill, just tension, morning sickness, but I began to realize you weren't going to call. You weren't coming back. I was angry for a while, acknowledging you just hadn't wanted me enough. Small-town girl."

"That's not true. That was never true."

She studied him a moment, almost dispassion- ately. The lights of the tree fell over his dark-blond hair, glimmered in the deep, deep eyes that had always held their own secrets. Restlessness. "Wasn't it?" she murmured. "It was certainly true that you wanted out. I was part of Quiet Valley and you wanted out."

"I wanted you with me."

"But not enough to let me go with you." She shook her head when he started to speak. "Not enough to let me come to you until you'd proved the things you needed to prove. I didn't always understand that, Jason, but I began to when you came back."

"You weren't ever going to tell me about Clara, were you?"

She heard the bitterness again and closed her eyes against it. "I don't know. I honestly don't."

He drank, hoping it would warm the ice in his veins. "Tell me the rest."

"I wanted the baby, but I was scared, too scared even to tell my mother."

She picked up the brandy again but merely warmed her hands with it. "I should have of course, but I wasn't thinking clearly."

"Why did you marry Tom?" But even as he asked, he realized the old jealousies were fading. He only wanted to understand.

"Tom would come by almost every night. We'd talk. He didn't seem to mind me talking about you and God knows I needed to. Then one night we were sitting on the porch and I just broke down. I was three months pregnant and my body was changing. That morning I hadn't been able to snap my jeans." With a shaky laugh, she ran a hand over her face. "It sounds so silly, but I hadn't been able to snap my jeans and it was terrifying. It made me realize there was no going back. Everything just poured out while we sat there. He said he'd marry me. Of course I said no, but he began to reason it all out. You weren't coming back and I was pregnant. He loved me and wanted to marry me. The baby would have a name, a home, a family. It sounded so right the way he said it and I wanted the baby to be safe. I wanted to be safe."

She drank now because her throat ached. "It was wrong, right from the beginning. He knew I didn't love him, but he just wanted me, or thought he did. The first few months he tried, we both really tried. But after Clara came, he couldn't handle it. I could see every time he looked at her he thought of you. There was nothing I could do to change the fact that she was yours." She paused and found it easier to say it all. "There was nothing I would have done to change that. As long as I had her, I had part of you. Tom knew it, no matter how much I tried to be what he wanted. He started drinking, picking fights, staying out. It was as though he wanted me to ask for a divorce."

"But you didn't."

"I didn't because I…well, I felt I owed him. Then one day I came home from taking Clara out and he was gone. Divorce papers came in the mail, and that was that."

"Why didn't you ever try to contact me, Faith, through one of the magazines or newspapers?"

"And say what? Jason, remember me? By the way, you have a daughter back here in Quiet Valley. Drop in some time."

"One word—one word from you and I'd have left everything and come back. I never stopped loving you."

She closed her eyes. "I watched you walk away from me. I watched you get on the bus and leave me without a trace. I stood there for hours, half believing you'd get off at the next stop and come back. I was the one who had to stay behind, Jason."

"I called. Damn it, Faith, it only took me six months to get something started."

She smiled. "And when you called I was seven months pregnant. My mother didn't tell me for a

long time, not until after Tom had left. She said you
made her promise."

"I needed my pride."

"I know."

That she didn't question. He saw the way she
smiled as she said it, as if she'd always understood.
"You must have been terrified."

Her smile softened. "There were moments."

"You must have hated me."

"Never. How could I? You went away but you
left me with the most beautiful thing in my life.
Maybe you were right, maybe I was. Maybe we
were both wrong, but there was Clara. Every time I
looked at her, I could remember how much I loved
you."

"How do you feel now?"

"Shaky." She laughed a little, then folded her
hands, determined to do what was right. "Clara
should be told. I'd prefer doing it myself."

The idea made him reach for the brandy again.
"How do you think she'll take it?"

"She's learned to get along without a father. It
doesn't mean she hasn't needed one." She sat up
straight and raised her chin. "You have a right, of

course, to see her whenever you like, but I won't have her bounced around. I also realize you can't be here for her all the time because of your work, but don't think you can just pop into her life and out again. You'll have to make an effort, to keep in touch with her, Jason."

So this was another fear she'd lived with, he realized. Maybe he deserved it. "You don't trust me, do you?"

"Clara's too important." She let out a little sigh. "So are you."

"If I told you I fell for her before I knew, would it make a difference?"

She thought of the toboggan, of the way he'd looked when Clara had thrown her arms around his neck. "She needs all the love she can get. We all do. She's so much like you, I—" She broke off when her eyes filled. "Damn, I don't want to do this." Impatient, she brushed tears away. "I'll tell her tomorrow, Jason. On Christmas. You and I can work out the arrangements. I know you're leaving soon, but if you could stay a few more days, give her some time, it would make it easier for all of us."

He rubbed at the tension at the back of his neck.

"You never asked me for much of anything, did you?"

She smiled. "I asked you for everything. We were both too young to realize it."

"You always believed in magic, Faith." He pulled a box out of his pocket. "It's nearly midnight. Open it now."

"Jason." She pushed her hands through her hair. How could he think of presents now? "I don't think this is the time."

"It's ten years past time."

When he thrust the box at her she found herself gripping it with both hands. "I don't have anything to give you."

He touched her face, almost hesitantly. "You've just given me a daughter."

Relief poured through her. Instead of bitterness, she heard gratitude. Love, never dimmed, shimmered in her eyes. "Jason—"

"Please, open it."

She pulled off the glossy red paper and revealed the black velvet box beneath. With fingers not quite steady she opened it. The ring was a teardrop, frozen in place, glorious with the reflected lights from the tree.

"Paul told me it was the best he had."

"You bought this before you knew—"

"Yeah, before I knew I was going to ask the mother of my child to marry me. We'll be legal, the three of us." He took her hand and waited. "How about a second chance? I won't let you down, Faith."

"You never did." Close to tears again, she reached out her hand to his cheek. "It wasn't you, it wasn't me, it was life. Oh, Jason, I want this. Understand, all I've ever really wanted was to be married to you, have a family with you."

"Then let me put the ring on."

"Jason, it's not just me. If it were I'd leave with you this instant. We'd go to Hong Kong, Siberia, Peking. Anywhere. But it's not just me; I have to stay."

"It's not just you," he repeated. He took the ring and tossed the box aside. "And *I* have to stay. Do you think I'd leave you again? Do you think I could leave what's upstairs or the chance to have more that I can watch grow up? I'm not going anywhere."

"But you said—Hong Kong."

"I quit." When he grinned he felt the pressure of years melt away. "Today. That was one of the things I took care of this afternoon. I'm going to write a book." He took her by the shoulders. "I'm out of a job, I'm living in a room at the inn and asking you to marry me."

The breath backed up in her lungs. Her heart was pounding. Yes, she'd always believed in magic. It was standing in front of her. "Ten years ago, I thought I loved you as much as it was possible to love. You were a boy. In the last few days I've learned that loving a man is something quite different." She paused and saw the ring in his hand explode with the joyful lights on the tree. "If you'd asked me ten years ago I'd have said yes."

"Faith—"

With a laugh, she threw her arms around his neck. "You're going to get the same answer now. Oh, I love you, Jason, more than ever."

"We've got years to make up for."

"Yes." She met his mouth with equal hunger, equal hope. "We will. The three of us."

"The three of us." He let his forehead rest against hers. "I want more."

"We've more than enough time to give Clara a baby brother or sister for next Christmas." Her lips sought his again. "We've got more than enough time for everything."

They both heard the bells peal out from the town hall. Midnight.

"Merry Christmas, Faith."

She felt the ring slide onto her finger. All wishes were granted. "Welcome home, Jason."

★ ★ ★ ★ ★

Search for Love

Chapter One

The train ride seemed endless, and Serenity was tired. The argument the night before with Tony had not helped her disposition, plus the long flight from Washington to Paris, and now the arduous hours in the stuffy train had her gritting her teeth to hold back the groan. All in all, she decided miserably, she was a poor traveler.

The trip had been the excuse for the last, terminal battle between Serenity and Tony, their relationship having been strained and uneven for weeks. Her continued refusal to be pressured into marriage had provoked several minor tiffs, but Tony had wanted her, and his patience seemed inexhaustible. Not until her announcement of the intended trip had his forebearance cracked, and the war had begun.

"You can't go rushing off this way to France to see some supposed grandmother you never knew existed until a couple of weeks ago." Tony had paced, his agitation obvious by the way he allowed his hand to disturb his well-styled fair hair.

"Brittany," Serenity had elaborated. "And it doesn't matter when I found out she existed; I know now."

"This old lady writes you a letter, tells you she's your grandmother and wants to see you, and off you go, just like that." He had been totally exasperated. She knew his logical mind was unable to comprehend her impulse, and she had hung on to the threads of her own temper and had attempted to speak calmly.

"She's my mother's mother, Tony, the only family I have left, and I intend to see her. You know I've been making plans to go since her letter arrived."

"The old girl lets twenty-four years go by without a word, and now suddenly, this big summons." He had continued to pace the large, high-ceilinged room before whirling back to her. "Why in heaven's name did your parents never speak of her? Why did she wait until they were dead to contact you?"

Serenity had known he had not meant to be cruel; it was not in Tony's nature to be cruel, merely logical, his lawyer's mind dealing constantly in facts and figures. Even he could not know the slow, deadly ache that remained, lingering after two months, the time since her parents' sudden, unexpected deaths. Knowing that his words had not been intended to hurt did not prevent her from lashing out, and the argument had grown in proportion until Tony had stomped out and left her alone, seething and resentful.

Now, as the train chugged its way across Brittany, Serenity was forced to admit that she, too, had doubts. Why had her grandmother, this unknown Comtesse Françoise de Kergallen, remained silent for nearly a quarter of a century? Why had her mother, her lovely, fragile, fascinatingly different mother, never mentioned a relative in far-off Brittany? Not even her father, as volatile, outspoken, and direct as he had been, had ever spoken of ties across the Atlantic.

They had been so close, Serenity mused with a

sigh of memory. The three of them had done so much together. Even when she had been a child, her parents had included her when they visited senators, congressmen, and ambassadors.

Jonathan Smith had been a much-sought-after artist; a portrait created by his talented hand, a prized possession. Those in Washington society had clamored for his commissions for more than twenty years. He had been well liked and respected as a man as well as an artist, and the gentle charm and grace of Gaelle, his wife, had made the couple a highly esteemed addition to the capital set.

When Serenity had grown older, and her natural artistic abilities became apparent, her father's pride had known no bounds. They had sketched and painted together, first as tutor and pupil, then as man and woman, and they drew even closer with the shared joy of art.

The small family had shared an idyllic existence in the elegant rowhouse in Georgetown, a life full of love and laughter, until Serenity's world had crashed in around her, along with the plane which had been carrying her parents to California. It had been impossible to believe they were dead, and she still lived on. The high-ceilinged rooms would no longer echo with her father's booming voice or her mother's gentle laughter. The house was empty but for memories that lay like shadows in each corner.

For the first two weeks, Serenity could not bear the sight of a canvas or brush, or the thought of entering the third-floor studio where she and her father had spent so many hours, where her mother would enter and remind them that even artists had to eat.

When she had finally gathered up the courage to climb the stairs and enter the sun-filled room, she found, rather than unbearable grief, a strange, healing peace. The skylight showered the room with the sun's warmth, and the walls retained the love and laughter which had once existed there. She had begun to live again, paint again, and Tony had been kind and gentle, helping to fill the hollowness left by loss. Then, the letter had come.

Now she had left Georgetown and Tony behind in a quest for the part of her that belonged to Brittany and an unknown grandmother. The strange, formal letter which had brought her from the familiarity of Washington's crowded streets to the

unaccustomed Breton countryside lay safely tucked
in the smooth leather bag at her side. There had
been no affection in the missive, merely facts and
an invitation, more like a royal command, Serenity
mused, half-annoyed, half-amused. But if her pride
would have scoffed at the command, her curiosity,
her desire to know more of her mother's family,
had accepted. With her innate impulsiveness and
organization, she had arranged her trip, closed up
the beloved house in Georgetown, and burned her
bridges with Tony.

The train groaned and screeched in protest as it
dragged into the station at Lannion. Tingling excitement warred with jet lag as Serenity gathered
her hand luggage and stepped onto the platform,
taking her first attentive look at her mother's native
country. She stared around her with an artist's eyes,
lost for a moment in the simple beauty and soft,
melding colors that were Brittany.

The man watched her concentration, the small
smile playing on her parted lips, and his dark
brow rose slightly in surprise. He took his time surveying her, a tall, willow-slim figure in a powder-
blue traveling suit, the soft skirt floating around

long, shapely legs. The soft breeze ran easy fingers through her sunlit hair, feathering it back to frame the delicate-boned, oval face. The eyes, he noted, were large and wide, the color of brandy, surrounded by thick lashes shades darker than her pale hair. Her skin looked incredibly soft, smooth like alabaster, and the combination lent an ethereal appearance: a delicate, fragile orchid. He would all too soon discover that appearances are often deceptive.

He approached her slowly, almost reluctantly. "You are Mademoiselle Serenity Smith?" he inquired in lightly accented English.

Serenity started at the sound of his voice, so absorbed in the countryside she had not noted his nearness. Brushing back a lock of hair, she turned her head and found herself looking up, much higher than was her habit, into dark, heavy-lidded brown eyes.

"Yes," she answered, wondering why those eyes made her feel so strange. "Are you from the Château Kergallen?"

The slow lifting of one dark brow was the only

change in his expression. "*Oui,* I am Christophe de Kergallen. I have come to take you to the countess."

"De Kergallen?" She repeated with some surprise. "Not another mysterious relative?"

The brow remained lifted, and full, sensuous lips curved so slightly as to be imperceptible. "One could say, Mademoiselle, that we are, in an obscure manner, cousins."

"Cousins," she murmured as they studied each other, rather like two prizefighters sizing each other up before a bout.

Rich black hair fell thick and straight to his collar, and the dark eyes which continued to remain steady seemed nearly as black against his deep bronze skin. His features were sharp, hawklike, somewhat piratical, and he exuded a basic masculine aura which both attracted and repelled her. She immediately wished for her sketch pad, wondering if she could possibly capture his aristocratic virility with pencil and paper.

Her lengthy scrutiny left him unperturbed, and he held her gaze, his eyes cool and aloof. "Your trunks will be delivered to the château." He bent down, picking up the bags she had set on the platform. "If you will come with me, the countess is anxious to see you."

He led her to a gleaming black sedan, assisted her into the passenger's side, and stowed her bags in the back, his manner so cold and impersonal that Serenity felt both annoyed and curious. He began to drive in silence, and she turned in her seat and examined him with open boldness.

"And how," she demanded, "are we cousins?" *What do I call him?* she wondered. *Monsieur? Christophe? Hey, you?*

"The countess's husband, your mother's father, died when your mother was a child." He began his explanation in polite, faintly bored tones, and she was tempted to tell him not to strain himself. "Several years later, the countess married my grandfather, the Comte de Kergallen, whose wife had died and left him with a son, my father." He turned his head and spared her a brief glance. "Your mother and my father were raised as brother and sister in the château. My grandfather died, my father married, lived long enough to see me born, and then promptly killed himself in a hunting accident. My mother pined for him for three years, then joined him in the family crypt."

The story had been recited in remote, unemotional tones, and the sympathy Serenity would have normally felt for the child left orphaned never materialized. She watched his hawk-like profile for another moment.

"So, that makes you the present Comte de Kergallen and my cousin through marriage."

Again, a brief, negligent glance. *"Oui."*

"I can't tell you how both facts thrill me," she stated, a definite edge of sarcasm in her tone. His brow rose once more as he turned to her, and she thought for an instant that she had detected laughter lighting the cool, dark eyes. She decided against it, positive that the man sitting next to her never laughed. "Did you know my mother?" she inquired when the silence grew.

"Oui. I was eight when she left the château."

"Why did she leave?" Serenity demanded, turning to him with direct amber eyes. He twisted his head and met them with equal directness, and she was assaulted by their power before he turned his attention back to the road.

"The countess will tell you what she wishes you to know."

"What she wishes?" Serenity sputtered, angered by the deliberate rebuff. "Let's understand each other, Cousin. I fully intend to find out exactly why my mother left Brittany, and why I've spent my life ignorant of my grandmother."

With slow, casual movements, Christophe lit a cheroot, expelling smoke lazily. "There is nothing I can tell you."

"You mean," she corrected, narrowing her eyes, "there is nothing you *will* tell me."

His broad shoulders moved in a purely Gallic shrug, and Serenity turned to stare out the front window, copying his movement with the American version, missing the slight smile which played on his mouth at her gesture.

They continued to drive in sporadic silence, with Serenity occasionally inquiring about the scenery, Christophe answering in polite monosyllables, making no effort to expand the conversation. Golden sun and pure sky might have been sufficient to soothe the disposition ruffled by the journey, but his continued coolness outbalanced nature's gift.

"For a count from Brittany," she observed with deceptive sweetness after being spared another two syllables, "you speak remarkably fine English."

Sarcasm rolled off him like a summer's breeze, and his response was lightly patronizing. "The countess also speaks English quite well, Mademoiselle. The servants, however, speak only French or Breton. If you find yourself in difficulty, you have only to ask the countess or myself for assistance."

Serenity tilted her chin and turned her rich golden eyes on him with haughty disdain. *"Ce n'est pas nécessaire,* Monsieur le Comte. *Je parle bien le français."*

One dark brow lifted in harmony with his lips. *"Bon,"* he replied in the same language. "That will make your visit less complicated."

"Is it much farther to the château?" she inquired, continuing to speak in French. She felt hot, crumpled, and tired. Due to the long trip and the time change, it seemed as if she had been in some kind of vehicle for days, and she longed for a stationary tub filled with hot, soapy water.

"We have been on Kergallen land for some time, Mademoiselle," he replied, his eyes remaining on

the winding road. "The château is not much farther."

The car had been climbing slowly to a higher
elevation. Serenity closed her eyes on the headache
which had begun to throb in her left temple, and
wished fervently that her mysterious grandmother
lived in a less complicated place, like Idaho or New
Jersey. When she opened her eyes again, all aches,
fatigue, and complaints vanished like a mist in the
hot sun.

"Stop!" she cried, reverting to English, unconsciously laying a hand on Christophe's arm.

The château stood high, proud, and solitary: an
immense stone edifice from another century with
drum towers and crenellated walls and a tiled conical roof glowing warm and gray against a cerulean-blue sky. The windows were many, high and
narrow, reflecting the diminishing sunlight with
a myriad of colors. It was ancient, arrogant, confident, and Serenity fell immediately in love.

Christophe watched the surprise and pleasure
register on her unguarded face, her hand still warm
and light on his arm. A stray curl had fallen loose
onto her forehead, and he reached out to brush it

back, catching himself before he reached her and staring at his own hand in annoyance.

Serenity was too absorbed with the château to notice his movement, already planning what angles she would use for sketches, imagining the moat that might have encircled the château at one time in the past.

"It's fabulous," she said at last, turning to her companion. Hastily, she removed her hand from his arm, wondering how it could have gotten there. "It's like something out of a fairy tale. I can almost hear the sound of trumpets, see the knights in armor, and ladies in full, floating dresses and high, pointed hats. Is there a neighborhood dragon?" She smiled at him, her face illuminated and incredibly lovely.

"Not unless one counts Marie, the cook," he answered, lowering the cool, polite wall for a moment and allowing her a quick glimpse of the wide, disarming smile which made him seem younger and approachable.

So, *he's human, after all,* she concluded. But as her pulse leaped in response to the sudden smile, she realized that when human, he was infinitely more dangerous. As their eyes met and held, she had the strange sensation of being totally alone with him, the rest of the world only a backdrop as they sat alone in private, enchanted solitude, and George-town seemed a lifetime away.

The stiffly polite stranger soon replaced the charming escort, and Christophe resumed the drive in silence, all the more thick and cold after the brief friendly interlude.

Watch it, Serenity, she cautioned herself. *Your imagination's running rampant again. This man is most definitely not for you. For some unknown reason, he doesn't even like you, and one quick smile doesn't change him from a cold, condescending aristocrat.*

Christophe pulled the car to a halt in a large, circular drive bordered by a flagstone courtyard, its low stone walls spilling over with phlox. He alighted from the car with swift, agile grace, and Serenity copied him before he had rounded the hood to assist her, so enchanted by the storybook atmosphere that she failed to note the frown which creased his brow at her action.

Taking her arm, he led her up stone steps to a massive oaken door, and, pulling a gleaming brass handle, inclined his head in a slight bow and motioned her to enter.

The entrance hall was huge. The floors were buffed to a mirrorlike shine and scattered with exquisite hand-hooked rugs. The walls were paneled, hung with tapestries, wide and colorful and incredibly old. A large hall rack and hunt table, both oak and glowing with the patina of age, oaken chairs with hand-worked seats, and the scent of fresh flowers graced the room, which seemed oddly familiar to her. It was as if she had known what to expect when she had crossed the threshold into the château, and the room seemed to recognize her, and welcome her.

"Something is wrong?" Christophe asked, noting her expression of confusion.

She shook her head with a slight shiver. *"Déjà vu,"* she murmured, and turned to him. "It's very strange; I feel as though I've stood right here before." She caught herself with a jolt of shock before she added, "with you." Letting out a deep breath, she made a restless movement with her shoulders. "It's very odd."

"So, you have brought her, Christophe."

Serenity turned away from suddenly intense brown eyes to watch her grandmother approach.

La Comtesse de Kergallen was tall and nearly as slender as Serenity. Her hair was a pure, brilliant white, lying like clouds around a sharp, angular face that defied the network of wrinkles age had bestowed on it. The eyes were clear, a piercing blue under well-arched brows, and she carried herself regally, as one who knows that more than six decades had not dimmed her beauty.

No Mother Hubbard, this, Serenity thought quickly. *This lady is a countess right down to her fingertips.*

The eyes surveyed Serenity slowly, completely, and she observed a flicker of emotion cross the angular face before it once again became impassive and guarded. The countess extended a well-shaped, ringed hand.

"Welcome to the Château Kergallen, Serenity Smith. I am Madame la Comtesse Françoise de Kergallen."

Serenity accepted the offered hand in her own, wondering whimsically if she should kiss it and curtsy. The clasp was brief and formal—no affectionate embrace, no smile of welcome. She swallowed disappointment and spoke with equal formality.

"Thank you, Madame. I am pleased to be here."

"You must be tired after your journey," the countess stated. "I will show you to your room myself. You will wish to rest before you change for dinner."

She moved to a large, curving staircase, and Serenity followed. Pausing on the landing, she glanced back to find Christophe watching her, his face creased in a brooding frown. He made no effort to smooth it away or remove his eyes from hers, and Serenity found herself turning swiftly and hurrying after the countess's retreating back.

They walked down a long, narrow corridor with brass lights set at intervals into the walls, replacing, she imagined, what would have once been torches. When the countess stopped at a door, she turned once more to Serenity, and after giving her another quick study, she opened the door and motioned her to enter.

The room was large and open, yet somehow retained an air of delicate grace. The furniture was glossy cherry, and a large four-poster canopied bed dominated the room, its silk coverlet embroidered with time-consuming stitches. A stone fireplace was set in the wall opposite the foot of the bed, its mantle carved and ornate, a collection of Dresden figures reflecting in the large framed mirror over it. One end of the room was curved and glassed, an upholstered windowseat inviting one to sit and ponder the breathtaking view.

Serenity felt the uncontrollable pull of the room, an aura of love and happiness, the gentle elegance well remembered. "This was my mother's room."

Again, the quick play of emotion flickered, like a candle caught in a draft. "*Oui.* Gaelle decorated it herself when she was sixteen."

"Thank you for giving it to me, Madame." Even the cool reply could not dispel the warmth the room brought her, and she smiled. "I shall feel very close to her during my stay."

The countess merely nodded and pressed a small button next to the bed. "Bridget will draw your bath. Your trunks will arrive shortly, and she will see to your unpacking. We dine at eight, unless you would care for some refreshment now."

"No, thank you, Countess," Serenity replied,

beginning to feel like a boarder in a very well-run hotel. "Eight will be fine."

The countess moved to the doorway. "Bridget will show you to the drawing room after you have rested. We have cocktails at seven-thirty. If there is anything you require, you have only to ring."

The door closed behind her, and Serenity took a deep breath and sat heavily on the bed.

Why did I come? she asked herself, closing her eyes on a sudden surge of loneliness. *I should have stayed in Georgetown, stayed with Tony, stayed with what I could understand. What am I searching for here?* Taking a long breath, she fought the encompassing depression and surveyed her room again. *My mother's room,* she reminded herself and felt the soothing hands of comfort. *This is something I can understand.*

Moving to the window, Serenity watched day soften into twilight, the sun flashing with final, brilliant fire before surrendering to slumber. A breeze stirred the air, and the few scattered clouds moved with it, rolling lazily across the darkening sky.

A château on a hill in Brittany. Shaking her head at the thought, she knelt on the windowseat and watched evening's nativity. *Where does Serenity Smith fit into this?* Somewhere. She frowned at the knowledge which sprang from her heart. *Somehow I belong here, or a part of me does. I felt it the moment I saw those incredible stone walls, and again when I walked into the hall.* Pushing the feeling to the depths of her brain, she concentrated on her grandmother.

She certainly wasn't overwhelmed by the reunion, Serenity decided with a rueful smile. Or perhaps it was just the European formality that made her seem so cold and distant. It hardly seems reasonable that she would ask me to come if she hadn't wanted to see me. I suppose I expected more because I wanted more. Lifting her shoulders, she allowed them to fall slowly. *Patience has never been one of my virtues, but I suppose I'd better develop it. Perhaps if my greeting at the station had been a bit more welcoming...* Her frown appeared again as she replayed Christophe's attitude.

I could swear he would have liked to bundle me back on the train the minute he set eyes on me. Then, that infuriating conversation in the car. Frown deepened into scowl, and she ceased to focus on the quiet dimness of dusk. *That is a very frustrating man,* and she added, her scowl softening into thoughtfulness, *the very epitome of a Breton count. Perhaps that's why he affected me so strongly.* Resting her chin on her palm, she recalled the awareness which had shimmered between them as they had sat alone in the lengthening shadow of the château. *He's unlike any man I've ever known: elegant and vital at the same time. There's a potency there, a virility wrapped inside the sophistication.* Power. The word flashed into her brain, drawing her brows close. *Yes,* she admitted with a reluctance she could not quite understand, *there's power there, and an essence of self-assurance.*

From an artist's standpoint, he's a remarkable study. He attracts me as an artist, she told herself, *certainly not as a woman. A woman would have to be mad to get tangled up with a man like that. Absolutely mad,* she repeated to herself firmly.

Chapter Two

The oval, free-standing gilt-framed mirror reflected a slim, fair-haired woman. The flowing, high-necked gown in a muted "ashes of roses" shade lent a glow to the creamy skin, leaving arms and shoulders bare. Serenity met the reflection's amber eyes, held them, and sighed. It was nearly time to go down and again meet her grandmother—the regal, reserved countess—and her cousin, the formal, oddly hostile count.

Her trunks had arrived while she was enjoying the bath drawn by the small, dark Breton maid. Bridget had unpacked and put away her clothes, shyly at first, then chattering and exclaiming over the articles as she hung them in the large wardrobe or folded them in the antique bureau. The simple friendliness had been a marked contrast to the attitude of those who were her family.

Serenity's attempts to rest between the cool linen sheets of the great canopied bed had been futile, all her emotions in turmoil. The strange awareness she had experienced upon entering the château, the stiff, formal welcome of her grandmother, and the strong, physical response to the remote count had all banded together to make her unaccustomedly nervous and unsure of herself. She found herself wishing again she had allowed Tony to sway her, and had remained among the things and people she knew and understood.

Letting out a deep breath, she straightened her shoulders and lifted her chin. She was not a naïve schoolgirl to be awed by castles and overdone formality, she reminded herself. She was Serenity Smith, Jonathan and Gaelle Smith's daughter, and she would hold her head up and deal with counts and countesses.

Bridget knocked softly at her door, and Serenity followed her down the narrow corridor and began her descent down the curved staircase, cloaked in confidence.

"*Bonsoir,* Mademoiselle Smith." Christophe greeted her with his usual formality as she reached the bottom landing, and Bridget made a quick, unobtrusive exit.

"*Bonsoir,* Monsieur le Comte," Serenity returned, equally ritualistic, as they once more surveyed each other closely.

The black dinner suit lent a certain Satanic appearance to his aquiline features, the dark eyes glistening to near jet-black, the skin against the black and stark white of his shirt gleaming dusky-bronze. If there were pirates in his lineage, Serenity decided, they were elegant ones—and, she concluded further, as his eyes lingered on her, probably highly successful in all aspects of piratical pursuits.

"The countess awaits us in the drawing room," he announced when he had looked his fill, and with unexpected charm, he offered her his arm.

The countess watched as they entered the room, the tall, haughty man and the slim, golden-haired woman, a perfect foil at his side. A remarkably handsome couple, she reflected, one that would cause heads to turn wherever they went. "*Bonsoir,*

Serenity, Christophe." She greeted them, regally resplendent in a gown of sapphire-blue, diamonds shooting fire from her throat. "*Mon apéritif,* Christophe, *s'il te plaît.* And for you, Serenity?"

"Vermouth, thank you, Madame," she replied, the practiced social smile on her lips.

"You rested well, I hope," the older woman inquired as Christophe handed her the small crystal glass.

"Yes, very well, Madame." She turned to accept the offered wine. "I…" The inane words she was about to utter stuck in her throat as the portrait caught her eye, and she turned around fully and faced it.

A cream-skinned, pale-haired woman looked back at her, the face the mirror image of her own. But for the length of the light gold mist of hair, falling to the shoulders, and the eyes that shone deep blue rather than amber, the portrait was Serenity: the oval face, delicate, with interesting hollows, the full, shapely mouth, the fragile, elusive beauty of her mother, reproduced in oil a quarter of a century earlier.

Her father's work—Serenity knew this immediately and unmistakably. The brush strokes, the use of color, the individual technique that shouted Jonathan Smith as surely as if she had read the small signature in the bottom corner. Her eyes filled, and she blinked back the threatening mist. Seeing the portrait had brought her parents close for a moment, and she was saturated with a deep sense of warmth and belonging that she had just been learning to live without.

She continued to study the painting, allowing herself to take in the details of her father's work, the folds of the oyster-white gown which seemed to float on a hidden breeze, the rubies at her mother's ears, a sharp contrast of color, the stone repeated in the ring on her finger. During the survey, something nagged at the back of her mind, some small detail out of place which refused to bring itself out of her consciousness, and she let it fade and merely experienced.

"Your mother was a very beautiful woman," the countess remarked after a time, and Serenity answered absently, still absorbed by the glowing look of love and happiness in her mother's eyes.

"Yes, she was. It's amazing how little she changed since my father painted this. How old was she?"

"Barely twenty," the countess replied, cultured tones edging with curtness. "You recognized your father's work quickly."

"Of course," Serenity agreed, not noticing the tones, and turning, she smiled with honest warmth. "As his daughter and a fellow artist, I recognize his work as quickly as his handwriting." Facing the portrait again, she gestured with a slim, long-fingered hand. "That was painted twenty-five years ago, and it still breathes with life, almost as if they were both right here in this room."

"Your resemblance to her is very strong," Christophe observed as he sipped his wine from his place by the mantel, capturing her attention as completely as if he had put his hands on her. "I was quite struck by it when you stepped from the train."

"But for the eyes," the countess pronounced before Serenity could form a suitable comment. "The eyes are his."

There was no mistaking the bitterness which vibrated in her voice, and narrowing the eyes under discussion, Serenity spun around, the skirt of her gown following lazily. "Yes, Madame, I have my father's eyes. Does that displease you?"

Elegant shoulders moved in dismissal, and the countess lifted her glass and sipped.

"Did my parents meet here, in the château?" Serenity demanded, patience straining. "Why did they leave and never come back? Why did they never speak to me of you?" Glancing from her grandmother to Christophe, she met two cool, expressionless faces. The countess had lifted a shield, and Serenity knew Christophe would help her maintain it. He would tell her nothing; any answers must come from the woman. She opened her mouth to speak again when she was cut off with a wave of a ringed hand.

"We will speak of it soon enough." The words were spoken like a royal decree as the countess rose from her chair. "Now, we will go in to dinner."

The dining room was massive, but Serenity had decided everything was massive in the château. High-beamed ceilings towered like those in a cathedral, and the dark wainscotted walls were broken by high windows framed with rich velvet drapes, the color of blood. A fireplace large enough to stand in commanded an entire wall, and she thought, when lit, it must be an awesome sight. A heavy chandelier gave the room its lights, its crystals trembling in a glistening rainbow of colors on the suite of dark majestic oak.

The meal began with an onion soup, thick, rich, and very French, and the trio maintained a polite conversation throughout the course. Serenity glanced at Christophe, intrigued against her will by his darkly handsome looks and haughty bearing.

He certainly doesn't like me, she concluded with a puzzled frown. *He didn't like me the moment he set eyes on me. I wonder why.* With a mental shrug, she began to eat her creamed salmon. *Perhaps he doesn't like women in general.* Looking over, his eyes met hers with a force that rivaled an electric storm, and her heart leaped suddenly, as if seeking to escape from behind her ribs. *No,* she amended quickly, tearing her eyes from his and studying the clear white wine in her glass, *he's no woman hater; those eyes are full of knowledge and experience. Tony never made me react like this.* Lifting her glass, she sipped with determination. *No one ever made me react like this.*

"Stevan," the countess commanded, "*du vin pour* Mademoiselle."

The countess's order to the hovering servant brought Serenity back from her contemplations. "*Mais non, merci. C'est bien.*"

"You speak French very well for an American, Serenity," the dowager observed. "I am grateful your education was complete, even in that barbarous country."

The disdain in the last few words was so blatant that Serenity was unsure whether to be insulted or amused by the slight on her nationality. "That 'barbarous' country, Madame," she said dryly, "is called America, and it's nearly civilized these days. Why, we go virtually weeks between Indian attacks."

The proud head lifted imperiously. "There is no need for impudence, young woman."

"Really?" Serenity asked with a guileless smile. "Strange, I was sure there was." Lifting her wineglass, she saw, to her surprise, Christophe's teeth flash white against his dark skin in a wide, quick grin.

"You may have your mother's gentle looks,"

the countess observed, "but you have your father's tongue."

"Thank you." She met the clear blue eyes with an acknowledging nod. "On both counts."

The meal concluded, the conversation was allowed to drift back into generalities. And if the interlude took on the aspect of a truce, Serenity was still floundering as to the reason for the war. They adjourned once more to the main drawing room, Christophe lounging idly in an overstuffed chair swirling his after-dinner brandy while the countess and Serenity sipped coffee from fragile china cups.

"Jean-Paul le Goff, Gaelle's fiancé, met Jonathan Smith in Paris." The countess began to speak without preamble, and Serenity's cup halted on its journey to her lips, her eyes flying to the angular face. "He was quite taken with your father's talent and commissioned him to paint Gaelle's portrait as a wedding gift."

"My mother was engaged to another man before she married my father?" Serenity asked, setting down her cup with a great deal of care.

"*Oui*. The betrothal had been understood between the families for years; Gaelle was content with the arrangement. Jean-Paul was a good man, of good background."

"It was to be an arranged marriage, then?"

The countess waved away Serenity's sense of distaste with a gesture of her hand. "It is an old custom, and as I said, Gaelle was content. Jonathan Smith's arrival at the château changed everything. Had I been more alert, I would have recognized the danger, the looks which passed between them, the blushes which rose to Gaelle's cheeks when his name was spoken."

Françoise de Kergallen sighed deeply and gazed up at the portrait of her daughter. "Never did I imagine Gaelle would break her word, disgrace the family honor. Always she was a sweet, obedient child, but your father blinded her to her duty." The blue eyes shifted from the portrait to the living image. "I had no knowledge of what had passed between them. She did not, as she had always done before, confide in me, seek my advice. The day the portrait was completed, Gaelle fainted in the garden. When I insisted on summoning a doctor, she told me there was no need—she was not ill, but with child."

The countess stopped speaking, and the silence spread like a heavy cloak through the room. "Madame," Serenity said, breaking the silence in clear, even tones, "if you are attempting to shock my sensibilities by telling me I was conceived before my parents were married, I must disappoint you. I find it irrelevant. The days of stone-throwing and branding have passed, in my country at least. My parents loved each other; whether they expressed that love before or after they exchanged vows does not concern me."

The countess sat back in her chair, laced her fingers, and studied Serenity intently. "You are very outspoken, *n'est-ce pas?*"

"Yes, I am." She gave the woman a level look. "However, I try to prevent my honesty from causing injury."

"Touché," Christophe murmured, and the arched white brows rose fractionally before the countess gave her attention back to Serenity.

"Your mother had been married a month before you were conceived." The statement was given without a change of expression. "They were married in secret in a small chapel in another village, intending to keep the knowledge to themselves until your father was able to take Gaelle to America with him."

"I see." Serenity sat back with a slight smile. "My existence brought matters into the open a bit sooner than expected. And what did you do, Madame, when you discovered your daughter married and carrying the child of an obscure artist?"

"I disowned her, told them both to leave my home. From that day, I had no daughter." The words were spoken quickly, as if to throw off a burden no longer tolerable.

A small sound of anguish escaped Serenity, and her eyes flew to Christophe only to meet a blank, brooding wall. She rose slowly, a deep ache assailing her, and turning her back on her grandmother, she faced the gentle smile in her mother's portrait.

"I'm not surprised they put you out of their lives and kept you out of mine." Whirling back, she confronted the countess, whose face remained impassive, the pallor of her cheeks the only evidence of emotion. "I'm sorry for you, Madame. You robbed yourself of great happiness. It is you who have been isolated and alone. My parents shared a deep, encompassing love, and you cloistered yourself with pride and bruised honor. She would have forgiven you; if you knew her at all, then you know that. My father would have forgiven you for her sake, for he could deny her nothing."

"Forgive me?" High color replaced the pallor, and rage shook the cultured voice. "What need I with the forgiveness of a common thief and a daughter who betrayed her heritage?"

Amber eyes grew hot, like golden flames against flushed cheeks, and Serenity shrouded her fury in frigidity. "Thief? Madame, do you say my father stole from you?"

"*Oui,* he stole from me." The answering voice was hard and steady, matching the eyes. "He was not content to steal my child, a daughter I loved more than life. He added to his loot the Raphael Madonna which had belonged to my family for generations. Both priceless, both irreplaceable, both lost to a man I foolishly welcomed into my home and trusted."

"A Raphael?" Serenity repeated, lifting a hand to her temple in confusion. "You're implying my father stole a Raphael? You must be mad."

"I imply nothing," the countess corrected, lifting her head like a queen about to pronounce sentence. "I am stating that Jonathan Smith took both Gaelle and the Madonna. He was very clever. He knew it was my intention to donate the painting to the Louvre and he offered to clean it. I trusted him." The angular face was once more a grim mask of composure. "He exploited my trust, blinded my daughter to her duty, and left the château with both my treasures."

"It's a lie!" Serenity raged, anger welling up inside her with a force of a tidal wave. "My father would never steal—never! If you lost your daughter, it was because of your own pride, your own blindness."

"And the Raphael?" The question was spoken softly, but it rang in the room and echoed from the walls.

"I have no idea what became of your Raphael." She looked from the rigid woman to the impassive man and felt very much alone. "My father didn't take it; he was not a thief. He never did one dishonest thing in his life." She began to pace the room, battling the urge to shout and shatter their wall of composure. "If you were so sure he had your precious painting, why didn't you have him arrested? Why didn't you prove it?"

"As I said, your father was very clever," the countess rejoined. "He knew I would not involve Gaelle in such a scandal, no matter how she had betrayed me. With or without my consent, he was her husband, the father of the child she carried. He was secure."

Stopping her furious pacing, Serenity turned, her face incredulous. "Do you think he married her for security? You have no conception of what they had. He loved her more than his life, more than a hundred Raphaels."

"When I found the Raphael missing," the dowager continued, as if Serenity had not spoken, "I went to your father and demanded an explanation. They were already preparing to leave. When I accused him of taking the Raphael, I saw the look which passed between them—this man I had trusted, and my own daughter. I saw that he had taken the painting, and Gaelle knew him to be a thief but would stand with him against me. She betrayed herself, her family, and her country." The speech ended on a weary whisper, a brief spasm of pain appearing on the tightly controlled face.

"You have talked of it enough tonight," Christophe stated and rose to pour a brandy from a decanter, bringing the countess the glass with a murmur in Breton.

"They did not take it." Serenity took a step closer to the countess, only to be intercepted by Christophe's hand on her arm.

"We will speak of it no more at this time."

Jerking her arm away from his hold, she emptied her fury on him. "You won't tell me when I will speak! I will not tolerate my father being branded a thief! Tell me, Monsieur le Comte, if he had taken it, where is it? What did he do with it?"

Christophe's brow lifted, and his eyes held hers, the meaning in his look all too clear. Serenity's color ebbed, then flowed back in a rush, her mouth opening helplessly, before she swallowed and spoke in calm, distinct tones.

"If I were a man, you would pay for insulting both my parents and me."

"*Alors,* Mademoiselle," he returned with a small nod, "it is my good fortune you are not."

Serenity turned from the mockery in his tone and addressed the countess, who sat watching their exchange in silence. "Madame, if you sent for me because you believed I might know of the where-abouts of your Raphael, you will be disappointed. I know nothing. In turn, I have my own disappoint-ment, because I came to you thinking to find a family tie, another bond with my mother. We must both learn to live with our disappointments."

Turning, she left the room without so much as a backward glance.

Giving the door to her bedroom a satisfactory slam, Serenity dragged her cases from the wardrobe and dropped them onto the bed. Mind whirling in near-incoherent fury, she began pulling neatly hung clothing from its sanctuary and tossing it into the mouth of the open suitcases in a colorful jumble of confusion.

"Go away!" she called out with distinct rudeness as a knock sounded on her door, then turned and spared Christophe a lethal glare as he ignored the command.

He gave her packing technique a raised-brow

study before closing the door quietly behind him. "So, Mademoiselle, you are leaving."

"Perfect deduction." She tossed a pale pink blouse atop the vivid mountain on her bed and proceeded to ignore him.

"A wise decision," he stated as she pointedly kept her back to him. "It would have been better if you had not come."

"Better?" she repeated, turning to face him as the slow, simmering rage began to boil. "Better for whom?"

"For the countess."

She advanced on him slowly, eyes narrowing as one prepared for battle, giving one brief mental oath on his advantage of height. "The countess invited me to come. Summoned," she corrected, allowing her tone to edge. "Summoned is more accurate. How dare you stand there and speak to me as if I had trampled on sacred ground! I never even knew the woman existed until her letter came, and I was blissfully happy in my ignorance."

"It would have been more prudent if the countess had left you to your bliss."

"That, Monsieur le Comte, is a brilliant example

of understatement. I'm glad you understand I could have struggled through life without ever knowing any of my Breton connections." Turning in dismissal, Serenity vented her anger on innocent clothing.

"Perhaps you will find the struggle remains simple since the acquaintance will be brief."

"You want me out, don't you?" Spinning, she felt the last thread of dignity snap. "The quicker the better. Let me tell you something, Monsieur le Comte de Kergallen, I'd rather camp on the side of the road than accept your gracious hospitality. Here." She tossed a flowing flowered skirt in his general direction. "Why don't you help me pack?"

Stooping, he retrieved the skirt and laid it on a graceful upholstered chair, his cool, composed manner infuriating Serenity all the more. "I will send Bridget to you." The astringent politeness of his tone caused Serenity to glance quickly for something more solid to hurl at him. "You do seem to require assistance."

"Don't you dare send anyone!" she shouted as he turned for the door, and he faced her again, inclining his head at the order.

"As you wish, Mademoiselle. The state of your attire is your own concern."

Detesting his unblemished formality, Serenity found herself forced to provoke him. "I'll see to my own packing, Cousin, when I decide to leave." Deliberately, she turned and lifted a garment from the heap. "Perhaps I'll change my mind and stay for a day or two, after all. I've heard the Breton countryside has much charm."

"It is your privilege to remain, Mademoiselle." Catching the faint tint of annoyance in his tone, Serenity found it imperative to smile in victory. "I would, however, not recommend it under the circumstances."

"Wouldn't you?" Her shoulders moved in a small, elegant shrug, and she tilted her face to his in provocation. "That is yet another inducement for remaining." She saw both her words and actions had touched a chord of response as his eyes darkened with anger. His expression, however, remained calm and composed, and she wondered what form his temper would take when and if he unleashed it.

"You must do as you wish, Mademoiselle." He surprised her by closing the distance between them and capturing the back of her neck with strong fingers. At the touch, she realized his temper was not as far below the surface as she had imagined. "You may, however, find your visit not as comfortable as you might like."

"I'm well able to deal with discomfort." Attempting to pull away, she found the hand held her stationary with little effort.

"Perhaps, but discomfort is not something sought by a person of intelligence." The politeness of Christophe's smile was more arrogant than a sneer, and Serenity stiffened and endeavored to draw away again. "I would have said you possessed intelligence, Mademoiselle, if not wisdom."

Determined not to surrender to slowly growing fear, Serenity kept both eyes and voice level. "My decision to go or stay is not something I need to discuss with you. I will sleep on it and make the suitable arrangements in the morning. Of course, you can always chain me to a wall in the dungeon."

"An interesting alternative." His smile became both mocking and amused, his fingers squeezing lightly before they finally released her. "I will sleep on it." He moved to the door, giving her a brief bow as he turned the knob. "And make the suitable arrangements in the morning."

Frustrated by being outmaneuvered, Serenity hurled a shoe at the panel which closed behind him.

Chapter Three

The quiet awoke Serenity. Opening her eyes, she stared without comprehension at the sun-filled room before she remembered where she was. She sat up in bed and listened. Silence, the deep, rich quality of silence, broken only by the occasional music of a bird. A quiet lacking the bustling, throbbing city noises she had known all of her life, and she decided she liked it.

The small, ornate clock on the cherry writing desk told her it was barely six, so she lay back for a moment in the luxury of elegant pillows and sheets and wallowed in laziness. Though her mind had been crowded with the facts and accusations her grandmother had disclosed, the fatigue from the long journey had taken precedence, and she had slept instantly and deeply, oddly at peace in the bed which had once been her mother's. Now, she stared up at the ceiling and ran through the previous evening again in her mind.

The countess was bitter. All the layers of practiced composure could not disguise the bitterness, or, Serenity admitted, the pain. Even through her own anger she had glimpsed the pain. Though she had banished the daughter, she had kept the portrait, and perhaps, Serenity concluded, the contradiction meant the heart was not as hard as the pride.

Christophe's attitude, however, still left her simmering. It seemed he had stood towering over her like a biased judge, ready to condemn without trial. *Well,* she determined, *I have my own share of pride, and I won't cower and shrink while my father's name is muddied, and my head put on the block. I can play the game of cold politeness, as well. I'm not running home like a wounded puppy; I'm going to stay right here.*

Gazing at the streaming sunlight, she gave a deep sigh. "*C'est un nouveau jour,* Maman," she said aloud. And, slipping from the bed, she walked over to the window. The garden spread out below her like a precious gift. "I'll go for a walk in your garden, Maman, and later I'll sketch your home." Sighing, she reached for her robe. "Then perhaps the countess and I can come to terms."

She washed and dressed quickly, choosing a pastel-printed sundress which left her arms and shoulders bare. The château remained in tranquil silence as she made her way to the main floor and stepped out into the warmth of the summer morning.

Strange, she mused, turning in a large circle. How strange not to see another building or cars or even another human being. The air was fresh and mildly scented, and she took a deep breath, consuming it before she began to circle the château on her way to the garden.

It was even more astonishing at close range than it had been from her window. Lush blooms exploded in an incredible profusion of colors, scents mixing and mingling into one exotic fragrance, at once tangy and sweet. There were a variety of paths cutting through the well-tended arrangements, smooth flagstones catching the morning sun and holding it glistening on their surface. Choosing one path at random, she strolled in idle contentment, enjoying the solitude, the artist in her reveling in the riot of hues and shapes.

"*Bonjour,* Mademoiselle." A deep voice broke the quiet, and Serenity whirled around, startled at the intrusion on her solitary contemplations. Christophe approached her slowly, tall and lean, his movements reminding her of an arrogant Russian dancer she had met at a Washington party. Graceful, confident, and very male.

"*Bonjour,* Monsieur le Comte." She did not waste a smile, but greeted him with careful cordiality. He was casually dressed in a buff-colored shirt and sleek-fitting brown jeans, and if she had felt the breeze of the buccaneer before, she was now caught in the storm.

He reached her and stared down with his habitual thorough survey. "You are an early riser. I trust you slept well."

"Very well, thank you," she returned, angry at having to battle not only animosity, but also attraction. "Your gardens are beautiful and very appealing."

"I have a fondness for what is beautiful and appealing." His eyes were direct, the dark brown smothering the amber, until she felt unable to breathe, dropping her eyes from the power of his.

"Oh, well, hello." They had been speaking in French, but at the sight of the dog at Christophe's heels, Serenity reverted back to English. "What's his name?" She crouched down to ruffle the thick, soft fur.

"Korrigan," he told her, looking down at her bent head as the sun streamed down, making a halo of pale curls.

"Korrigan," she repeated, enchanted by the dog and forgetting her annoyance with his master. "What breed is he?"

"Brittany spaniel."

Korrigan began to reciprocate her affection with tender licks on smooth cheeks. Before Christophe could command the dog to stop, Serenity laughed and buried her face against the animal's soft neck.

"I should have known. I had a dog once; it followed me home." Glancing up, she grinned as Korrigan continued to love her with a moist tongue. "Actually, I gave him a great deal of encouragement. I named him Leonardo, but my father called him

Horrible, and that's the name that stuck. No amount of washing or brushing ever improved his inherent scruffiness."

As she went to rise, Christophe extended his hand to assist her to her feet, his grasp firm and disturbing. Checking the urge to jerk away from him, she disengaged herself casually and continued her walk. Both master and dog fell into step beside her.

"Your temper has cooled, I see. I found it surprising that such a dangerous temper exists inside such a fragile shell."

"I'm afraid you're mistaken." She twisted her head, giving him a brief but level glance. "Not about the temper, but the fragility. I'm really quite sturdy and not easily dented."

"Perhaps you have not yet been dropped," he countered, and she gave her attention to a bush pregnant with roses. "You have decided to stay for a time?"

"Yes, I have," she admitted and turned to face him directly, "although I get the distinct impression you'd rather I didn't."

His shoulders moved in an eloquent shrug. "*Mais,*

non, Mademoiselle. You are welcome to remain as long as it pleases you to do so."

"Your enthusiasm overwhelms me," muttered Serenity.

"Pardon?"

"Nothing." Letting out a quick breath, she tilted her head and gave him a bold stare. "Tell me, Monsieur, do you dislike me because you think my father was a thief, or is it just me personally?"

The cool, set expression did not alter as he met her stare. "I regret to have given you such an impression. Mademoiselle, my manners must be at fault. I will attempt to be more polite."

"You're so infernally polite at times it borders on rudeness," she snapped, losing control and stomping her foot in exasperation.

"Perhaps you would find rudeness more to your taste?" His brow lifted as he regarded her temper with total nonchalance.

"Oh!" Turning away, she reached out angrily to pluck a rose. "You infuriate me! Darn!" she swore as a thorn pricked her thumb. "Now look what you made me do." Lifting her thumb to her mouth, she glared.

"My apologies," Christophe returned, a mocking light in his eyes. "That was most unkind of me."

"You are arrogant, patronizing, and stuffy," Serenity accused, tossing her curls.

"And you are bad-tempered, spoiled, and stubborn," he rejoined, narrowing his gaze and folding his arms across his chest. They stared at each other for a moment, his polite veneer slipping, allowing her a glimpse of the ruthless and exciting man beneath the coolly detached covering.

"Well, we seem to hold high opinions of each other after so short an acquaintance," she observed, smoothing back displaced curls. "If we know each other much longer, we'll be madly in love."

"An interesting conclusion, Mademoiselle." With a slight bow, he turned and headed back toward the château. Serenity felt an unexpected but tangible loss.

"Christophe," she called on impulse, wanting inexplicably to clear the air between them. He turned back, brow lifted in question, and she took a step toward him. "Can't we just be friends?"

He held her eyes for a long moment, so deep and intense a look that she felt he stripped her to the soul. "No, Serenity, I am afraid we will never just be friends."

She watched his tall, lithe figure stride away, the spaniel once more at his heels.

An hour later, Serenity joined her grandmother and Christophe at breakfast, with the countess making the usual inquiries as to how she had spent her night. The conversation was correct, if uninspired, and Serenity felt the older woman was making an effort to ease the tension brought on by the previous evening's confrontation. Perhaps, Serenity decided, it was not considered proper to squabble over croissants. *How amazingly civilized we are!* Suppressing an ironical smile, she mirrored the attitude of her companions.

"You will wish to explore the château, Serenity, *n'est-ce pas?*" Lifting her eyes as she set down the creamer, the countess stirred her coffee with a perfectly manicured hand.

"Yes, Madame, I would enjoy that," Serenity agreed with the expected smile. "I should like to make some sketches from the outside later, but I would love to see the inside first."

"*Mais, oui*. Christophe," she said, addressing the

dark man who was idly sipping his coffee, "we must escort Serenity through the château this morning."

"Nothing would give me greater pleasure, Grand-mère," he agreed, placing his cup back in its china saucer. "But I regret I shall be occupied this morning. The new bull we imported is due to arrive, and I must supervise its transport."

"Ah, the cattle," the countess sighed and moved her shoulders. "You think too much about the cattle."

It was the first spontaneous statement Serenity had noted, and she picked it up automatically. "Do you raise cattle, then?"

"Yes," Christophe confirmed, meeting her inquiring gaze. "The raising of cattle is the château's business."

"Really?" she countered with exaggerated surprise. "I didn't think the de Kergallens bothered with such mundane matters. I imagined they just sat back and counted their serfs."

His lips curved slightly and he gave a small nod. "Only once a month. Serfs do tend to be highly prolific."

She found herself laughing into his eyes. Then as

his quick, answering grin pounded a warning in her brain, she gave her attention to her own coffee.

In the end, the countess herself escorted Serenity on her tour of the rambling château, explaining some of its history as they moved from one astonishing room to another.

The château had been built in the late seventeenth century, and being in existence for just slightly less than three hundred years, it was not considered old by Breton standards. The château itself and the estates which belonged to it had been handed down from generation to generation to the oldest son, and although some modernizations had been made, it remained basically the same as it had been when the first Comte de Kergallen brought his bride over the drawbridge. To Serenity it was the essence of a lost and timeless charm, and the immediate affection and enchantment she had felt at first sight only grew with the explorations.

In the portrait gallery, she saw Christophe's dark fascination reproduced over the centuries. Though varied from generation to generation, the inveterate pride remained, the aristocratic bearing, the elusive air of mystery. She paused in front of one eighteenth-century ancestor whose resemblance was so striking that she took a step nearer to make a closer study.

"You find Jean-Claud interesting, Serenity?" the countess questioned, following her gaze. "Christophe is much like him in looks, *n'est-ce pas?*"

"Yes, it's remarkable." The eyes, she decided, were much too assured, and much too alive, and unless she were very much mistaken, the mouth had known a great many women.

"He is reputed to have been a bit, uh, *sauvage,*" she continued with a hint of admiration. "It is said smuggling was his pastime; he was a man of the sea. The story is told that once when in England, he fell enamored of a woman of that country, and not having the patience for a long, formal, old-fashioned courtship, he kidnapped her and brought her to the château. He married her, of course; she is there." She pointed to a portrait of a rose-and-cream-fleshed English girl of about twenty. "She does not look unhappy."

With this comment, she strolled down the corridor, leaving Serenity staring up at the smiling face of a kidnapped bride.

The ballroom was huge, the far wall being opened with lead-paned windows adding to the space. Another wall was entirely mirrored, reflecting the brilliant prisms of the trio of chandeliers which would throw their sparkling light like silent stars from the high-beamed ceiling. Stiff-backed Regency chairs with elegant tapestry seats were strategically arranged for those who merely wished to look on as couples whirled across the highly polished floor. She wondered if Jean-Claud had given a wedding ball for his Sabine wife, and decided he undoubtedly had.

The countess led Serenity down another narrow corridor to a set of steep stone steps, winding spiral-like to the topmost tower. Although the room they entered was bare, Serenity immediately gave a cry of pleasure, moving to its center and gazing about as though it had been filled with treasures. It was large and airy and completely circular, and the high windows which encompassed it allowed the streaming sunlight to kiss every inch of space. Without effort, she pictured herself painting here for hours in blissful solitude.

"Your father used this room as his studio," the

countess informed her, the stiffness returning to her voice, and Serenity broke off her fantasies and turned to confront her grandmother.

"Madame, if it is your wish that I remain here for a time, we must come to an understanding. If we cannot, I will have no choice but to leave." She kept her voice firm and controlled and astringently polite, but the eyes betrayed the struggle with temper. "I loved my father very much, as I did my mother. I will not tolerate the tone you use when you speak of him."

"Is it customary in your country for a young woman to address her elders in such a manner?" The regal head was held high, temper equally apparent.

"I can speak only for myself, Madame," she returned, standing straight and tall in the glow of sunlight. "And I am not of the opinion that age always equates with wisdom. Nor am I hypocrite enough to pay you lip service while you insult a man I loved and respected above all others."

"Perhaps it would be wiser if we refrained from discussing your father while you are with us." The request was an unmistakable command, and Serenity bristled with anger.

"I intend to mention him, Madame. I intend to discover precisely what became of the Raphael Madonna and clear the black mark you have put on his name."

"And how do you intend to accomplish this?"

"I don't know," she tossed back, "but I will." Pacing the room, she spread her hands unconsciously in a completely French gesture. "Maybe it's hidden in the château; maybe someone else took it." She whirled on the other woman with sudden fury. "Maybe you sold it and placed the blame on my father."

"You are insulting!" the countess returned, blue eyes leaping with fire.

"You brand my father a thief, and you say that *I* am insulting?" Serenity retorted, meeting her fire for fire. "I knew Jonathan Smith, Countess, and he was no thief, but I do not know you."

The countess regarded the furious young woman silently for several moments, blue flames dying, replaced by consideration. "That is true," she acknowledged with a nod. "You do not know me, and I do not know you. And if we are strangers, I cannot place the blame on your head. Nor can I blame you for what happened before you were born."

Moving to a window, she stared out silently. "I have not changed my opinion of your father," she said at length, and turning, she held up a hand to silence Serenity's automatic retort. "But I have not been just where his daughter is concerned. You come to my home, a stranger, at my request, and I have greeted you badly. For this much, I apologize." Her lips curved in a small smile. "If you are agreeable, we will not speak of the past until we know each other."

"Very well, Madame," Serenity agreed, sensing both request and apology were an olive branch of sorts.

"You have a soft heart to go with a strong spirit," the dowager observed, a faint hint of approval in her tone. "It is a good match. But you also have a swift temper, *n'est-ce pas?*"

"*Évidemment,*" Serenity acknowledged.

"Christophe is also given to quick outbursts of temper and black moods," the countess informed her in a sudden change of topic. "He is strong and stubborn and requires a wife of equal strength, but with a heart that is soft."

Serenity stared in confusion at her grandmother's ambiguous statement. "She has my sympathy," she began, then narrowed her eyes as a small seed of doubt began to sprout. "Madame, what have Christophe's needs to do with me?"

"He has reached the age when a man requires a wife," the countess stated simply. "And you are past the age when most Breton women are well married and raising a family."

"I am only half-Breton," she asserted, distracted for a moment. Her eyes widened in amazement. "Surely you don't…you aren't thinking that Christophe and I…? Oh, how beautifully ridiculous!" She laughed outright, a full, rich sound that echoed in the empty room. "Madame, I am sorry to disappoint you, but the count does not care for me. He didn't like me the moment he set eyes on me, and I'm forced to admit that I'm not overly fond of him, either."

"What has liking to do with it?" the countess demanded, her hands waving the words away.

Serenity's laughter stilled, and she shook her head in disbelief even as realization seeped through. "You've spoken to him of this already?"

"Oui, d'accord," the countess agreed easily.

Serenity shut her eyes, nearly swamped with humiliation and fury. "No wonder he resented me on sight—between this and thinking what he does of my father!" She turned away from her grandmother, then back again full of righteous indignation. "You overreach your bounds, Comtesse. The time of arranged marriages has long since passed."

"Poof!" It was a dismissive exclamation. "Christophe is too much his own man to agree to anything arranged by another, and I see you are too headstrong to do so. But—" a slow smile creased the angular face as Serenity looked on with wide, incredulous eyes—"you are very lovely, and Christophe is an attractive and virile man. Perhaps nature will—what is it? Take its course."

Serenity could only gape open-mouthed into the calm, inscrutable face.

"Come." The countess moved easily toward the door. "There is more for you to see."

Chapter Four

The afternoon was warm, and Serenity was simmering. Indignation had spread from her grandmother to encompass Christophe, and the more she simmered, the more it became directed at him.

Insufferable, conceited aristocrat! she fumed. Her pencil ran violently across her pad as she sketched the drum towers of the château. *I'd rather marry Attila the Hun than be bound to that stiff-necked boor!* She broke the midday hush with a short burst of laughter. *Madame is probably picturing dozens of miniature counts and countesses playing formal little games in the courtyard and growing up to carry on the imperial line in the best Breton style!*

What a lovely place to raise children, she thought, pencil pausing, and eyes softening. *It's so clean and quiet and beautiful.* A deep sigh filled the air, and she started. Then realizing that it had emitted from her own lips, she frowned furiously. *La Comtesse Serenity de Kergallen,* she said silently and frowned with more feeling. *That'll be the day!*

A movement caught her attention, and she twisted her head, squinting against the sun to watch Christophe approach. His strides were long and sure, and he crossed the lawn with an effortless rhythm of limbs and muscles. *He walks as if he owns the world,* she observed, part in admiration, part in resentment. By the time he reached her, resentment had emerged victorious.

"You!" she spat without preamble, rising from the soft tuft of grass and standing like a slender, avenging angel, gold and glowing.

His gaze narrowed at her tone, but his voice remained cool and controlled. "Something disturbs you, Mademoiselle?"

The ice in his voice only fanned the fire of anger, and dignity was abandoned. "Yes, I'm disturbed! You know very well I'm disturbed! Why in heaven's name didn't you tell me about this ludicrous idea of the countess's?"

"Ah." Brows rose, and lips curved in a sardonic smile. "*Alors,* Grandmère has informed you of the plans for our marital bliss. And when, my beloved, shall we have the banns announced?"

"You conceited..." she sputtered, unable to dream up an appropriately insulting term. "You know what you can do with your banns! I wouldn't have you on a bet!"

"*Bon,*" he replied with a nod. "Then we are at last in full agreement. I have no desire to tie myself to a wasp-tongued brat. Whoever christened you Serenity had very little foresight."

"You're the most detestable man I have ever met!" she raged, her temper a direct contrast to his cool composure. "I can't abide the sight of you."

"Then you have decided to cut your visit short and return to America?"

She tilted her chin and shook her head slowly. "Oh, no, Monsieur le Comte, I shall remain right here. I have inducements for staying which outweigh my feelings for you."

The dark eyes narrowed into slits as he studied

her face. "It would appear the countess has added a few francs to make you more agreeable."

Serenity stared at him in puzzlement until his meaning slowly seeped through, draining her color and darkening her eyes. Her hand swung out and struck him with full force in a loud, stinging slap, and then she spun on her heel and began to run toward the château. Hard hands dug into her shoulders and whirled her around, crushing her against the firm length of his body as his lips descended on hers in a brutal, punishing kiss.

The shock was electric, like a brilliant light flashed on, then extinguished. For a moment, she was limp against him, unable to surface from a darkness teeming with heat and demand. Her breath was no longer her own; she realized suddenly he was stealing even that, and she began to push at his chest, then pound with helpless, impotent fists, terrified she would be captured forever in the swirling, simmering darkness.

His arms banded around her, molding her soft slenderness to the hard, unyielding lines of his body, merging them into one passionate form. His hand slid up to cup the back of her neck with firm fingers, forcing her head to remain still, his other arm encircling her waist, maintaining absolute possession.

Her struggles slipped off him as though they were not taking place, emphasizing his superior strength and the violence which bubbled just beneath the surface. Her lips were forced apart as his mouth continued its assault, exploring hers with an intimacy without mercy or compassion. The musky scent of his maleness was assailing her senses, numbing both brain and will, and dimly she heard her grandmother describing the long-dead count with Christophe's face. *Sauvage,* she had said. *Sauvage.*

He gave her mouth its freedom, his grip returning to her shoulders as he looked down into clouded, confused eyes. For a moment, the silence hung like a shimmering wall of heat.

"Who gave you permission to do that?" she demanded unevenly, a hand reaching to her head to halt its spinning.

"It was either that or return your slap, Mademoiselle," he informed her, and from his tone and expression, she could see he had not yet completed the transformation from pirate to aristocrat. "Unfortunately, I have a reluctance to strike a woman, no matter how richly she may deserve it."

Serenity jerked away from his restraint, feeling the treacherous tears stinging, demanding release. "Next time, slap me. I'd prefer it."

"If you ever raise your hand to me again, my dear cousin, rest assured I will bruise more than your pride," he promised.

"You had it coming," she tossed back, but the temerity of her words was spoiled by wide eyes shimmering like golden pools of light. "How dare you accuse me of accepting money to stay here? Did it ever occur to you that I might *want* to know the grandmother I was denied all my life? Did you ever think that I might *want* to know the place where my parents met and fell in love? That I need to stay and prove my father's innocence?" Tears escaped and rolled down smooth cheeks, and Serenity despised each separate drop of weakness. "I only wish I could have hit you harder. What would you have done if someone had accused *you* of being bought like a side of beef?"

He watched the journey of a tear as it spilled from her eye and clung to satin skin, and a small smile tilted one corner of his mouth. "I would have beat them soundly, but I believe your tears are a more effective punishment than fists."

"I don't use tears as a weapon." She wiped at them with the back of her hand, wishing she could have stemmed the flow.

"No; they are therefore all the more potent." A long bronzed finger brushed a drop from ivory skin, the contrast of colors lending her a delicate, vulnerable appearance, and he removed his hand quickly, addressing her in a casual tone. "My words were unjust, and I apologize. We have both received our punishment, so now we are—how do you say?—quits."

He gave her his rare, charming smile, and she stared at him, drawn by its power and enchanted by the positive change it lent to his appearance. Her own smile answered, the sudden shining of the sun through a veil of rain. He made a small, impatient sound, as though he regretted the momentary lapse, and nodding, he turned on his heel and strode away, leaving Serenity staring after him.

During the evening meal, the conversation was once more strictly conventional, as if the astonishing conversation in the tower room and the tempestuous encounter on the château grounds had not taken place. Serenity marveled at the composure of her companions as they carried on a light umbrella of table talk over *langoustes à la crème*. If it had not been for the fact that her lips still felt the imprint, she would have sworn she had imagined the stormy, breathtaking kiss Christophe had planted there. It had been a kiss which had stirred some deep inner feeling of response and had jolted her cool detachment more than she cared to admit.

It meant nothing, she insisted silently and applied herself to the succulent lobster on her plate. She'd been kissed before and she would be kissed again. She would not allow any moody tyrant to give her one more moment's concern. Deciding to resume her role in the game of casual formality, she sipped from her glass and made a comment on the character of the wine.

"You find it agreeable?" Christophe picked up the trend of conversation in an equally light tone. "It is the château's own Muscadet. We produce a small quantity each year for our own enjoyment and for the immediate vicinity."

"I find it very agreeable," Serenity commented. "How exciting to enjoy wine made from your own vineyards. I've never tasted anything quite like it."

"The Muscadet is the only wine produced in Brittany," the countess informed Serenity with a smile. "We are primarily a province of the sea and lace."

Serenity ran a finger over the snowy-white cloth that adorned the oak table. "Brittany lace, it's exquisite. It looks so fragile, yet years only increase the beauty."

"Like a woman," Christophe murmured, and Serenity lifted her eyes to meet his dark regard.

"But then, there are also the cattle." She grabbed at the topic to cover momentary confusion.

"Ah, the cattle." His lips curved, and Serenity had the uncomfortable impression that he was well aware of his effect on her.

"Having lived in the city all my life, I'm totally ignorant when it comes to cattle." She floundered on, more and more disconcerted by the directness of his eyes. "I'm sure they make quite a picture grazing in the fields."

"We must introduce you to the Breton countryside," the countess declared, drawing Serenity's attention. "Perhaps you would care to ride out to-morrow and view the estate?"

"I would enjoy that, Madame. I'm sure it will be a pleasant change from sidewalks and government buildings."

"I would be pleased to escort you, Serenity," Christophe offered, surprising her. Turning back to him, her expression mirrored her thoughts. He smiled and inclined his head. "Do you have the suitable attire?"

"Suitable attire?" she repeated, surprise melting into confusion.

"But yes." He appeared to be enjoying her chang-ing expressions, and his smile spread. "Your taste in clothing is impeccable, but you would find it dif-ficult to ride a horse in a gown like that."

Her gaze lowered to the gently flowing lines of her willow-green dress before rising to his amused glance. "Horse?" she said, frowning.

"You cannot tour the estate in an automobile, *ma petite*. The horse is more adaptable."

At his laughing eyes, she straightened and drew out her dignity. "I'm afraid I don't ride."

"C'est impossible!" the countess exclaimed in disbelief. "Gaelle was a marvelous horsewoman."

"Perhaps equestrian abilities are not genetic, Madame," Serenity suggested, amused by her grandmother's incredulous expression. "I am no horsewoman at all. I can't control a merry-go-round pony."

"I will teach you." Christophe's words were a statement rather than a request, and she turned to him, amusement fading into hauteur.

"How kind of you to offer, Monsieur, but I have no desire to learn. Do not trouble yourself."

"Nevertheless," he stated and lifted his wineglass, "you shall. You will be ready at nine o'clock, *n'est-ce pas?* You will have your first lesson."

She glared at him, astonished by his arbitrary dismissal of her refusal. "I just told you…"

"Try to be punctual, *chérie,*" he warned with deceptive laziness as he rose from the table. "You will find it more comfortable to walk to the stables than to be dragged by your golden hair." He smiled as if the latter prospect held great appeal for him. "*Bonne nuit,* Grandmère," he added with affection before he disappeared from the room, leaving Serenity fuming, and his grandmother unashamedly pleased.

"Of all the insufferable nerve!" she sputtered when she located her voice. Turning angry eyes on the other woman, she added defiantly, "If he thinks I'm going to meekly obey and…"

"You would be wise to obey, meekly or otherwise," the dowager interrupted. "Once Christophe has set his mind…" With a small, meaningful shrug, she left the rest of the sentence to Serenity's imagination. "You have slacks, I presume. Bridget will bring you a pair of your mother's riding boots in the morning."

"Madame," Serenity began slowly, as if attempting to make each word understood, "I have no intention of getting on a horse in the morning."

"Do not be foolish child." A slender, ringed hand reached negligently for a wineglass. "He is more than capable of carrying out his threat. Christophe is a very stubborn man." She smiled, and for the first time Serenity felt genuine warmth. "Perhaps even more stubborn than you."

Muttering strong oaths, Serenity pulled on the sturdy boots that had been her mother's. They had been cleaned and polished to a glossy black shine and fit her small feet as if custom-made for them.

It seems even you are conspiring against me, Maman, she silently chided her mother in despair. Then she called out a casual *"Entrez"* as a knock sounded on her door. It was not the little maid, Bridget, who opened the door, however, but Christophe, dressed with insouciant elegance in fawn riding breeches and a white linen shirt.

"What do you want?" she asked with a scowl, pulling on the second boot with a firm tug.

"Merely to see if you are indeed punctual, Serenity," he returned with an easy smile, his eyes roaming over her mutinous face and the slim, supple body clad in a silkscreen-printed T-shirt and French tailored jeans.

Wishing he would not always look at her as if memorizing each feature, she rose in defense. "I'm ready, Captain Bligh, but I'm afraid you won't find me a very apt pupil."

"That remains to be seen, *ma chérie.*" His eyes swept over her again, as if considering. "You seem to be quite capable of following a few simple instructions."

Her eyes narrowed into jeweled slits, and she struggled with the temper he had a habit of provoking. "I am reasonably intelligent, thank you, but I don't like being bulldozed."

"Pardon?" His blank expression brought out a smug smile.

"I shall have to recall a great many colloquialisms, Cousin. Perhaps I can slowly drive you mad."

Serenity accompanied Christophe to the stables in haughty silence, determinedly lengthening her strides to match his gait and preventing the necessity of trailing after him like an obedient puppy. When they reached the outbuilding, a groom emerged leading two horses, bridled and saddled in anticipation. One was full black and gleaming, the other a creamy buckskin, and to Serenity's apprehensive eyes, both were impossibly large.

She halted suddenly and eyed the pair with a dubious frown. *He wouldn't really drag me by the hair,* she thought carefully. "If I just turned around and walked away, what would you do about it?" Serenity inquired aloud.

"I would only bring you back, *ma petite*." The

dark brow rose at her deepening frown, revealing he had already anticipated her question.

"The black is obviously yours, Comte," she concluded in a light voice, struggling to control a mounting panic. "I can already picture you gallop-ing over the countryside in the light of a full moon, the gleam of a saber at your hip."

"You are very astute, Mademoiselle." He nodded, and taking the buckskin's reins from the groom, he walked the mount toward her. She took an involun-tary step back and swallowed.

"I suppose you want me to get on him."

"Her," he corrected, mouth curving.

She flashed at him, angry and nervous and disgusted with her own apprehension. "I'm not really concerned about its sex." Looking over the quiet horse, she swallowed again. "She's…she's very large." Her voice was fathoms weaker than she had hoped.

"Babette is as gentle as Korrigan," Christophe as-sured her in unexpectedly patient tones. "You like dogs, *n'est-ce pas?*"

"Yes, but…"

"She is soft, no?" He took her hand and lifted it to

Babette's smooth cheek. "She has a good heart and wishes only to please."

Her hand was captured between the smooth flesh of the horse and the hard insistence of Christophe's palm, and she found the combination oddly enjoyable. Relaxing, she allowed him to guide her hand over the mare and twisted her head, smiling over her shoulder.

"She feels nice," she began, but as the mare blew from wide nostrils, she jumped nervously and stumbled back against Christophe's chest.

"Relax, *chérie*." He chuckled softly, his arms encircling her waist to steady her. "She is only telling you that she likes you."

"It just startled me," Serenity returned in defense, disgusted with herself, and decided it was now or never. She turned to tell him she was ready to begin, but found herself staring wordlessly into dark, enigmatic eyes as his arms remained around her.

She felt her heart stop its steady rhythm, remaining motionless for a stifling moment, then race sporadically at a wild pace. For an instant, she believed he would kiss her again, and to her own astonishment and confusion, she realized she wanted to feel his lips on hers above all else. A frown creased his brow suddenly, and he released her in a sharp gesture.

"We will begin." Cool and controlled, he stepped effortlessly into the role of instructor.

Pride took over, and Serenity became determined to be a star pupil. Swallowing her anxiety, she allowed Christophe to assist her in mounting. With some surprise, she noted that the ground was not as far away as she had anticipated, and she gave her full attention to Christophe's instructions. She did as he bade, concentrating on following his directions precisely, determined not to make a fool of herself again.

Serenity watched Christophe mount his stallion with a fluid grace and economy of movement she envied. The spirited black suited the dark, haughty man to perfection, and she reflected, with some distress, that not even Tony at his most ardent had ever affected her the way this strange, remote man did with his enveloping stares.

She couldn't be attracted to him, she argued fiercely. He was much too unpredictable, and she realized, with a flash of insight, that he could hurt her as no man had been able to hurt her before. *Besides,* she thought, frowning at the buckskin's mane, *I don't like his superior, dominating attitude.*

"Have you decided to take a short nap, Serenity?" Christophe's mocking voice brought her back with a snap, and meeting his laughing eyes, she felt herself flush to her undying consternation. *"Allons-y, chérie."* Her deepening color was noted with a curve of his lips, as he directed his horse away from the stables and proceeded at a slow walk.

They moved side by side, and after several moments Serenity found herself relaxing in the saddle. She passed Christophe's instructions on to the mare, which responded with smooth obedience. Confidence grew, and she allowed herself to view the scenery, enjoying the caress of the sun on her face and the gentle rhythm of the horse under her.

"Maintenant, we trot," Christophe commanded suddenly, and Serenity twisted her head to regard him seriously.

"Perhaps my French is not as good as I supposed. Did you say trot?"

"Your French is fine, Serenity."

"I'm quite content to amble along," she returned with a careless shrug. "I'm in no hurry at all."

"You must move with the jogging of the horse," he instructed, ignoring her statement. "Rise with every other jog. Press gently with your heels."

"Now, listen…"

"Afraid?" he taunted, his brow lifting high in mockery. Before common sense could overtake pride, Serenity tossed her head and pressed her heels against the horse's side.

This must be what it feels like to operate one of those damnable jackhammers they're forever tearing up the streets with, she thought breathlessly, bouncing without grace on the trotting mare.

"Rise with every other jog," Christophe reminded her, and she was too preoccupied with her own predicament to observe the wide grin which accompanied his words. After a few more awkward moments, she caught onto the timing.

"Comment ça va?" he inquired as they moved side by side along the dirt path.

"Well, now that my bones have stopped rattling, it's not so bad. Actually"—she turned and smiled at him—"it's fun."

"*Bon*. Now we canter," he said simply, and she sent him a withering glance.

"Really, Christophe, if you want to murder me, why not try something simpler like poison, or a nice clean stab in the back?"

He threw back his head and laughed, a full, rich sound that filled the quiet morning, echoing on the breeze. When he turned his head and smiled at her, Serenity felt the world tilt, and her heart, ignoring the warnings of her brain, was lost.

"*Allons, ma brave*." His voice was light, carefree, and contagious. "Press in your heels, and I will teach you to fly."

Her feet obeyed automatically, and the mare responded, quickening her gate to a smooth, easy canter. The wind played with Serenity's hair and brushed her cheeks with cool fingers. She felt as though she were riding on a cloud, unsure whether the lightness was a result of the rush of wind or the dizziness of love. Enthralled with the novelty of both, she did not care.

At Christophe's command, she drew back on the reins, slowing the mare from a canter to a trot to a walk before finally coming to a halt. Lifting her face to the sky, she gave a deep sigh of pleasure before turning to her companion. The wind and excitement had whipped a rose blush onto her cheeks, her eyes were wide, golden, and bright, and her hair was tousled, an unruly halo around her happiness.

"You enjoyed yourself, Mademoiselle?"

She flashed him a brilliant smile, still intoxicated with love's potent wine. "Go ahead; say 'I told you so.' It's perfectly all right."

"*Mais non, chérie,* it is merely a pleasure to see one's pupil progress with such speed and ability." He returned her smile, the invisible barrier between them vanishing. "You move naturally in the saddle; perhaps the talent is genetic, after all."

"Oh, Monsieur." She fluttered her lashes over a gleam of mischief. "I must give the credit to my teacher."

"Your French blood is showing, Serenity, but your technique needs practice."

"Not so good, huh?" Pushing back disheveled hair, she gave a deep sigh. "I suppose I'll never get it right. Too much American Puritan from my father's ancestors."

"Puritan?" Christophe's full laugh once more disturbed the quiet morning. "*Chérie,* no Puritan was ever so full of fire."

"I shall take that as a compliment, though I sincerely doubt it was intended as one." Turning her head, she looked down from the hilltop to the spreading valley below. "Oh, how beautiful."

A scene from a postcard slumbered in the distance, gentle hills dotted with grazing cattle against a backdrop of neat cottages. Farther in the distance, she observed a tiny village, a small toy town set down by a giant hand, dominated by a white church, its spire reaching heavenward.

"It's perfect," she decided. "Like slipping back in time." Her eyes roamed back to the grazing cattle. "Those are yours?" she asked, gesturing with her hand.

"*Oui,*" he asserted.

"This is all your property, then?" she asked again, feeling a sudden sinking sensation.

"This is part of the estates." He answered with a careless movement of his shoulders.

We've been riding for so long, she thought with a frown, *and we're still on his land. Lord knows how far it spreads in other directions. Why can't he be an ordinary man?* Turning her head, she studied his hawklike profile. *But he is not an ordinary man,* she reminded herself. *He is the Comte de Kergallen, master of all he surveys, and I must remember that.* Her gaze moved back to the valley, her frown deepening. *I don't want to be in love with him.* Swallowing the sudden dryness of her throat, she used her words as a defense against her heart.

"How wonderful to possess so much beauty."

He turned to her, brow raising at her tone. "One cannot possess beauty, Serenity, merely care for and cherish it."

She fought against the warmth his soft words aroused, keeping her eyes glued to the valley. "Really? I was under the impression that young aristocrats took such things for granted." She made a wide, sweeping gesture. "After all, this is only your due."

"You have no liking for aristocracy, Serenity, but you have aristocratic blood, as well." Her blank look brought a slow smile to his chiseled features, and his tone was cool. "Yes, your mother's father was a count, though his estates were ravaged during the war. The Raphael was one of the few treasures your grandmother salvaged when she escaped."

The damnable Raphael again! Serenity thought dismally. He was angry; she determined this from the hard light in his eyes, and she found herself oddly pleased. It would be easier to control her feelings for him if they remained at odds with each other.

"So, that makes me half-peasant, half-aristocrat," she retorted, moving her slim shoulders in dismissal. "Well, *mon cher cousin,* I much prefer the peasant half myself. I'll leave the blue blood in the family to you."

"You would do well to remember there is no blood between us, Mademoiselle." Christophe's voice was low, and meeting his narrowed eyes, Serenity felt a trickle of fear. "The de Kergallens are notorious for taking what they want, and I am no exception. Take care how you use your brandy eyes."

"The warning is unnecessary, Monsieur. I can take care of myself."

He smiled, a slow, confident smile, more unnerving than a furious retort, and turned his mount back toward the château.

The return ride was accomplished in silence, broken only by Christophe's occasional instructions. They had crossed swords again, and Serenity was forced to admit he had parried her thrust easily.

When they reached the stables, Christophe dismounted with his usual grace, handing the reins to a groom and moving to assist her before she could copy his action.

Defiantly, she ignored the stiffness in her limbs as she eased herself from the mare's back and Christophe's hands encircled her waist. They remained around her for a moment, and he brooded down at her before releasing the hold that seemed to burn through the light material of her shirt.

"Go have a hot bath," he ordered. "It will ease the stiffness you are undoubtedly feeling."

"You have an amazing capacity for issuing orders, Monsieur."

His eyes narrowed before his arm went around her with incredible speed, pulling her close and crushing her lips in a hard, thorough kiss that left no time for struggle or protest, but drew a response as easily as a hand turning a water tap.

For an eternity he kept her the prisoner of his will,

plunging her deeper and deeper into the kiss. Its bruising intensity released a new and primitive need in her, and abandoning pride for love, she surrendered to demands she could not conquer. The world evaporated, the soft Breton landscape melting like a watercolor left out in the rain, leaving nothing but warm flesh and lips which sought her surrender. His hand ran over the slim curve of her hip, then up her spine with sure authority, crushing her against him with a force which would have cracked her bones had they not already dissolved in the heat.

Love. Her mind whirled with the word. Love was walks in soft rain, a quiet evening beside a crackling fire. How could it be a throbbing, turbulent storm which left you weak and breathless and vulnerable? How could it be that one would crave the weakness as much as life itself? Was this how it had been for Maman? Was this what put the dreamy mists of knowledge in her eyes? *Will he never set me free?* she wondered desperately, and her arms encircled his neck, body contradicting will.

"Mademoiselle," he murmured with soft mockery, keeping his mouth a breath from hers, his fingers teasing the nape of her neck, "you have an amazing capacity for provoking punishment. I find the need to discipline you imperative."

Releasing her, he turned and strode carelessly away, stopping to acknowledge the greeting of Korrigan, who trotted faithfully at his heels.

Chapter Five

Serenity and the countess shared their lunch on the terrace, surrounded by sweet-smelling blossoms. Refusing the offered wine, Serenity requested coffee instead, enduring the raised white brow with tranquil indifference.

I suppose this makes me an undoubted Philistine, she concluded, suppressing a smile as she enjoyed the strong black liquid along with the elegant shrimp bisque.

"I trust you found your ride enjoyable," the countess stated after they had exchanged comments on the food and weather.

"To my utter amazement, Madame," Serenity admitted, "I did. I only wished I had learned long ago. Your Breton scenery is magnificent."

"Christophe is justifiably proud of his land," the countess asserted, studying the pale wine in her glass. "He loves it as a man loves a woman, an intense sort of passion. And though the land is eternal, a man needs a wife. The earth is a cold lover."

Serenity's brows rose at her grandmother's frankness, the sudden abandonment of formality. Her shoulders moved in a faintly Gallic gesture. "I'm sure Christophe has little trouble finding warm ones." *He probably merely snaps his fingers and dozens tumble into his arms,* she added silently, almost wincing at the fierce stab of jealousy.

"Naturellement," the countess agreed, a glimmer of amusement lighting up her eyes. "How could it be otherwise?" Serenity digested this with a scowl, and the dowager lifted her wineglass. "But men like Christophe require constancy rather than variety after a time. Ah, but he is so like his grandfather." Looking over quickly, Serenity saw the soft expression transform the angular face. "They are wild, these Kergallen men, dominant and arrogantly masculine. The women who are given their love

are blessed with both heaven and hell." Blue eyes focused on amber once more and smiled. "Their women must be strong or be trampled beneath them, and they must be wise enough to know when to be weak."

Serenity had been listening to her grandmother's words as if under a spell. Shaking herself, she pushed back the plate of shrimp for which her appetite had fled. "Madame," she began, determined to make her position clear, "I have no intention of entering into the competition for the present count. As I see it, we are incredibly ill matched." She recalled suddenly the feel of his lips against hers, the demanding pressure of his hard body, and she trembled. Raising her eyes to her grandmother's, she shook her head in fierce denial. "No." She did not stop to reason if she was speaking to her heart or the woman across from her, but stood and hurried back into the château.

The full moon had risen high in the star-studded sky, its silver light streaming through the high windows as Serenity awoke, miserable, sore, and disgusted. Though she had retired early, latching on to the inspiration of a fictitious headache to separate herself from the man who clouded her thoughts, sleep had not come easily. Now, just a few short hours since she had captured it, it had escaped. Turning in the oversized bed, she moaned aloud at her body's revolt.

I'm paying the price for this morning's little adventure. She winced and sat up with a deep sigh. *Perhaps I need another hot bath,* she decided with dim hope. *Lord knows it couldn't make me any stiffer.* She eased herself from the mattress, legs and shoulders protesting violently. Ignoring the robe at the foot of the bed, she made her way across the dimly lit room toward the adjoining bath, banging her shin smartly against an elegant Louis XVI chair.

She swore, torn between anger and pain. Still muttering, she nursed her leg, pulling the chair back into position and leaning on it. "What?" she called out rudely as a knock sounded on her door.

It swung open, and Christophe, dressed casually in a robe of royal-blue silk, stood observing her. "Have you injured yourself, Serenity?" It was not necessary to see his expression to be aware of his mockery.

"Just a broken leg," she snapped. "Pray, don't trouble yourself."

"May one inquire as to why you are groping about in the dark?" He leaned against the doorframe, cool, calm, and in total command, his arrogance all the catalyst Serenity's mercurial temper required.

"I'll tell you why I'm groping about in the dark, you smug, self-assured beast!" she began, her voice a furious whisper. "I was going to drown myself in the tub to put myself out of the misery you inflicted on me today!"

"I?" he said innocently, his eyes roaming over her, slim and golden in the shimmering moonlight, her long, shapely legs and pure alabaster-toned skin exposed by the briefness of her flimsy nightdress. She was too angry to be aware of her dishabille or his appreciation, oblivious to the moonlight which seeped through the sheerness of her gown and left her curves delectably shadowed.

"Yes, you!" she shot back at him. "It was you who got me up on that horse this morning, wasn't it? And now each individual muscle in my body despises me." Groaning, she rubbed her palm against the small of her back. "I may never walk properly again."

"Ah."

"Oh, what a wealth of meaning in a single syllable." She glared at him, doing her best to stand with some dignity. "Could you do it again?"

"Ma pauvre petite," he murmured in exaggerated sympathy. *"Je suis désolé."* He straightened and began to move toward her. Then, suddenly recalling her state of dress, her eyes grew wide.

"Christophe, I..." she began as his hands descended on her bare shoulders, but the words ended in a sigh as his fingers massaged the strain.

"You have discovered new muscles, yes? And they are not being agreeable. It will not be so difficult the next time." He led her to the bed and pressed her shoulders so that she sat, unresisting, savoring the firm movements on her neck and shoulders. Easing down behind her, his long fingers continued down her back, kneading away the ache as if by magic.

She sighed again, unconsciously moving against him. "You have wonderful hands," she murmured, a blessed lethargy seeping into her as the soreness disappeared and a warm contentment took its place. "Marvelous strong fingers; I'll be purring any minute."

She was not aware when the transition occurred, when the gentle relaxation became a slow kindling in her stomach, his objective massage an insistent caress, but she felt her head suddenly spinning with the heat.

"That's better, much better," she faltered and made to move away, but his hands went quickly to her waist, holding her immobile as his lips sought the soft vulnerability of her neck in a gentle feather of a kiss. She trembled, then started like a frightened doe, but before she could escape, he had twisted her to face him, his lips descending in possession on hers, stilling all protests.

Struggle died before it became a reality, the kindling erupting into a burst of flame, and her arms encircled his neck as she was pressed against the mattress. His mouth seemed to devour hers, hard and assured, and his hands followed the curves of her body as if he had made love to her countless times. Impatiently, he pushed aside the thin strap on her shoulder, seeking and finding the satin smoothness of her breast, his touch inciting a tempest of desire, and she began to move under him. His demands became more urgent, his hands more insistent as they moved down the whisper of silk, his lips leaving hers to assault her neck with an insatiable hunger.

"Christophe," she moaned, knowing she was incapable of combating both him and her own weakness. "Christophe, please, I can't fight you here. I could never win."

"Do not fight me, *ma belle,*" he whispered into her neck. "And we shall both win."

His mouth took hers again, soft and lingering, causing desire to swell, then soar. Slowly, his lips explored her face, brushing along the hollows of her cheeks, teasing the vulnerability of parted lips before moving on to other conquests. A hand cupped her breast in lazy possession, fingers tracing its curve, tarrying over the nipple until a dull, throbbing ache spread through her. The sweet, weakening pain brought a moan, and her hands began to seek the rippling muscles of his back, as if to accentuate his power over her.

His lazy explorations altered to urgency once

more, as if her submission had fanned the fires of his own passions. Hands bruised soft flesh, and her mouth was savaged by his, the teeth which had nibbled along her bottom lip replaced by a mouth which ravaged her senses, and demanded more than surrender, but equal passion.

The hand left her breast to run down her side, pausing over her hip before he continued on, claiming the smooth, fresh skin of her thigh, and her breath came only in shuddering sighs as his lips moved lower along her throat to taste the warm hollow between her breasts.

With one final flash of lucidity, she knew she stood on the edge of a precipice, and one more step would plunge her into an everlasting void.

"Christophe, please." She began to tremble, though nearly suffocating with the heat. "Please, you frighten me, I frighten me. I've never…I've never been with a man before."

His movements stopped, and the silence became thick as he lifted his face and stared down at her. Slivers of moonlight slept on her pale hair, tousled on the snowy pillow, her eyes smoky with awakened passion and fear.

With a short, harsh sound, he lifted his weight from her. "Your timing, Serenity, is incredible."

"I'm sorry," she began, sitting up.

"For what do you apologize?" he demanded, anger just below the surface of icy calm. "For your innocence, or for allowing me to come very close to claiming it?"

"That's a rotten thing to say!" she snapped, fighting to steady her breathing. "This happened so quickly, I couldn't think. If I had been prepared, you would never have come so close."

"You think not?" He dragged her up until she was kneeling on the surface of the bed, once more molded against him. "You are prepared now. Do you think I could not take you this minute with you more than willing to allow it?"

He glared down at her, the air around him tingling with assurance and fury, and she could say nothing, knowing she was helpless against his authority and her own surging need. Her eyes were huge in her pale face, fear and innocence shining like beacons, and he swore and pushed her away.

"*Nom de Dieu!* You look at me with the eyes of a child. Your body disguises your innocence well; it is a dangerous masquerade." Moving to the door, he turned back to survey the lightly clad form made small by the vastness of the bed. "Sleep well, *mignonne*," he said with a touch of mockery. "The next time you choose to run into the furniture, it would be wise if you lock your door; I will not walk away again."

Serenity's cool greeting to Christophe over breakfast was returned in kind, his eyes meeting hers briefly, showing no trace of the passion or anger they had held the previous night. Perversely, she was annoyed at his lack of reaction as he chatted with the countess, addressing Serenity only when necessary, and then with a strict politeness which could be detected only by the most sensitive ear.

"You have not forgotten Geneviève and Yves are dining with us this evening?" the countess asked Christophe.

"*Mais non,* Grandmère," he assured her, replacing his cup in its saucer. "It is always a pleasure to see them."

"I believe you will find them pleasant company, Serenity." The countess turned her clear blue eyes on her granddaughter. "Geneviève is very close to your age, perhaps a year younger, a very sweet, well-mannered young woman. Her brother, Yves, is very charming and quite attractive." A smile was born on her lips. "You will find his company, uh, *diverting.* Do you not agree, Christophe?"

"I am sure Serenity will find Yves highly entertaining."

Serenity glanced over quickly at Christophe. Was there a touch of briskness to his tone? He was sipping his coffee calmly, and she decided she had been mistaken.

"The Dejots are old family friends," the countess went on, drawing Serenity's attention back to her. "I am sure you will find it pleasant to have company near your own age, *n'est-ce pas?* Geneviève is often a visitor to the château. As a child she trotted after Christophe like a faithful puppy. *Bien sûr,* she is not a child any longer." She threw a meaningful glance at the man at the head of the long oak table, and Serenity used great willpower not to wrinkle her nose in disdain.

"Geneviève grew from an awkward pigtailed child into an elegant, lovely woman," Christophe replied, and the affection in his voice was unmistakable.

Good for her, Serenity thought, struggling to keep an interested smile in place.

"She will make a marvelous wife," the countess predicted. "She has a quiet beauty and natural grace. We must persuade her to play for you, Serenity. She is a highly skilled pianist."

Chalk up one more for the paragon of virtue, Serenity brooded to herself silently, miserably jealous of the absent Geneviève's relationship with Christophe. Aloud, she said, "I shall look forward to meeting your friends, Madame." Silently, she assured herself that she would dislike the perfect Geneviève on sight.

The golden morning passed quietly, a lazy mid-morning hush falling over the garden as Serenity sketched. She had exchanged a few words with the gardener before they had both settled down to their respective tasks. Finding him an interesting study, she sketched him as he bent over the bushes, trimming the overblown blossoms and chattering, scolding and praising his colorful, scented friends.

His face was timeless, weathered and lined with

character, unexpectedly bright blue eyes shining against a ruddy complexion. The hat covering his shock of steel-gray hair was black, a wide, flat-brimmed cap with velvet ribbons streaming down the back. He wore a sleeveless vest and aged knickers, and she marveled at his agility in the wooden *sabots*.

So deep was her concentration on capturing his Old World aura with her pencil that she failed to hear the footsteps on the flagstones behind her. Christophe watched her for some moments as she bent over her work, the graceful curve of her neck calling to his mind an image of a proud white swan floating on a cool, clear lake. Only when she tucked her pencil behind her ear and brushed an absent hand through her hair did he make his presence known.

"You have captured Jacques admirably, Serenity." His brow rose in amusement at the startled jump she made and the hand that flew to her heart.

"I didn't know you were there," she said, cursing the breathlessness of her voice and the pounding of her pulse.

"You were deep in your work," he explained, casually sitting next to her on the white marble bench. "I did not wish to disturb you."

Ho, she amended silently, *you'd disturb me if you were a thousand miles away.* Aloud, she spoke politely: "*Merci.* You are most considerate." In defense, she turned her attention to the spaniel at their feet. "Ah, Korrigan, *comment ça va?*" She scratched behind his ear, and he licked her hand with loving kisses.

"Korrigan is quite taken with you," Christophe remarked, watching the long, tapering fingers being bathed. "He is normally much more reserved, but it appears you have captured his heart." Korrigan collapsed in an adoring heap over her feet.

"A very sloppy lover," she remarked, holding out her hand.

"A small price to pay, *ma belle,* for such devotion."

He drew a handkerchief from his pocket, captured her hand, and began to dry it. The effect on Serenity was violent. Sharp currents vibrated from the tips of her fingers and up her arm, spreading a tingling heat through her body.

"That's not necessary. I have a rag right here." She indicated her case of chalks and pencils and attempted to pull her hand away from his.

His eyes narrowed, his grip increasing, and she found herself outmatched in the short, silent struggle. With a sigh of angry exasperation, she allowed her hand to lay limp in his.

"Do you always get your own way?" she demanded, eyes darkening with suppressed fury.

"Bien sûr," he replied with irritating confidence, releasing her now-dry hand and giving her a long, measuring look. "I feel you are also used to having your own way, Serenity Smith. Will it not be interesting to see who, how do you say, 'comes out on top' during your visit?"

"Perhaps we should put up a scoreboard," she suggested, retreating behind the armor of frigidity. "Then there would be no doubt as to who comes out on top."

He gave her a slow, lazy smile. "There will be no doubt, *cousine.*"

Her retort was cut off by the appearance of the countess, and Serenity automatically smoothed her features into relaxed lines to avoid the other woman's speculation.

"Good morning, my children." The countess greeted them with a maternal smile that surprised her granddaughter. "You are enjoying the beauty of the garden. I find it at its most peaceful at this time of day."

"It's lovely, Madame," Serenity concurred. "One feels there is no other world beyond the colors and scents of this one solitary spot."

"I have often felt that way." The angular lines softened. "The hours I have spent here over the years are uncountable." She seated herself on a bench across from the dark man and fair-skinned woman and sighed. "What have you drawn?" Serenity offered her pad, and the countess studied the drawing before raising her eyes to study the woman in turn. "You have your father's talent." At the grudging admission, Serenity's eyes sharpened, and her mouth opened to retort. "Your father was a very talented artist," the countess continued. "And I begin to see he had some quality of goodness to have earned Gaelle's love and your loyalty."

"Yes, Madame," Serenity replied, realizing she had been awarded a difficult concession. "He was a very good man, both a constant loving father and husband."

She resisted the urge to bring up the Raphael,

unwilling to break the tenuous threads of understanding being woven. The countess nodded. Then, turning to Christophe, she made a comment about the evening's dinner party.

Picking up drawing paper and chalks Serenity began idly to draw her grandmother. The voices hummed around her, soothing, peaceful sounds suited to the garden's atmosphere. She did not attempt to follow the conversation, merely allowing the murmuring voices to wash over her as she began to concentrate on her work with more intensity.

In duplicating the fine-boned face and the surprisingly vulnerable mouth, she saw more clearly the countess's resemblance to her mother, and so, in fact, to herself. The countess's expression was relaxed, an ageless beauty that instinctively held itself proud. But somehow now, Serenity saw a glimpse of her mother's softness and fragility, the face of a woman who would love deeply—and therefore be hurt deeply. For the first time since she had received the formal letter from her unknown grandmother, Serenity felt a stirring of kinship, the first trickle of love for the woman who had borne her mother, and so had been responsible for her own existence.

Serenity was unaware of the variety of expressions flitting across her face, or of the man who sat beside her, observing the metamorphosis while he carried on his conversation. When she had finished, she lay down her chalks and wiped her hands absently, starting when she turned her head and encountered Christophe's direct stare. His eyes dropped to the portrait in her lap before coming back to her bemused eyes.

"You have a rare gift, *ma chérie*," he murmured. And she frowned in puzzlement, unsure from his tone whether he was speaking of her work or something entirely different.

"What have you drawn?" the countess inquired. Serenity tore her eyes from his compelling regard and handed her grandmother the portrait.

The countess studied it for several moments, the first expression of surprise fading into something Serenity could not comprehend. When the eyes rose and rested on her, the face altered with a smile.

"I am honored and flattered. If you would permit me, I would like to purchase this." The smile increased. "Partly for my vanity, but also because I would like a sample of your work."

Serenity watched her for a moment, hovering on the line between pride and love. "I'm sorry, Madame." She shook her head and took the drawing. "I cannot sell it." She glanced down at the paper in her hand before handing it back and meeting the blue eyes. "It is a gift for you, Grandmère." She watched the play of emotion move both mouth and eyes before speaking again. "Do you accept?"

"Oui." The word came on a sigh. "I shall treasure your gift, and this"—she looked down once more at the chalk portrait—"shall be my reminder that one should never allow pride to stand in the way of love." She rose and touched her lips to Serenity's cheeks before she moved down the flagstone path toward the château.

Standing, Serenity moved away from the bench. "You have a natural ability to invite love," Christophe observed, and she rounded on him, her emotions highly tuned.

"She's my grandmother, too."

He noted the veil of tears shimmering in her eyes and rose to his feet in an easy movement. "My statement was a compliment."

"Really? I thought it a condemnation." Despising

the mist in her eyes, she wanted both to be alone and to lean against his broad shoulder.

"You are always on the defensive with me, are you not, Serenity?" His eyes narrowed as they did when he was angry, but she was too involved with battling her own emotions to care.

"You've given me plenty of cause," she tossed back. "From the moment I stepped off the train, you made your feelings clear. You'd condemned both my father and me. You're cold and autocratic and without a bit of compassion or understanding. I wish you'd go away and leave me alone. Go flog some peasants or something; it suits you."

He moved so quickly that she had no chance to back away, his arms nearly splitting her in two as they banded around her. "Are you afraid?" he demanded, and his lips crushed hers before she could answer, and all reason was blotted out.

She moaned against the pain and pleasure his mouth inflicted, going limp as his hold increased, conquering even her breath.

How is it possible to hate and love at the same time? her heart demanded of her numbed brain, but the answer was lost in a flood of turbulent, triumphant passion. Fingers tangled ruthlessly in her hair, pulling her head back to expose the creamy length of her neck, and he claimed the vulnerable skin with a mouth hot and hungry. The thinness of her blouse was no defense against the sultry heat of his body, but he disposed of the brief barrier, his hand sliding under, then up along her flesh to claim the swell of her breast with a consummate and absolute possession.

His mouth returned to ravage hers, bruising softness with a demand she could not deny. No longer did she question the complexity of her love, but yielded like a willow in a storm to the entreatment of her own needs.

He lifted his face, and his eyes were dark, the fires of anger and passion burning them to black. He wanted her, and her eyes grew wide and terrified at the knowledge. No one had ever wanted her this intensely, and no one had ever possessed the power to take her this effortlessly. For even without his love, she knew she would submit, and even without her submission, he would take.

He read the fear in her eyes, and his voice was low and dangerous. "*Oui, petite cousine,* you have cause to be afraid, for you know what will be. You are safe for the moment, but take care how and where you provoke me again."

Releasing her, he walked easily up the path his grandmother had chosen, and Korrigan bounded up, sent Serenity an apologetic glance, and then followed close on his master's heels.

Chapter Six

Serenity dressed with great care for dinner that evening, using the time to put her feelings in order and decide on a plan of action. No amount of arguments or reasoning could alter the fact that she had plunged headlong into love with a man she had known only a few days, a man who was as terrifying as he was exciting.

An arrogant, domineering, audaciously stubborn man, she added, pulling up the zipper at the back of her dress. And one who had condemned her father as a thief. *How could I let this happen?* she berated herself. *How could I have prevented it?* she reflected with a sigh. *My heart may have deserted me, but my head is still*

*on my shoulders, and I'm going to have to use it. I refuse
to allow Christophe to see that I've fallen in love with him
and subject myself to his mockery.*

Seated at the cherrywood vanity, she ran a brush
through soft curls and touched up her light ap-
plication of makeup. War paint, she decided, and
grinned at the reflection. *It fits; I'd rather be at war
with him than in love. Besides*—the grin turned into a
frown—*there is also Mademoiselle Dejot to contend with
tonight.*

Standing, she surveyed her full reflection in the
free-standing mirror. The amber silk echoed the
color of her eyes and added a warm glow to her
creamy skin. Thin straps revealed smooth shoulders,
and the low, rounded bodice teased the subtle curve
of breast. The knife-pleated skirt floated gently to
her ankles, the filminess and muted color adding to
her fragile, ethereal beauty.

She frowned at the effect, seeing fragility when
she had desired poise and sophistication. The clock
informed her that there was no time to alter gowns,
so slipping on shoes and spraying a cloud of scent
around her, she hurried from the room.

The murmur of voices emitting from the main

drawing room made Serenity realize, to her irritation, that the dinner guests had already arrived. Her artist's eye immediately sketched the tableau which greeted her as she entered the room: the gleaming floor and warm polished paneling, the high, lead-paned windows, the immense stone fireplace with the carved mantel—all set the perfect backdrop for the elegant inhabitants of the château's drawing room, with the countess the undisputed queen in regal red silk.

The severe black of Christophe's dinner suit threw the snow-white of his shirt into relief and accented the tawny color of his skin. Yves Dejot was also in black, his skin more gold than bronze, his hair an unexpected chestnut. But it was the woman between the two dark men who caught both Serenity's eye and reluctant admiration. If her grandmother was the queen, here was the crown princess. Jet-black hair framed a small, elfin face of poignant beauty. Almond-shaped eyes of pansy-brown dominated the engaging face, and the gown of forest-green glowed against the rich golden skin.

Both men rose as she entered the room, and Serenity gave her attention to the stranger, all too aware of Christophe's habitual all-encompassing survey. As introductions were made, she found herself looking into chestnut eyes, the same shade as his hair, which held undeniable masculine approval and an unmistakable light of mischief.

"You did not tell me, *mon ami,* that your cousin was a golden goddess." He bent over Serenity's fingers, brushing them with his lips. "I shall have to visit the château more often, Mademoiselle, during your stay."

She smiled with honest enjoyment, summing up Yves Dejot as both charming and harmless. "I am sure my stay will be all the more enjoyable with that prospect in mind, Monsieur," she responded, matching his tone, and she was rewarded with a flashing smile.

Christophe continued his introductions, and Serenity's hand was clasped in a small, hesitant grip. "I am so happy to meet you at last, Mademoiselle Smith." Geneviève greeted her with a warm smile. "You are so like your mother's portrait, it is like seeing the painting come to life."

The voice was sincere, and Serenity concluded that no matter how hard she tried, it would be impossible to dislike the pixielike woman who gazed at her with the liquid eyes of a cocker spaniel.

The conversation continued light and pleasant throughout *apéritifs* and dinner, delectable oysters in champagne setting the mood for an elegantly prepared and served meal. The Dejots were curious about America and Serenity's life in its capital, and she attempted to describe the city of contrasts as the small group enjoyed *le ris de veau au Chablis.*

She began to draw a picture with words of stately old government buildings, the graceful lines and columns of the White House. "Unfortunately, there has been a great deal of modernization, with huge steel and glass monstrosities replacing some of the old buildings. Neat, vast, and charmless. But there are dozens of theatres, from Ford's, where Lincoln was assassinated, to the Kennedy Center."

Continuing, she took them from the stunning elegance of Embassy Row to the slums and tenements outside the federal enclave, through museums and galleries and the bustle of Capitol Hill.

"But we lived in Georgetown, and this is a world apart from the rest of Washington. Most of the homes are row houses or semi-detached, two or three stories, with small bricked-in yards edged with azaleas and flowerbeds. Some of the side streets are still cobblestoned, and it still retains a rather old-fashioned charm."

"Such an exciting city," Geneviève commented. "You must find our life here very quiet. Do you miss the animation, the activity of your home?"

Serenity frowned into her wineglass, then shook her head, "No," she answered, somewhat surprised by her own admission. "That's strange, I suppose." She met the brown eyes across from her. "I spent my entire life there, and I was very happy, but I don't miss it at all. I had the strangest feeling of affinity when I first walked into the château, a feeling of recognition. I've been very content here."

Glancing over, she found Christophe's eyes on her, brooding and penetrating, and she felt a quick surge of panic. "Of course, it's a relief not to enter into the daily contest for a parking space," she added with a smile, attempting to shake off the mood of seriousness. "Parking spaces are more precious than gold in Washington, and behind the wheel even the most mild-mannered person would commit murder and mayhem to obtain one."

"Have you resorted to such tactics, *ma chérie?*" Christophe asked. Raising his wineglass, he kept his eyes on her.

"I shudder to think of my crimes," she answered, relieved by the light turn of topic. "I dare not confess what lengths I've gone to in order to secure a few feet of empty space. I can be terribly aggressive."

"It is not possible to believe that aggression is a quality of such a delicate willow," Yves declared, blanketing her in his charming smile.

"You would be surprised, *mon ami,*" Christophe commented with an inclination of his head. "The willow has many unexpected qualities."

Serenity continued to frown at him as the countess skillfully changed the subject.

The drawing room was gently lit, lending an air of intimacy to the vast room. As the group enjoyed after-dinner coffee and brandy, Yves seated himself next to Serenity and began dispensing his abundant supply of Gallic charm. She noted, with a great deal of discomfort around her heart, which she was forced to recognize as pure, honest jealousy, that Christophe devoted himself to entertaining Geneviève. They spoke of her parents, who were touring the Greek islands, of mutual acquaintances and old friends. He listened attentively as Geneviève related an anecdote, flattered, laughed, teased, his attitude being one of overall gentleness, a softness Serenity had not seen in him before. Their relationship was so obviously special, so close and long standing, that Serenity felt a swift pang of despair.

He treats her as though she were made of fine, delicate crystal, small and precious, and he treats me as though I were made of stone, sturdy, strong, and dull.

It would have been infinitely easier if Serenity could have disliked the other woman, but natural friendliness overcame jealousy, and as time went by, she found herself liking both Dejots more and more.

Geneviève consented, after some gentle prompting by the countess, to play a few selections on the piano. The music floated through the room as sweet and fragile as its mistress.

I suppose she's perfect for him, Serenity concluded dismally. *They have so much in common, and she brings out a tenderness in him that will keep him from hurting her.* She glanced over to where Christophe sat, relaxed against the cushions of the sofa, his dark, fascinating eyes fixed on the woman at the piano. A swift variety of emotions ran through her—longing, despair, resentment, settling into a hopeless fog of depression as she realized no matter how perfect Geneviève might be for him, she could never happily watch Christophe court another woman.

"As an artist, Mademoiselle," Yves began as the music ended and conversation resumed, "you require inspiration, *n'est-ce pas?*"

"Of one kind or another," she agreed and smiled at him.

"The gardens of the château are immensely inspirational in the moonlight," he pointed out with an answering smile.

"I am in the mood for inspiration," she decided on quick impulse. "Perhaps I could impose on you to escort me."

"Mademoiselle," he answered happily, "I would be honored."

Yves informed the rest of the party of their intention, and Serenity accepted his proffered arm without seeing the dark look thrown at her by the remaining male member.

The garden was indeed an inspiration, the brilliance of colors muted in the silver shimmer of moonlight. The scents intertwined into a heady perfume, mellowing the warm summer evening into a night for lovers. She sighed as her thoughts strayed back to the man in the château's drawing room.

"You sigh from pleasure, Mademoiselle?" Yves questioned as they strolled down a winding path.

"Bien sûr," she answered lightly, shaking off her somber mood and granting her escort one of her best smiles. "I'm overcome by the overwhelming beauty."

"Ah, Mademoiselle." He lifted her hand to his lips and kissed it with much feeling. "The beauty of each blossom pales before yours. What rose could compare with such lips, or gardenia with such skin?"

"How do French men learn to make love with words?"

"It is taught from the cradle, Mademoiselle," he informed her with suspicious sobriety.

"How difficult for a woman to resist such a setting." Serenity took a deep, consuming breath. "A moonlit garden outside a Breton château, the air filled with perfume, a handsome man with poetry on his lips."

"Hélas!" Yves gave a heavy sigh. "I fear you will find the strength to do so."

She shook her head with mock sorrow. "I am unfortunately extremely strong, and you," she added with a grin, "are a charming Breton wolf."

His laughter broke the night's stillness. "Ah, already you know me too well. If it were not for the feeling I had when we met that we were destined to be friends and not lovers, I would pursue my campaign with more feeling. But, we Bretons are great believers in destiny."

"And it is so difficult to be both friends and lovers."

"Mais, oui."

"Then friends it shall be," Serenity stated, extending her hand. "I shall call you Yves, and you shall call me Serenity."

He accepted her hand and held it a moment. *"C'est extraordinaire* that I should be content with friendship with one like you. You possess an elusive beauty that locks into a man's mind and keeps him constantly aware of you." His shoulders moved in a Gallic shrug which said more than a three-hour speech. "Well, such is life," he remarked fatalistically. Serenity was still laughing when they re-entered the château.

The following morning, Serenity accompanied her grandmother and Christophe to Mass in the village she had viewed from the hilltop. A light, insistent rain had begun during the pre-dawn hours, its soft hissing against her window awakening her until its steady rhythm had lulled her back to sleep.

The rain continued as they drove to the village, drenching leaves and causing flowers in the cottage's neat garden to droop heavy-headed, lending them an air of a colorful congregation at prayer. She had noticed, with some puzzlement, that Christophe had maintained a strange silence since the previous evening. The Dejots had departed soon after Serenity and Yves had rejoined the group in the drawing room, and though Christophe's farewells to his guests were faultlessly charming, he had avoided addressing Serenity directly. The only communication between them had been a brief—and, she had imagined—forbidding glance, quickly veiled.

Now, he spoke almost exclusively to the countess, with occasional comments or replies made directly to Serenity, polite, with a barely discernible hostility which she decided to ignore.

The focal point of the small village was the chapel, a tiny white structure with its neatly trimmed grounds an almost humorous contrast to its slightly apologetic, crumbling state. The roof had had more than one recent repair, and the single oak door at the entrance was weathered and battered from age and constant use.

"Christophe has offered to have a new chapel built," the countess commented. "But the villagers will not have it. This is where their fathers and grandfathers have worshipped for centuries, and they will continue to worship here until it crumbles about their ears."

"It's charming," Serenity decided, for somehow the tiny chapel's faintly dilapidated air gave it a certain steadfast dignity, a sense of pride at having witnessed generations of christenings, weddings, and funerals.

The door groaned in apology as Christophe opened it, allowing the two women to precede him.

The interior was dark and quiet, the high-beamed ceiling adding an illusion of space. The countess glided to the front pew, taking her place in the seats which had been reserved for the Château Kergallen for nearly three centuries. Spying Yves and Geneviève across the narrow aisle, Serenity threw them both a full smile and was rewarded with an answering one from Geneviève and a barely discernible wink from Yves.

"This is hardly the proper setting for your flirtations, Serenity," Christophe whispered in her ear as he assisted her out of her damp trenchcoat.

Her color rose, making her feel like a child caught giggling in the sacristy, and she turned her head to retort as the priest, who seemed as old as the chapel, approached the altar, and the service began.

A feeling of peace drifted over her like a soft, down-filled quilt. The rain insulated the congregation from the outside, its soft whispering on the roof adding to the quiet rather than detracting from it. The low drone of Breton from the ancient priest, and the light rumble of response, an occasional whimper from an infant, a muffled cough, the dark stained glass with rivulets of rain running down its surface—all combined into a quiet timelessness. Sitting in the well-worn pew, Serenity felt the chapel's magic and understood the villagers' refusal to give up the crumbling building for a more substantial structure, for here was peace, and the serenity for which she had been named. A continuity with the past, and a link with the future.

As the service ended, so did the rain, and a vague beam of sunlight filtered through the stained glass, introducing a subtle, elusive glow. When they emerged outside, the air was fresh, sparkling from the clean scent of rain. Drops still clung to the newly washed leaves, glistening like tears against the bright green surfaces.

Yves greeted Serenity with a courtly bow and a lingering kiss on the fingers. "You have brought out the sun, Serenity."

"Mais, oui," she agreed, smiling into his eyes. "I have ordered all my days in Brittany to be bright and sunny."

Removing her hand, she smiled at Geneviève, who resembled a dainty primrose in a cool yellow dress and narrow-brimmed hat. Greetings were exchanged, and Yves leaned down toward Serenity like a conspirator.

"Perhaps you would care to take advantage of the sunshine, *chérie,* and come for a drive with me. The countryside is exquisite after a rain."

"I'm afraid Serenity will be occupied today," Christophe answered before she could accept or decline, and she glared at him. "Your second lesson," he said smoothly, ignoring the battle lights in her amber eyes.

"Lesson?" Yves repeated with a crooked smile. "What are you teaching your lovely cousin, Christophe?"

"Horsemanship," he responded with a like smile, "at the moment."

"Ah, you could not find a finer instructor," Geneviève observed with a light touch on Christophe's arm. "Christophe taught me to ride when Yves and my father had given me up as hopelessly inadequate. You are so patient." Her cocker spaniel eyes gazed up at the lean man, and Serenity stifled an incredulous laugh.

Patient was the last word she would use to describe Christophe. Arrogant, demanding, autocratic, overconfident—she began silently listing qualities she attributed to the man at her side. Cynical and overbearing, also. Her attention wandered from the conversation, her gaze lighting on a small girl sitting on a patch of grass with a frisky black puppy. The dog was alternately bathing the child's face with enthusiastic kisses and running in frantic circles around her as the child's high, sweet laughter floated on the air. It was such a relaxing, innocent picture that it took Serenity a few extra seconds to react to what happened next.

The dog suddenly darted across the grass toward the road, and the child scrambled up, dashing after it, calling the dog's name in stern disapproval. Serenity watched without reaction as a car approached. Then a cold draft of fear overtook her as she observed the child's continuing flight toward the road.

Without thought, she streaked in pursuit, frantically calling in Breton for the child to stop, but the girl's attention was riveted on her pet, and she rushed over the grass, stepping out in the path of the oncoming car.

Serenity heard the squeal of breaks as her arms wrapped around the child, and she felt the rush of wind and slight bump of the fender against her side as she hurled both herself and the girl across the road, landing in a tangled heap on its surface. There was absolute silence for a split-second, and then pandemonium broke loose as the puppy, which Serenity was now sitting on rather heavily, yelped in rude objection, and the child's loud wails for her mother joined the animal's indignation.

Suddenly, excited voices in a mixture of languages joined the wailing and yelping, adding to Serenity's dazed, befuddled state. She could find no strength to remove her weight from the errant puppy, and the girl struggled from her now-limp grasp and ran into the arms of her pale, tearful mother.

Strong, hard arms lifted Serenity to her feet, holding her shoulders and tilting back her head so that she met Christophe's dark, stormy eyes. "Are you hurt?" When she shook her head, he continued in a tight, angry voice: "*Nom de Dieu!* You must be mad!" He shook her slightly, increasing the dizziness. "You could have been killed! How you missed being struck is a miracle."

"They were playing so sweetly," she recalled in a vague voice. "Then that silly dog goes tearing off into the street. Oh, I wonder if I hurt it; I sat right on it. I don't think the poor animal liked it."

"Serenity." Christophe's furious voice and the vigorous shaking brought her attention back to him. "*Mon Dieu!* I begin to believe you really are mad!"

"Sorry," she murmured, feeling empty and light-headed. "Silly to think of the dog first and the child later. Is she all right?"

He let out a soft stream of curses on a long breath. "*Oui,* she is with her mother. You moved like a cheetah; otherwise, both of you would not be standing up babbling now."

"Adrenaline," she muttered and swayed. "It's gone now."

His grip increased on her shoulders as he surveyed her face. "You are going to faint?" The question was accompanied by a deep frown.

"Certainly not," she replied, attempting to sound firm and dignified, but succeeding in a rather wavering denial.

"Serenity." Geneviève reached her, taking her hand and abandoning formality. "That was so brave." Tears swam in the brown eyes, and she kissed both of Serenity's pale cheeks.

"Are you hurt?" Yves echoed Christophe's question, his eyes concerned rather than angry.

"No, no, I'm fine," she assured him, unconsciously leaning on Christophe for support. "The puppy got the worst of it when I landed on it." *I just want to sit down,* she thought wearily, *until the world stops spinning.*

Suddenly, she found herself being addressed in rapid, tearful Breton by the child's mother. The words were slurred with emotion, and the dialect was so thick she had difficulty following the stream of conversation. The woman continually wiped brimming eyes with a wrinkled ball of handkerchief, and Serenity made what she hoped were the correct responses, feeling incredibly tired and faintly embarrassed as the mother's hands grabbed and kissed with fervent gratitude. At a low order from Christophe, they were relinquished, and she retreated, gathering up her child and melting away into the crowd.

"Come." He slipped an arm around Serenity's waist, and the mass of people parted like the waves of the Red Sea as he led her back toward the chapel. "I think both you and the mongrel should be put on a short leash."

"How kind of you to lump us together," she muttered, then caught sight of her grandmother sitting on a small stone bench, looking pale and suddenly old.

"I thought you would be killed," the countess stated in a thick voice, and Serenity knelt in front of her.

"I'm quite indestructible, Grandmère," she claimed with a confident smile. "I inherited it from both sides of my family."

The thin, bony hand gripped Serenity's tightly. "You are very impudent and stubborn," the countess declared in a firmer voice. "And I love you very much."

"I love you, too," Serenity said simply.

Chapter Seven

Serenity insisted on receiving her riding lesson after the midday meal, vetoing both the suggested prescription of a long rest and the prospect of summoning a doctor.

"I don't need a doctor, Grandmère, and I don't need a rest. I'm perfectly all right." She shrugged aside the morning's incident. "A few bumps and bruises; I told you I'm indestructible."

"You are stubborn," the countess corrected, and Serenity merely smiled and shrugged again.

"You have had a frightening experience," Christophe inserted, studying her with critical eyes. "A less strenuous activity would be more suitable."

"For heaven's sake, not you, too!" She pushed away her coffee impatiently. "I'm not some mid-Victorian weakling who subsides into fits of vapors and needs to be coddled. If you don't want to take me riding, I'll call Yves and accept his invitation for the drive which you refused for me." Her fine-boned face was set, and her chin lifted. "I am not going to go to bed in the middle of the day like a child."

"Very well." Christophe's eyes darkened. "You will have your ride, though perhaps your lesson will not be as stimulating as what Yves intended."

She stared at him for a moment in bewilderment before color seeped into her cheeks. "Oh, really, what a ridiculous thing to say."

"I will meet you at the stables in half an hour." He interrupted her protestations, rose from the table, and strode from the room before she could formulate a suitable rebuttal.

Turning to her grandmother, her face was a picture of indignation. "Why is he so insufferably rude to me?"

The countess's slim shoulders moved expressively,

and she looked wise. "Men are complicated crea-
tures, *chérie.*"

"One day," Serenity predicted with an ominous
frown, "one day he's not going to walk away until
I've had my say."

Serenity met Christophe at the appointed time,
determined to focus every ounce of energy into de-
veloping the proper riding technique. She mounted
the mare with concentrated confidence, then followed her silent instructor as he pointed his horse
in the opposite direction from that which they had
taken on their last outing. When he broke into a
light canter, she copied his action, and she experienced the same intoxicating freedom as she had
before. There was, however, no sudden, exciting
flash of smile on his features, no laughter or teasing words, and she told herself she was better off
without them. He called out an occasional instruc-
tion, and she obeyed immediately, needing to prove
both to him and herself that she was capable. So,
she contented herself with the task of riding and an
infrequent glance at his dark, hawklike profile.

Lord help me, she sighed in defeat, taking her eyes

from him and staring straight ahead. *He's going to haunt me for the rest of my life. I'll end up a crotchety old maid, comparing every man I see to the one I couldn't have. I wish to God I'd never laid eyes on him.*

"Pardon?" Christophe's voice broke into her silent meditations, and she started, realizing she must have muttered something aloud.

"Nothing," she stammered, "it was nothing." Taking a deep breath, she frowned. "I could swear I smell the sea." He slowed his mount to a walk, and she reined in beside him as a faint rumble broke the silence. "Is that thunder?" She gazed up into a clear blue sky, but the rumble continued. "It *is* the sea!" she exclaimed, all animosity forgotten. "Are we near it? Will I be able to see it?" He merely halted his horse and dismounted. "Christophe, for heaven's sake!" She watched in exasperation as he tied his mount's reins to a tree. "Christophe!" she repeated, struggling from the saddle with more speed than grace. He took her arm as she landed awkwardly and tied her mount beside his before leading her farther down the path. "Choose whatever language you like," she invited magnanimously, "but talk to me before I go crazy!"

He stopped, turned, and drew her close, covering her mouth with a brief, distracting kiss. "You talk too much," he stated simply and continued on his way.

"Really," she began, but subsided when he turned and looked down at her again. Satisfied with her silence, he led her on, the distant rumbling growing nearer and more insistent. When he stopped again, Serenity caught her breath at the scene below.

The sea stretched as far as she could see, the sun's rays dancing on its deep green surface. The surf rolled in to caress the rocks, its foam resembling frothy lace on a deep velvet gown. Teasingly, it flowed back from the shore, only to roll back like a coquettish lover.

"It's marvelous," she sighed, reveling in the sharp salt-sprayed air and the breeze which ruffled her hair. "I suppose you must be used to this by now; I doubt I ever could be."

"I always enjoy looking at the sea," he answered, his eyes focused on the distant horizon, where the clear blue sky kissed the deep green. "It has many moods; perhaps that is why the fishermen call it a woman. Today she is calm and gentle, but when she is angry, her temper is a magnificent thing to see."

His hand slid down her arm to clasp her in a simple, intimate gesture she had not expected from him, and her heart did a series of somersaults. "When I was a boy, I thought to run away to the sea, live my life on the water, and sail with her moods." His thumb rubbed against the tender skin of her palm, and she swallowed before she could speak.

"Why didn't you?"

His shoulders moved, and she wondered for a moment if he remembered she was there. "I discovered that the land has its own magic—vivid-colored grass, rich soil, purple grapes, and grazing cattle. Riding a horse over the long stretches of land is as exciting as sailing over the waves of the sea. The land is my duty, my pleasure, and my destiny."

He looked down into the amber eyes, fixed wide and open on his face, and something passed between them, shimmering and expanding until Serenity felt submerged by its power. Then, she was crushed against him, the wind swirling around them like ribbons to bind them closer as his mouth demanded an absolute surrender. She clung to him as the roar of the sea swelled to a deafening pitch, and suddenly she was straining against him and demanding more.

If the mood of the sea was calm and gentle, his did not mirror it. Helpless against her own need, she reveled in the savage possession of his mouth, the urgent insistence of the hands which claimed her, as if by right. Trembling, not with fear, but with the longing to give, she pressed yet closer, willing him to take what she offered.

His mouth lifted once, briefly, and she shook her head against the liberation, pulling his face back to hers, lips begging for the merging. Her fingers dug into the flesh of his shoulders at the force of the new embrace, his mouth seeking hers with a new hunger, as if he would taste her or starve. His hand slipped under the silk of her blouse to claim the breast which ached for his touch, the warmth of his fingers searing like glowing embers against her skin, and though her mouth was conquered, his tongue demanding the intimacy of velvet moisture, her mind murmured his name over and over until there was nothing else.

Arms banded around her again, hands abandoning their explorations, and breath flew away and was forgotten in the new, crushing power. Soft breasts pressed against the hard leanness of his chest, thigh straining against thigh, heart pounding against heart, and Serenity knew she had taken the step from the precipice and would never return to the solidity of earth.

He released her so abruptly, she would have stumbled had his hand not gripped her arm to steady her. "We must go back," he stated as if the moment had never been. "It grows late."

Her hands reached up to push the tumbled curls from her face, her eyes lifting to his, wide and full of confused pleading. "Christophe." She said his name on a whisper, unable to form any other sound, and he stared down at her, the brooding look familiar and, as always, unfathomable.

"It grows late, Serenity," he repeated, and the underlying anger in his tone brought only more bewilderment.

Suddenly cold, her arms wrapped around her body to ward off the chill. "Christophe, why are you angry with me? I haven't done anything wrong."

"Haven't you?" His eyes narrowed and darkened

with familiar temper, and through the ache of rejection, her own rose to meet it.

"No. What could I do to you? You're so infuriatingly superior, up there on your little golden throne. A partial aristocrat like myself could hardly climb up to your level to cause any damage."

"Your tongue will cause you endless trouble, Serenity, unless you learn to control it." His voice was precise and much too controlled, but Serenity found discretion buried under a growing mountain of fury.

"Well, until I choose to do so, perhaps I'll use it to tell you precisely what I think about your arrogant, autocratic, domineering, and infuriating attitude toward life in general, and myself in particular."

"A woman," he began, in a voice she noted was entirely too soft and too silky, "with your temperament, *ma petite cousine,* must be continually shown there is only one master." He took her arm in a firm hold and turned away from the sea. "I said we will go."

"*You,* Monsieur," she returned, holding her

ground and sending him a look of smoldering amber, "can go whenever you want."

Her exit of furious dignity took her three feet before her shoulders were captured in a viselike grip, then whirled around to face a fury which made her own temper seem tranquil. "You cause me to think again about the wisdom of beating a woman." His mouth took hers swiftly, hard and more punishing than a fist, and Serenity felt a quick surge of pain, tasting only anger on his lips, and no desire. Fingers dug into her shoulders, but she allowed herself neither struggle nor response, remaining passive in his arms as courage fled into hopelessness.

Set free, she stared up at him, detesting the veil of moistness which clouded her eyes. "You have the advantage, Christophe, and will always win a physical battle." Her voice was calm and carefully toned, and she watched his brows draw close, as if her reaction puzzled him. His hand lifted to brush at a drop which had escaped to flow down her cheek, and she jerked away, wiping it away herself and blinking the rest back.

"I've had my quota of humiliations for one day, and I will not dissolve into a pool of tears for your benefit." Her voice became firmer as she gained control, and her shoulders straightened as Christophe watched the transformation in silence. "As you said, it's getting late." Turning, she walked back up the path to where the horses waited.

The days passed quietly, soft summer days filled with the sun and the sweet perfume of flowers. Serenity devoted most of the daylight hours to painting, reproducing the proud, indomitable lines of the château on canvas. She had noted, at first with despair and then with increasing anger, Christophe's calculated avoidance of her. Since the afternoon when they had stood on the cliff above the sea, he had barely spoken to her, and then only with astringent politeness. Pride soon covered her hurt like a bandage over an open wound, and painting became a refuge against longing.

The countess never mentioned the Raphael, and Serenity was content for the time to drift, wanting to strengthen the bond between them before delving further into its disappearance and the accusation against her father.

She was immersed in her work, clad in faded

jeans and a paint-splattered smock, her hair disheveled by her own hand, when she spotted Geneviève approaching across the smooth carpet of lawn. A beautiful Breton fairy, Serenity imagined, small and lovely in a buff-colored riding jacket and dark brown breeches.

"*Bonjour,* Serenity," she called out when Serenity raised a slim hand in greeting. "I hope I am not disturbing you."

"Of course not. It's good to see you." The words came easily because she meant them, and she smiled and put down her brush.

"Oh, but I have made you stop," Geneviève began in apology.

"You've given me a marvelous excuse to stop," she corrected.

"May I see?" Geneviève requested. "Or do you not like your work viewed before it is finished?"

"Of course you may see. Tell me what you think."

She moved around to stand beside Serenity. The background was completed: the azure sky, lamb's-wool clouds, vivid green grass, and stately trees. The château itself was taking shape gradually: the gray walls glowing pearly in the sunlight, high glistening windows, the drum towers. There was much left to complete, but even in its infancy, the painting captured the fairy-tale aura Serenity had envisioned.

"I have always loved the château," Geneviève stated, her eyes still on the canvas. "Now I see you do, as well." Pansy eyes lifted from the half-completed painting and sought Serenity's. "You have captured its warmth, as well as its arrogance. I am glad to know you see it as I do."

"I fell in love with it the first moment I saw it," Serenity admitted. "The longer I stay, the more hopelessly I'm lost." She sighed, knowing her words described the man, as well as his home.

"You are lucky to have such a gift. I hope you will not think less of me if I confess something."

"No, of course not," Serenity assured her, both surprised and intrigued.

"I am terribly envious of you," she blurted out quickly, as if courage might fail her.

Serenity stared down at the lovely face incredulously. "You, envious of me?"

"*Oui.*" Geneviève hesitated for a moment, and then began to speak in a rush. "Not only of your talent as an artist, but of your confidence, your independence." Serenity continued to gape, her mouth wide open in astonishment. "There is something about you which draws people to you—an openness, a warmth in your eyes that makes one want to confide, feeling somehow you will understand."

"How extraordinary," Serenity murmured, astonished. "But, Geneviève," she began in a lighter tone, "you're so lovely and warm, how could you envy anyone, least of all me? You make me feel like a veritable Amazon."

"Men treat you as a woman," she explained, her voice faintly desperate. "They admire you not only for the way you look, but for what you are." She turned away, then back again quickly, a hand brushing at her hair. "What would you do if you loved a man, had loved him all of your life, loved with a woman's heart, but he saw you only as an amusing child?"

Serenity felt a cloud of despair envelop her heart. *Christophe,* she concluded. *Dear Lord, she wants my advice about Christophe.* She stifled the urge to give a shout of hysterical laughter. *I'm supposed to give her pointers on the man I love. Would she seek me out if she knew what he thinks of me...of my father?* Her eyes met

Geneviève's dark ones, filled with hope and trust. She sighed.

"If I were in love with such a man, I would take great pains to let him know I was a woman, and that was how I wanted him to see me."

"But how?" Geneviève's hand spread in a helpless gesture. "I am such a coward. Perhaps I would lose even his friendship."

"If you really love him, you'll have to risk it or face the rest of your life as only his friend. You must tell...your man, the next time he treats you as a child, that you are a woman. You must tell him so that there is no doubt in his mind what you mean. Then, the move is his."

Geneviève took a deep breath and squared her shoulders. "I will think about what you have said." She turned her warm eyes on Serenity's amber ones once more. "Thank you for listening, for being a friend."

Serenity watched the small, graceful figure retreat across the grass. *You're a real martyr,* Serenity, she told herself. *I thought self-sacrifice was supposed to make one glow with inner warmth; I just feel cold and miserable.* She began packing up her paints, no longer finding pleasure in the sunshine. *I think I'll give up martyrdom and take up foreclosing on widows and orphans; it couldn't make me feel any worse.*

Depressed, Serenity wandered up to her room to store her canvas and paints. With what she considered a herculean effort, she managed to produce a smile for the maid, who was busily folding freshly laundered lingerie into the bureau drawer.

"*Bonjour,* Mademoiselle." Bridget greeted Serenity with a dazzling smile of her own, and amber eyes blinked at the power.

"*Bonjour,* Bridget. You seem in remarkably good spirits." Glancing at the shafts of sunlight which flowed triumphantly through the windows, Serenity sighed and shrugged. "I suppose it is a beautiful day."

"*Oui,* Mademoiselle. *Quel jour!*" She gestured toward the sky with a hand filled with filmy silk. "I think I have never seen the sun smile more sweetly."

Unable to cling to depression under the attack of blatant good humor, Serenity plopped into a chair and grinned at the small maid's glowing face. "Unless I read the signs incorrectly, I would say it's love which is smiling sweetly."

Heightened color only added more appeal to the young face as Bridget paused in her duties to beam yet another smile over Serenity. "*Oui*, Mademoiselle, I am very much in love."

"And I gather from the look of you"—Serenity continued battling a sweet surge of envy of the youthful confidence—"that you are very much loved."

"*Oui*, Mademoiselle." Sunlight and happiness formed an aura around her. "On Saturday, Jean-Paul and I will be married."

"Married?" Serenity repeated, faintly astonished as she studied the tiny form facing her. "How old are you, Bridget?"

"Seventeen," she stated with a sage nod for her vast collection of years.

Seventeen, Serenity mused with an unconscious sigh. "Suddenly, I feel ninety-two."

"We will be married in the village," Bridget continued, warming to Serenity's interest. "Then everyone will come back to the château, and there will be singing and dancing in the garden. The count is very kind and very generous. He says we will have champagne." Serenity watched as joy turned to awe.

"Kind," she murmured, turning the adjective over in her mind. *Kindness is not a quality I would have attributed to Christophe.* Letting out a long breath, she recalled his gentle attitude toward Geneviève. *Obviously, I simply don't bring it out in him.*

"Mademoiselle has so many lovely things." Glancing up, Serenity saw Bridget fondling a flowing white negligée, her eyes soft and dreamy.

"Do you like it?" Rising, she fingered the hem, remembering the silky texture against her skin, then let it drift like a pure fall of snow to the floor.

"It's yours," Serenity declared impulsively, and the maid turned back, soft eyes now as wide as dark saucers.

"*Pardon,* Mademoiselle?"

"It's yours," she repeated, smiling into astonishment. "A wedding present."

"Oh, *mais non,* I could not…it is too lovely." Her voice faltered to a whisper as she gazed at the gown with wistful desire, then turned back to Serenity. "Mademoiselle could not bear to part with it."

"Of course I can," Serenity corrected. "It's a gift, and it would please me to know you were enjoying it." Studying the simple white silk which Bridget clutched to her breast, she sighed with a mixture of envy and hopelessness. "It was made for a bride, and you will look beautiful in it for your Jean-Paul."

"Oh, Mademoiselle!" Bridget breathed, blinking back tears of gratitude. "I will treasure it always." She followed this declaration with a joyful stream of Breton thanks, the simple words lifting Serenity's spirits. She left the future bride gazing into the mirror, negligée spread over apron as she dreamed of her wedding night.

The sun again smiled sweetly on Bridget's wedding day, the sky a cerulean-blue touched with a few friendly white wisps of clouds.

As the days had passed, Serenity's depression had altered to a frigid resentment. Christophe's aloof demeanor fanned the fires of temper, but determinedly, she had buried them under equally haughty ice. As a result, their conversations had been limited to a few stony, formally polite sentences.

She stood, flanked by him and the countess on the tiny lawn of the village church awaiting the bridal procession. The raw-silk suit she had chosen deliberately for its cool, untouchable appearance had been categorically dismissed by a wave of her grandmother's regal hand. Instead, she had been presented with an outfit of her mother's, the scent of lavender still clinging, as fresh as yesterday. Instead of appearing sophisticated and distant, she now appeared like a young girl awaiting a party.

The full gathered skirt just brushed bare calves, its brilliant vertical stripes of red and white topped with a short white apron. The peasant scoop-necked blouse was tucked into the tiny waist, its short puffed sleeves leaving arms bare to the sun. A black sleeveless vest fitted trimly over the subtle curve of breast, her pale halo of curls topped with a beribboned straw hat.

Christophe had made no comment on her appearance, merely inclining his head when she had descended the stairs, and now Serenity continued the silent war by addressing all her conversation exclusively to her grandmother.

"They will come from the house of the bride," the countess informed her, and though Serenity was uncomfortably aware of the dark man who stood behind her, she gave the appearance of polite attentiveness. "All of her family will walk with her on her last journey as a maiden. Then, she will meet the groom and enter the chapel to become a wife."

"She's so young," Serenity murmured in a sigh, "hardly more than a child."

"*Alors,* she is old enough to be a woman, my aged one." With a light laugh, the countess patted Serenity's hand. "I was little more when I married your grandfather. Age has little to do with love. Do you not agree, Christophe?"

Serenity felt, rather than saw, his shrug. "So it would seem, Grandmère. Before she is twenty, our Bridget will have a little one tugging on her apron and another under it."

"*Hélas!*" the countess sighed with suspicious wistfulness, and Serenity turned to regard her with careful curiosity. "It appears neither of my grandchildren see fit to provide me with little ones to spoil." She gave Serenity a sad, guileless smile. "It is difficult to be patient when one grows old."

"But it becomes simpler to be shrewd," Christophe commented in a dry voice, and Serenity could

not prevent herself from glancing up at him. He gave
her a brief, raised-brow look, and she met it steadily,
determined not to falter under its spell.

"To be wise, Christophe," the countess corrected,
unperturbed and faintly smug. "This is a truer statement. *Voilà!*" she announced before any comment
could be made. "They come!"

Soft new flower petals floated and danced to
earth as small children tossed them from wicker
baskets. They laid a carpet of love for the bride's
feet. Innocent petals, wild from the meadow and
forest, and the children danced in circles as they
offered them to the air. Surrounded by her family,
the bride walked like a small, exquisite doll. Her
dress was traditional, and obviously old, and Serenity knew she had never seen a bride more radiant or
a dress more perfect.

Aged white, the full, pleated skirt flowed from the
waist to dance an inch from the petal-strewn road.
The neck was high and trimmed with lace, and the
bodice was fitted and snug, touched with delicate
embroidery. She wore no veil, but instead had on a
round white cap topped with a stiff lace headdress

which lent the tiny dark form an exotic and ageless beauty.

The groom joined her, and Serenity noted, with a near-maternal relief, that Jean-Paul looked both kind and nearly as innocent as Bridget herself. He, too, was attired traditionally: white knickers tucked into soft boots, and a deep blue double-breasted jacket over an embroidered white shirt. The narrow-brimmed Breton cap with its velvet ribbons accentuated his youth, and Serenity surmised he was little older than his bride.

Shining young love glowed around them, pure and sweet as the morning sky, and the sudden, unexpected pang of longing caused Serenity to draw in her breath, then clutch her hands together tightly to combat a convulsive shudder. *Just once,* she thought, and swallowed against the dryness of her throat, *just once I would have Christophe look at me that way, and I could live on it for the rest of my life.*

Starting as a hand touched her arm, she looked up to find his eyes on her, faintly mocking and altogether cool. Tilting her chin, she allowed him to lead her inside the chapel.

★ ★ ★

The château's garden was a perfect world in which to celebrate a new marriage, vivid and fresh and alive with scents and hues. The terrace was laden with white-clothed tables brimming over with food and drink. The château had laid on its finest for the village wedding, silver and crystal gleaming with the pride of age in the glory of sunlight. And the village, Serenity observed, accepted it as their due. As they belonged to the château, so it belonged to them. Music rose over the mixture of voices and laughter: the sweet, lilting strain of violins and the softly nasal call of bagpipes.

Serenity watched from the terrace as bride and groom performed their first dance as man and wife, a folk dance, full of charm and saucy movements, and Bridget flirted with her husband with tossing head and teasing eyes, much to the approval of the audience. Dancing continued, growing livelier, and Serenity found herself being pulled into the crowd by a charmingly determined Yves.

"But I don't know how," she protested, unable to prevent the laugh his persistence provoked.

"I will teach you," he returned simply, taking

both her hands in his. "Christophe is not the only one with the ability to instruct." He inclined his head in acknowledgment of her frown. "Ah-ha! I thought as much." Her frown deepened at the ambiguity, but he merely smiled, lifted one hand to his lips briefly, and continued. "*Maintenant,* first we step to the right."

Caught up first in her lesson, then in the pleasure of the simple music and movements, Serenity found the tensions of the past days drifting away. Yves was attentive and charming, taking her through the steps of the dances and bringing her glasses of champagne. Once seeing Christophe dancing with a small, graceful Geneviève, a cloud of despair threatened her sun, and she turned away quickly, unwilling to fall back into the well of depression.

"You see, *chérie,* you take to the dance naturally." Yves smiled down at her as the music paused.

"Assuredly, my Breton genes have come to the fore to sustain me."

"So," he said in mock censure, "will you not give credit to your instructor?"

"*Mais, oui.*" She gave him a teasing smile and a small curtsy. "My instructor is both charming and brilliant."

"True," he agreed, chestnut eyes twinkling against the gravity of his tone. "And my student is both beautiful and enchanting."

"True," she agreed in turn, and laughing, she linked her arm through his.

"Ah, Christophe." Her laughter froze as she saw Yves's gaze travel above her head. "I have usurped your role as tutor."

"It appears you are both enjoying the transition." Hearing the icy politeness in his voice, Serenity turned to him warily. He looked entirely too much like the seafaring count in the portrait gallery for her comfort. The white silk shirt opened carelessly to reveal the strong, dark column of throat, the sleeveless black vest a startling contrast. The matching black pants were mated to soft leather boots, and Serenity decided he looked more dangerous than elegant.

"A delightful student, *mon ami,* as I am sure you agree." Yves's hand rested lightly on Serenity's shoulder as he smiled into the set, impassive face. "Perhaps you would care to test the quality of my instructions for yourself."

"Bien sûr." Christophe acknowledged the offer

with a slight inclination of his head. Then, with a graceful, rather old-fashioned gesture, he held out his hand, palm up for Serenity's acquiescence.

She hesitated, both fearing and longing for the contact of flesh. Then seeing the challenge in his dark eyes, she placed her palm in his with aristocratic grace.

Serenity moved with the music, the steps of the old, flirting dance coming easily. Swaying, circling, joining briefly, the dance began as a confrontation, a formalized contest between man and woman. Their eyes held, his bold and confident, hers defiant, and they moved in alternating circles, palms touching. As his arm slipped lightly around her waist, she tossed her head back to keep the gaze unbroken, ignoring the sudden thrill as their hips brushed.

Steps quickened with the music, the melody growing more demanding, the ancient choreography growing more enticing, the contact of bodies lengthening. She kept her chin tilted insolently, her eyes challenging, but she felt the heat begin its insistent rise as his arm became more possessive of her waist, drawing her closer with each turn. What had begun as a duel was now a seduction, and she felt his silent power taking command of her will as surely as if his lips had claimed hers. Drawing on one last shred of control, she stepped back, seeking the safety of distance. His arm pulled her against him, and helplessly, her eyes sought the mouth which hovered dangerously over hers. Her lips parted, half in protest, half in invitation, and his lowered until she could taste his breath on her tongue.

The silence when the music ended was like a thunderclap, and she watched wide-eyed as he drew the promise of his mouth away with a smile of pure triumph.

"Your teacher is to be commended, Mademoiselle." His hands dropped from her waist, and with a small bow, he turned and left her.

The more remote and taciturn Christophe became, the more open and expansive became the countess, as though sensing his mood and seeking to provoke him.

"You seem preoccupied, Christophe," the countess stated artlessly as they dined at the large oak table. "Are your cattle giving you trouble, or perhaps an *affaire de coeur?*"

Determinedly, Serenity kept her eyes on the wine she swirled in her glass, patently fascinated by the gently moving color.

"I am merely enjoying the excellent meal, Grandmère," Christophe returned, not rising to the bait. "Neither cattle nor women disturb me at the moment."

"Ah." The countess breathed life into the syllable. "Perhaps you group both together."

Broad shoulders moved in a typical gesture. "They both demand attention and a strong hand, *n'est-ce pas?*"

Serenity swallowed a bit of *canard à l'orange* before it choked her.

"Have you left many broken hearts behind in America, Serenity?" The countess spoke before Serenity could voice the murderous thoughts forming in her brain.

"Dozens," she returned, aiming a deadly glance at Christophe. "I have found that some men lack the intelligence of cattle, more often having the arms, if not the brains, of an octopus."

"Perhaps you have been dealing with the wrong men," Christophe suggested, his voice cool.

This time it was Serenity's shoulders which moved. "Men are men," she said in dismissal, seeking to annoy him with her own generalization. "They either want a warm body for groping in corners, or a piece of Dresden to sit on a shelf."

"And how, in your opinion, does a woman wish to be treated?" he demanded as the countess sat back and enjoyed the fruits of her instigation.

"As a human being with intellect, emotions, rights, needs." Her hands moved expressively. "Not as a happy convenience for a man's pleasure to be tucked away until the mood strikes him, or a child to be petted and amused."

"You seem to have a low opinion of men, *ma chérie,*" Christophe intimated, neither of them aware they were speaking more in this conversation than they had in days.

"Only of antiquated ideas and prejudice," she contradicted. "My father always treated my mother as a partner; they shared everything."

"Do you look for your father in the men you

meet, Serenity?" he asked suddenly, and her eyes widened, surprised and disconcerted.

"Why, no, at least I don't think so," she faltered, trying to see into her own heart. "Perhaps I look for his strength and his kindness, but not a replica. I think I look for a man who could love me as completely as he loved my mother—someone who could take me with all my faults and imperfections and love me for what I am, not what he might want me to be."

"And when you find such a man," Christophe asked, giving her an unfathomable stare, "what will you do?"

"Be content," she murmured, and made an effort to give her attention to the food on her plate.

Serenity continued her painting the following day. She had slept poorly, disturbed by the admission she had made to Christophe's unexpected question. She had spoken spontaneously, the words the fruit of a feeling she had not been aware of possessing. Now with the warmth of the sun at her back and brush and pallet in hand, she endeavored to lose her discomfort in the love of painting.

She found it difficult to concentrate, Christophe's

lean features invading her mind and blurring the sharp lines of the château. Rubbing her forehead, she finally threw down her brush in disgust and began to pack her equipment, mentally cursing the man who insisted on interfering with both her work and her life. The sound of a car cut into her eloquent swearing, and she turned, her hand shading her eyes from the sun, to watch the approaching vehicle wind down the long drive.

It halted a few yards from where she stood, and her mouth dropped open in amazement as a tall, fair man got out and began walking toward her.

"Tony!" she cried in surprise and pleasure, rushing across the grass to meet him.

His arms gripped her waist, and his lips covered hers in a brief but thorough kiss.

"What are you doing here?"

"I could say I was just in the neighborhood." He grinned down at her. "But I don't think you'd buy that." He paused and studied her face. "You look terrific," he decided, and bent to kiss her again, but she eluded him.

"Tony, you haven't answered me."

"The firm had some business to conduct in Paris,"

he explained. "So I flew over, and when I set things straight, I drove out here to see you."

"Two birds with one stone," she concluded wryly, feeling a vague disappointment. *It would have been nice,* she reflected, *if he had dropped his business and charged across the Atlantic because he couldn't bear to be parted from me.* But not Tony! She studied his good-looking, clear-cut features. *Tony's much too methodical for impulses, and that's been part of the problem.*

He brushed her brow with a casual kiss. "I missed you."

"Did you?"

He looked slightly taken aback. "Well, of course I did, Serenity." His arm slipped around her shoulders as he began walking toward her painting apparatus. "I'm hoping you'll come back with me."

"I'm not ready to go yet, Tony. I have commitments here. There are things I have to clear up before I can even think about going back."

"What things?" he asked with a frown.

"I can't explain, Tony," she evaded, unwilling to take him into her confidence. "But I've barely had time to know my grandmother; there are so many lost years to make up for."

"You can't expect to stay here for twenty-five years and make up for lost time." His voice was filled with exasperation. "You have friends back in Washington, a home, a career." He stopped and took her by the shoulders. "You know I want to marry you, Serenity. You've been putting me off for months."

"Tony, I never made any promises to you."

"Don't I know it." Releasing her, he stared around in abstraction. With a pang of guilt, she tried harder to make him understand.

"I've found part of myself here. My mother grew up here; her mother still lives here." She turned and faced the château, making a wide, sweeping gesture. "Just look at it, Tony. Have you ever seen anything to compare with it?"

He followed her gaze and studied the large stone structure with another frown. "Very impressive," he stated without enthusiasm. "It's also huge, rambling, and, more than likely, drafty. Give me a brick house on P Street any day."

She sighed, deflated, then turning to her companion, smiled with affection. "Yes, you're right, you don't belong here."

"And you do?" The frown deepened.

"I don't know," she murmured, her eyes roaming over the conical roof and down to the courtyard. "I just don't know."

He studied her profile a moment, then strategically changed the subject. "Old Barkley had some papers for you." He referred to the attorney who had handled her parents' affairs and for whom he worked as a junior partner. "So instead of trusting them to the mail, I'm delivering them in person."

"Papers?"

"Yes, very confidential." He grinned in his familiar way. "Wouldn't give me a clue as to what they were about; just said it was important that you get them as soon as possible."

"I'll look at them later," she said in dismissal, having had enough of papers and technical forms since her parents' death. "You must come inside and meet my grandmother."

If Tony had been unimpressed with the château, he was overwhelmed by the countess. Serenity hid her smile as she introduced Tony to her grandmother, noting the widening of his eyes as he accepted the offered hand. She was, Serenity thought with silent satisfaction, magnificent. Leading Tony into the main drawing room, the countess ordered refreshments and proceeded to pump Tony in the most charming way for every ounce of information about himself. Serenity sat back and observed the maneuver, proud of her straight face.

He doesn't stand a chance, she decided as she poured tea from the elegant silver pot. Handing the dainty china cup to her grandmother, their eyes met. The unexpected mischief in the blue eyes almost caused a burst of laughter to escape, so she busied herself with the pouring of more tea with intense concentration.

The old schemer! she thought, surprised that she was not offended. *She's determining if Tony's a worthy candidate for her granddaughter's hand, and poor Tony is so awed by her magnificence, he doesn't see what's going on.*

At the end of an hour's conversation, the countess had learned Tony's life history: his family background, education, hobbies, career, politics, many details of which Serenity had been ignorant herself. The inquisition had been skillful, so subtly accomplished that Serenity suppressed the urge to stand and applaud when it was completed.

"When do you have to get back?" she asked, feeling she should save Tony from disclosing his bank balance.

"I have to leave first thing in the morning," he told her, relaxed and totally oblivious to the gentle third degree to which he had been subjected. "I wish I could stay longer, but…" He shrugged.

"*Bien sûr,* your work comes first," the countess finished for him, looking understanding. "You must dine with us tonight, Monsieur Rollins, and stay with us until morning."

"I couldn't impose on your hospitality, Madame," he objected, perhaps halfheartedly.

"Impose? Nonsense!" His objection was dismissed with a regal wave of the hand. "A friend of Serenity's from so far away—I would be deeply offended if you would refuse to stay with us."

"You are very kind. I'm grateful."

"It is my pleasure," the countess stated as she rose. "You must show your friend around the grounds, and I will see that a room is prepared for him." Turning to Tony, she extended her hand once more. "We have cocktails at seven-thirty, Monsieur Rollins. I will look forward to seeing you then."

Chapter Eight

Serenity stood in front of the full-length mirror without seeing the reflection. The tall, slender woman in the amethyst gown, soft waves of crepe flowing like a jeweled breeze, might not have stared back from the highly polished glass. Serenity's mind was playing back the afternoon's events, her emotions running from pleasure, irritation, and disappointment to amusement.

After the countess had left them alone, Serenity had conducted Tony on a brief tour of the grounds. He had been vaguely complimentary about the garden, taking in its surface beauty, his logical, matter-of-fact mind unable to see beyond the roses and geraniums to the romance of hues and textures and scents. He was lightly amused by the appearance of the ancient gardener and slightly uncomfortable with the overwhelming spaciousness of the view from the terrace. He preferred, in his words, a few houses or at least a traffic light. Serenity had shaken her head at this in indulgent affection, but had realized how little she had in common with the man with whom she had spent so many months.

He was, however, completely overawed by the château's châtelaine. Anyone less like a grandmother, he had stated with great respect, he had never encountered. She was incredible, he had said, to which Serenity silently agreed, though perhaps for different reasons. She looked as if she belonged on a throne, indulgently granting audiences, and she had been so gracious, so interested in everything he had said. *Oh, yes,* Serenity had concurred silently, trying and failing to be indignant. *Oh yes, dear, gullible Tony, she had been vastly interested.* But what was the purpose of the game she was playing?

When Tony was settled in his room, strategically placed, Serenity noted, at the farthest end of the hall from herself, she had sought out her grandmother with the excuse of thanking her for inviting Tony to stay.

Seated in her room at an elegant Regency writing desk penning correspondence on heavy-crested stationery, the countess had greeted Serenity with an innocent smile, which somehow resembled the cat who swallowed the canary.

"Alors." She had put down her pen and gestured to a low brocade divan. "I hope your friend has found his room agreeable."

"Oui, Grandmère, I am very grateful to you for inviting Tony to stay for the night."

"Pas de quoi, ma chérie." The slender hand had gestured vaguely. "You must think of the château as your home, as well as mine."

"Merci, Grandmère," Serenity had said demurely, leaving the next move to the older woman.

"A very polite young man."

"Oui, Madame."

"Quite attractive…"—a slight pause—"…in an ordinary sort of way."

"Oui, Madame," Serenity had agreed conversationally, tossing the ball into her grandmother's court. The ball was received and returned.

"I have always preferred more unusual looks in a man, more strength and vitality. Perhaps"—a slight teasing curve of the lips—"more of the buccaneer, if you know what I mean."

"Ah, *oui,* Grandmère." Serenity had nodded, keeping a guileless open gaze on the countess. "I understand very well."

"Bien." The slim shoulders had moved. "Some prefer a tamer male."

"So it would seem."

"Monsieur Rollins is a very intelligent, well-mannered man, very logical and earnest."

And dull. Serenity had added the unspoken remark before speaking aloud in annoyance. "He helps little old ladies across the street twice a day."

"Ah, a credit to his parents, I am sure," the countess had decided, either unaware or unperturbed by Serenity's mockery. "I am sure Christophe will be most pleased to meet him."

A faint glimmer of uneasiness had been born in Serenity's brain. "I'm sure he will."

"Mais, oui." The countess smiled. "Christophe will be very interested to meet such a close friend of yours." The emphasis on "close" had been un-

mistakable, and Serenity's senses had sharpened as her uneasiness had grown.

"I fail to see why Christophe should be overly interested in Tony, Grandmère."

"Ah, *ma chérie,* I am sure Christophe will be fascinated by your Monsieur Rollins."

"Tony is not *my* Monsieur Rollins," Serenity had corrected, rising from the divan and advancing on her grandmother. "And I really don't see anything they have in common."

"No?" the countess asked with such irritating innocence that Serenity fought with amusement.

"You are a devious minx, Grandmère. What are you up to?"

Blue eyes met amber with the innocence of sweet childhood. "Serenity, *ma chérie,* I have no idea what you are talking about." As Serenity had opened her mouth to retort, the countess once more cloaked herself in her royalty. "I must finish my correspondence. I will see you this evening."

The command had been crystal clear, and Serenity had been forced to leave the room unsatisfied. The closing of the door with undue force had been her only concession to her rising temper.

★ ★ ★

Serenity's thoughts returned to the present. Slowly, her slim form, draped in amethyst, came into focus in the mirror. She smoothed her blond curls absently and erased the frown from her face. *We're going to play this very cool,* she informed herself as she fastened on pearl earrings. *Unless I am very much mistaken, my aristocratic grandmother would like to stir up some fireworks this evening, but she won't set off any sparks in this corner.*

She knocked on the door of Tony's room. "It's Serenity, Tony. If you're ready, I'll walk down with you." Tony's call bade her to enter, and she opened the door to see the tall, fair man struggling with a cufflink. "Having trouble?" she inquired with a wide grin.

"Very funny." He looked up from his task with a scowl. "I can't do anything lefthanded."

"Neither could my father," she stated with a quick, warm feeling of remembrance. "But he used to curse beautifully. It's amazing how many adjectives he used to describe a small pair of cufflinks." She moved to him and took his wrist in her hand. "Here, let me do it." She began to work the small object through his cuff. "Though what you would have done if I hadn't come along, I don't know." She shook her head and bent over his hand.

"I would have spent the evening with one hand thrust in my pocket," he answered smoothly. "Sort of a suave and continental stance."

"Oh, Tony." She looked up with a bright smile and shining eyes. "Sometimes you're positively cute."

A sound outside the door caught her attention, and she turned her head as Christophe walked by, paused for a moment to take in the intimate picture of the laughing woman fastening the man's cufflink, two fair heads close together. One dark brow raised fractionally, and with a small bow, Christophe continued on his way, leaving Serenity flushed and disconcerted.

"Who was that?" Tony asked with blatant curiosity, and she bent her head over his wrist to hide her burning cheeks.

"Le Comte de Kergallen," she answered with studied nonchalance.

"Not your grandmother's husband?" His voice was incredulous, and the question elicited a bright peal of laughter from Serenity, doing much to erase her tension.

"Oh, Tony, you are cute." She patted his wrist, the errant cufflink at last secured, and she looked up at him with sparkling eyes. "Christophe is the present count, and he's her grandson."

"Oh." Tony's brow creased in thought. "He's your cousin, then."

"Well…" She drew the word out slowly. "Not precisely." She explained the rather complicated family history and the resulting relationship between herself and the Breton count. "So, you see," she concluded, taking Tony's arm and walking from the room, "in a roundabout sort of way, we could be considered cousins."

"Kissing cousins," Tony observed with a definite frown.

"Don't be silly," she protested too quickly, unnerved by the memories of hard, demanding lips on hers.

If Tony noted the rushed denial and flushed cheeks, he made no comment.

They entered the drawing room arm in arm, and Serenity felt her flush deepen at Christophe's brief but encompassing appraisal. His face was smooth and unreadable, and she wished with sudden fervor that she could see the thoughts that lived behind his cool exterior.

Serenity watched his gaze shift to the man at her side, but his gaze remained impassive and correct.

"Ah, Serenity, Monsieur Rollins." The countess sat in the high-backed, richly brocaded chair framed by the massive stone fireplace, the image of a monarch receiving her subjects. Serenity wondered whether this placement had been deliberate or accidental. "Christophe, allow me to present Monsieur Anthony Rollins from America, Serenity's guest." The countess, Serenity noted with irony, had neatly categorized Tony as her personal property.

"Monsieur Rollins," she continued without breaking her rhythm, "allow me to present your host, Monsieur le Comte de Kergallen."

The title was emphasized delicately, and Christophe's position as master of the château was established. Serenity shot her grandmother a knowing glance.

The two men exchanged formalities, and Serenity was observant enough to note the age-old routine of sizing up, like two male dogs gauging the adversary before entering into combat.

Christophe served his grandmother an *apéritif,* then inquired as to Serenity's pleasure before continuing with his duties with Tony. He echoed Serenity's request for vermouth, and she stifled a smile, knowing Tony's taste ran strictly to dry vodka martinis or an occasional brandy.

The conversation flowed smoothly, the countess inserting several of the facts pertaining to Tony's background he had so conveniently provided her with that afternoon.

"It is so comforting to know that Serenity is in such capable hands in America," she stated with a gracious smile, and continued, ignoring the scowl Serenity threw at her. "You have been friends for some time, *non?*" The faint hesitation, barely perceptible, on the words "friends" caused Serenity's scowl to deepen.

"Yes," Tony agreed, patting Serenity's hand with affection. "We met about a year ago at a dinner party. Remember, darling?" He turned to smile at her, and she erased her scowl quickly.

"Of course. The Carsons' party."

"Now you have traveled so far just for a short visit." The countess smiled with fond indulgence. "Was that not considerate, Christophe?"

"Most considerate." With a nod, he lifted his glass.

Why, you artful minx, Serenity thought irreverently. *You know very well Tony came on business. What are you up to?*

"Such a pity you cannot remain longer, Monsieur Rollins. It is pleasant for Serenity to have company from America. Do you ride?"

"Ride?" he repeated, baffled for a moment. "No, I'm afraid not."

"*C'est dommage.* Christophe has been teaching Serenity. How is your pupil progressing, Christophe?"

"*Très bien,* Grandmère," he answered easily, his gaze moving from his grandmother to Serenity. "She has a natural ability, and now that the initial stiffness has passed"—a fleeting smile appeared, and her color rose in memory—"we are progressing nicely, eh, *mignonne?*"

"Yes," she agreed, thrown off balance by the casual endearment after days of cool politeness. "I'm glad you persuaded me to learn."

"It has been my pleasure." His enigmatic smile only served to increase her confusion.

"Perhaps you in turn will teach Monsieur Rollins, Serenity, when you have the opportunity." The countess drew her attention, and amber eyes narrowed at the innocence of the tone.

The meddler! she fumed inwardly. *She's playing the two against each other, dangling me in the middle like a meaty bone.* Irritation transformed into reluctant amusement as the clear eyes met hers, a devil of mischief dancing in their depths.

"Perhaps, Grandmère, though I doubt I shall be able to make the jump from student to instructor for some time. Two brief lessons hardly make me an expert."

"But you shall have others, *n'est-ce pas?*" She tossed off Serenity's counterploy and rose with fluid grace. "Monsieur Rollins, would you be so kind as to escort me to dinner?"

Tony smiled, greatly flattered, and took the countess's arm, though who was leading whom from the room was painfully obvious to the woman left behind.

"Alors, chérie." Christophe advanced on Serenity

and held out his hand to assist her to her feet. "It seems you must make do with me."

"I guess I can just about bear it," she retorted, ignoring the furious thumping of her heart as his hand closed over hers.

"Your American must be very slow," he began conversationally, retaining her hand and towering over her in a distracting manner. "He has known you for nearly a year, and still he is not your lover."

Her face flamed, and she glared up at him, grasping at her dignity. "Really, Christophe, you surprise me. What an incredibly rude observation."

"But a true one," he returned, unperturbed.

"Not all men think exclusively of sex. Tony is a very warm and considerate person, not overbearing like some others I could name."

He only smiled with maddening confidence. "Does your Tony make your pulse race as it does now?" His thumb caressed her wrist. "Or your heart beat like this?" His hand covered the heart that galloped like a mad horse, and his lips brushed hers in a gentle, lingering kiss so unlike any of the others he had given her that she could only stand swaying with dazed sensations.

Lips feathered over her face, teasing the corners of her mouth, withholding the promise with the experience of seduction. Teeth nibbled at the lobe of her ear, and she sighed as the small spark of pain shot inestimable currents of pleasure along her skin, drugging her with delight and slow, smoldering desire. Lightly, his fingers traced the length of her spine, then moved with devastating laziness along the bare flesh of her back until she was pliant and yielding in his arms, her mouth seeking his for fulfillment. He gave her only a brief taste of his lips before they roamed to the hollow of her throat, and his hands moved slowly from curve to curve, fingers teasing but not taking the fullness of breast before they began a circling, gentle massage at her hips.

Murmuring his name, she went limp against him, unable to demand what she craved, starving for the mouth he denied her. Wanting only to be possessed, needing what only he could give, her arms pulled him closer in silent supplication.

"Tell me," Christophe murmured, and through mists of languor, she heard the light mockery of his tone. "Has Tony heard you sigh his name, or felt your bones melt against him as he held you so?"

Stunned, she jerked back convulsively from his embrace, anger and humiliation warring with desire. "You are overconfident, Monsieur," she choked. "It's none of your business how Tony makes me feel."

"You think not?" he asked in a politely inquiring tone. "We must discuss that later, *ma belle cousine*. Now I think we had best join Grandmère and our guest." He gave her an engaging and exasperating grin. "They may well wonder what has become of us."

They need not have concerned themselves, Serenity noted as she entered the dining room on Christophe's arm. The countess was entertaining Tony beautifully, currently discussing the collection of antique Fabergé boxes displayed on a large mirrored buffet.

The meal commenced with vichyssoise, cold and refreshing, the conversation continuing in English for Tony's benefit. Talk was general and impersonal, and Serenity felt herself relaxing, commanding her muscles to uncoil as the soup course was cleared and the *homard grillé* was served. The lobster was nothing less than perfection, and she mused idly that, if the cook was indeed a dragon, as Christophe had joked on that first day, she was indeed a very skilled one.

"I imagine your mother made the transition from the château to your house in Georgetown very easily, Serenity," Tony stated suddenly, and she regarded him with a puzzled frown.

"I'm not sure I understand what you mean."

"There are so many basic similarities," he observed, and as she continued to look blank, he elaborated. "Of course, everything's on a much larger scale here, but there are the high ceilings, the fireplaces in every room, the style of furniture. Why, even the banisters on the stairs are similar. Surely you noticed?"

"Why, yes, I suppose I did," she answered slowly, "though I didn't realize it until now." Perhaps, she reasoned, her father had chosen the Georgetown house because he, too, had noted the similarities, and her mother had selected the furnishings from the memories of her childhood. The thought was somehow comforting. "Yes, even the banisters," she continued aloud with a smile. "I used to slide down them constantly, down from the third-floor studio, smack into the newel post, then slide to the ground floor and smack into the next one." The smile turned into a laugh. "Maman used to say that another part of my anatomy must be as hard as my head to take such punishment."

"She used to say the same to me," Christophe stated suddenly, and Serenity's eyes flew to him in surprise. *"Mais oui, petite."* He answered her look of surprise with one of his rare, full smiles. "What is the sense of walking if one can slide?"

A picture of a small, dark boy flying down the smooth rail, and her mother, young and lovely, watching and laughing, filled her mind. Her startled look faded slowly into a smile which mirrored Christophe's.

She helped herself to the raisin soufflé, light as a cloud, accompanied by a dry and sparkling champagne. She felt herself drifting through dinner in a warm, contented glow, happy to let the easy conversation flow around her.

When they moved to the drawing room after dinner, she decided to refuse the offer of a liqueur or brandy. The glow persisted, and she suspected that at least part of it (she was determined not to think about the other part and the quick, tantalizing embrace before dinner) was due to the wine served with each course. No one appeared to notice her bemused state, her flushed cheeks, and her almost mechanical answers. She found her senses almost unbearably sharpened as she listened to the music of the voices, the deep hum of the men's mingling with the lighter tones of her grandmother. She inhaled with sensuous pleasure the tangy smoke of Christophe's cheroot drifting toward her, and she breathed deeply of the women's mingled subtle perfumes overpowered by the sweet scent of the roses spilling from every porcelain vase. A pleasing balance, she decided, the artist in her responding to and enjoying the harmony, the fluid continuity of the scene. The soft lights, the night breeze gently lifting the curtains, the quiet clink of glasses being set on the table—all merged into an impressionistic canvas to be registered and stored in her mind's eye.

The dowager countess, magnificent on her brocade throne, presided, sipping crème de menthe from an exquisite gold-rimmed glass. Tony and Christophe were seated across from each other, like day and night, angel and devil. The last comparison brought Serenity up short. *Angel and Devil?* she repeated silently, surveying the two men.

Tony—sweet, reliable, predictable Tony, who applied the gentlest pressure. Tony of the infinite patience and carefully thought-out plans. What did she feel for him? Affection, loyalty, gratitude for being there when she needed him. A mild, comfortable love.

Her eyes moved to Christophe. Arrogant, dominating, exasperating, exciting. Demanding what he wanted, and taking it, bestowing his sudden, unexpected smile and stealing her heart like a thief in the night. He was moody, whereas Tony was constant; imperious, whereas Tony was persuasive. But if Tony's kisses had been pleasant and stirring, Christophe's had been wildly intoxicating, turning her blood to fire and lifting her into an unknown world of sensation and desire. And the love she felt for him was neither mild nor comfortable, but tempestuous and inescapable.

"Such a pity you do not play the piano, Serenity." The countess's voice brought her back with a guilty jerk.

"Oh, Serenity plays, Madame," Tony informed her with a wide grin. "Dreadfully, but she plays."

"Traitor!" Serenity gave him a cheerful grin.

"You do not play well?" the countess was clearly incredulous.

"I'm sorry to bring disgrace to the family once again, Grandmère," Serenity apologized. "But not only do I not play well, I play quite miserably. I even offend Tony, who is absolutely tone deaf."

"You'd offend a corpse with your playing, darling." He brushed a lock of hair from her face in a gesture of casual intimacy.

"Quite true." She smiled at him before glancing at her grandmother. "Poor Grandmère, don't look so stricken." Her smile faded somewhat as she met Christophe's frigid stare.

"But Gaelle played so beautifully," her grandmother countered with a gesture of her hand.

Serenity brought her attention back, attempting to shake off the chill of Christophe's eyes. "She could never understand the way I slaughtered music, either, but even with her abundant patience, she finally gave in and left me to my paints and easel."

"*Extraordinaire!*" The countess shook her head,

and Serenity shrugged and sipped her coffee. "Since you cannot play for us, *ma petite,*" she began in a change of mood, "perhaps Monsieur Rollins would enjoy a tour of the garden." She smiled wickedly. "Serenity enjoys the garden in the moonlight, *n'est-ce pas?*"

"That sounds tempting," Tony agreed before Serenity could respond. Sending her grandmother a telling look, Serenity allowed herself to be led outside.

Chapter Nine

For the second time Serenity strolled in the moon-lit garden with a tall, handsome man, and for the second time she wished dismally that it was Christophe by her side. They walked in companionable silence, enjoying the fresh night air and the pleasure of familiar linked hands.

"You're in love with him, aren't you?"

Tony's question broke the stillness like a rock being hurled through glass, and Serenity stopped and stared up at him with wide eyes.

"Serenity." He sighed and brushed a finger down her cheek. "I can read you like a book. You're doing your best to hide it, but you're crazy about him."

"Tony, I…" she stammered, feeling guilty and miserable. "I never meant to. I don't even like him, really."

"Lord." He gave a soft laugh and a grimace. "I wish you didn't like me that way. But then," he added, cupping her chin, "you never have."

"Oh, Tony."

"You were never anything but honest, darling," he assured her. "You've nothing to feel guilty about. I thought that with constant, persistent diligence I would wear you down." He slipped an arm around her shoulders as they continued deeper into the garden. "You know, Serenity, your looks are deceptive. You look like a delicate flower, so fragile a man's almost afraid to touch you for fear you'll break, but you're really amazingly strong." He gave her a brief squeeze. "You never stumble, darling. I've been waiting for a year to catch you, but you never stumble."

"My moods and temper would have driven you over the edge, Tony." Sighing, she leaned against his shoulder. "I could never be what you needed, and if I tried to mold myself into something else, it wouldn't have worked. We'd have ended up hating each other."

"I know. I've known for a long time, but I didn't want to admit it." He let out a long breath. "When you left for Brittany, I knew it was over. That's why I came to see you; I had to see you one more time." His words sounded so final that she looked up in surprise.

"But we'll see each other again, Tony; we're still friends. I'll be coming back soon."

He stopped again and met her eyes, the silence growing long between them. "Will you, Serenity?" Turning, he led her back toward the lights of the château.

The sun was warm on her bare shoulders as Serenity said her goodbyes to Tony the next morning. He had already made his farewells to the countess and Christophe, and Serenity had walked with him from the coolness of the main hall to the warmth of the flagstone courtyard. The little red Renault waited for him, his luggage already secured in the boot, and he glanced at it briefly before turning to her, taking both of her hands in his.

"Be happy, Serenity." His grip tightened, then relaxed on her hands. "Think of me sometimes."

"Of course I'll think of you, Tony. I'll write and let you know when I'll be back."

He smiled down at her, his eyes roaming over her face, as if imprinting every detail in his memory. "I'll think of you just as you are today, in a yellow dress with the sun in your hair and a castle at your back—the everlasting beauty of Serenity Smith of the golden eyes."

He lowered his mouth to hers, and she was swamped by a sudden surge of emotion, a strong premonition that she would never see him again. She threw her arms around his neck and clung to him and to the past. His lips brushed her hair before he drew her away.

"Goodbye darling." He smiled and patted her cheek.

"Goodbye, Tony. Take care." She returned his smile, determinedly battling back the tears which burned her eyes.

She watched as he walked to the car and got in, and with a wave headed down the long, winding drive. The car became a small red dot in the distance and then gradually faded from sight, and she continued to stand, allowing the silent tears to have their freedom. An arm slipped around her waist, and she turned to see her grandmother standing beside her, sympathy and understanding in the angular face.

"You are sad to see him go, *ma petite?*" The arm was comforting, and Serenity leaned her head against the slim shoulder.

"*Oui,* Grandmère, very sad."

"But you are not in love with him." It was a statement rather than a question, and Serenity sighed.

"He was very special to me." Pushing a tear from her cheek, she gave a childish sniffle. "I shall miss him very much. Now, I shall go to my room and have a good cry."

"*Oui,* that is wise." The countess patted her shoulder. "Few things clear the brain and cleanse the heart like a good cry." Turning, Serenity enveloped her in a hug. *"Allez, vite, mon enfant."* The countess held her close for a moment before disengaging herself. "Go shed your tears."

Serenity ran up the stone steps and entered through the heavy oak doors into the coolness of the château. Rushing toward the main staircase, she collided with a hard object. Hands gripped her shoulders.

"You must watch where you are going, *ma chérie,*" Christophe's voice mocked. "You will be running into walls and damaging your beautiful nose." She attempted to pull away, but one hand held her in place without effort as another came under her chin to tilt back her head. At the sight of brimming eyes, the mockery faded, replaced by surprise, then concern, and lastly an unfamiliar helplessness. "Serenity?" Her name was a question, the tone gentle as she had not heard it before, and the tenderness in the dark eyes broke what little composure she could still lay claim to.

"Oh, please," she choked on a desperate sob, "let me go." She struggled from his grasp, striving not to crumble completely, yet wanting to be held close by this suddenly gentle man.

"Is there something I can do?" He detained her by placing a hand on her arm.

Yes, you idiot! her brain screamed. *Love me!* "No," she said aloud, running up the stairs. "No, no, no!"

She streaked up the stairs, like a golden doe pursued by hunters, and finding her bedroom door, she opened it, then slammed it behind her, and threw herself on her bed.

The tears had worked their magic. Finally, Serenity was able to rinse them away and face the world and whatever the future had in store. She glanced at the manila envelope which she had tossed negligently on her bureau.

"Well, I suppose it's time to see what old Barkley sent me." Serenity got up reluctantly and went over to the bureau to pick up the envelope. She threw herself down on the bed again to break the seal, dumping its contents on the spread.

There was merely a page with the firm's impressive letterhead, which brought thoughts of Tony flooding back to her mind, and another sealed envelope. She picked up the neatly typewritten page listlessly, wondering what new form the family retainer had discovered for her to fill out. As she read the letter's contents, and the totally unexpected message it contained, she sat bolt upright.

Dear Miss Smith,
Enclosed you will find an envelope addressed to you containing a letter from your father. This

letter was left in my care to be given to you only if you made contact with your mother's family in Brittany. It has come to my attention through Anthony Rollins that you are now residing at the Château Kergallen in the company of your maternal grandmother, so I am entrusting same to Anthony to be delivered to you at the earliest possible date.

Had you informed me of your plans, I would have carried out your father's wishes at an earlier date. I, of course, have no knowledge of its contents, but I am sure your father's message will bring you comfort.

M. Barkley

Serenity read no farther, but put the lawyer's letter aside and picked up the message her father had left in his care. She stared at the envelope which had fallen face down on the bed, and, turning it over, her eyes misted at seeing the familiar handwriting. She broke the seal.

The letter was written in her father's bold, clear hand:

My own Serenity,
When you read this your mother and I will no longer be with you, and I pray you do not grieve too deeply,

for the love we feel for you remains true and strong as life itself.

As I write this, you are ten years old, already the image of your mother, so incredibly lovely that I am already fretting about the boys I will have to fight off one day. I watched you this morning as you sat sedately (a most unusual occupation for you, as I am more used to seeing you skating down the sidewalks at a horrifying speed or sliding without thought to bruised skin down the banisters). You sat in the garden, with my sketch book and a pencil, drawing with fierce concentration the azaleas that bloomed there. I saw in that moment, to both my pride and despair, that you were growing up, and would not always be my little girl, safe in the security your mother and I had provided for you. I knew then it was necessary to write down events you might one day have the need to understand.

I will give old Barkley (a small smile appeared on Serenity's face as she noted that the attorney had been known by that name even so many years ago) *instructions to hold this letter for you until such time as your grandmother, or some member of your mother's family, makes contact with you. If this does not occur, there will be no need to reveal the secret your mother and I have already kept for more than a decade.*

I was painting on the sidewalks of Paris in the full glory of spring, in love with the city and needing no mistress but my art. I was very young, and, I am afraid, very intense. I met a man, Jean-Paul le Goff, who was impressed by my, as he put it, raw young talent. He commissioned me to paint a portrait of his fiancée as a wedding present to her, and arranged for me to travel to Brittany and reside in the Château Kergallen. My life began the moment I entered that enormous hall and had my first glimpse of your mother.

It was not my intention to act upon the love I felt from the first moment I saw her, a delicate angel with hair like sunlight. I tried with all my being to put my art first. I was to paint her; she belonged to my patron; she belonged to the château. She was an angel, an aristocrat with a family lineage longer than time. All these things I told myself a hundred times. Jonathan Smith, itinerant artist, had no right to possess her in dreams, let alone reality. At times, when I made my preliminary sketches, I believed I would die for love of her. I told myself to go, to make some excuse and leave, but I could not find the courage. I thank God now that I could not.

One night, as I walked in the garden, I came upon her. I thought to turn away before I disturbed her, but she heard me, and when she turned, I saw in her eyes what I had not dared dream. She loved me. I could have shouted with the joy of it, but there were so many obstacles. She was betrothed, honor-bound to marry another man. We had no right to our love. Does one need a right to love, Serenity? Some would condemn us. I pray you do not. After much talk and tears, we defied what some would call right and honor, and we married. Gaelle begged me to keep the marriage a se-cret until she could find the right way to tell Jean-Paul and her mother. I wanted the world to know, but I agreed. She had given up so much for me, I could deny her nothing.

During this time of waiting, a more disturbing prob-lem came to light. The countess, your grandmother, had in her possession a Raphael Madonna, displayed in prominence in the main drawing room. It was a painting, the countess informed me, which had been in her family for generations. Next to Gaelle, she treasured this painting above all things. It seemed to

symbolize to her the continuity of her family, a shin-
ing beacon remaining constant after the hell of war
and loss. I had studied this painting closely and sus-
pected it was a forgery. I said nothing, at first think-
ing perhaps the countess herself had had a copy made
for her own needs. The Germans had taken so much
from her—husband, home—that perhaps they had
taken the original Raphael, as well. When she made
the announcement that she had decided to donate the
painting to the Louvre in order to share its greatness,
I nearly froze with fear. I had grown fond of this
woman, her pride and determination, her grace and
dignity. I had no desire to see her hurt, and I realized
that she believed the painting to be authentic. I knew
Gaelle would be tormented by the scandal if the paint-
ing was dismissed as a fraud, and the countess would
be destroyed. I could not let this happen. I offered to
clean the painting in order to examine it more criti-
cally, and I felt like a traitor.

I took the painting to my studio in the tower, and
under close study, I had no doubt that it was a very
well-executed copy. Even then, I do not know what
I would have done, if it had not been for the letter I
found hidden behind the frame. The letter was a con-

fession from the countess's first husband, a cry of despair for the treachery he had committed. He confessed he had lost nearly all of his possessions, and those of his wife. He was deep in debt, and having decided the Germans would defeat the Allies, he arranged to sell the Raphael to them. He had a copy made and replaced the original without the countess's knowledge, feeling the money would see him through the hardship of war, and the deal with the Germans would keep his estates secure. Too late, he despaired of his action, and hiding his confession in the frame of the copy, he went to face the men he had dealt with in the hopes of returning the money. The note ended with his telling of his intention, and pleading for forgiveness if he proved unsuccessful.

As I finished reading the letter, Gaelle came into the studio; I had not the foresight to bolt the door. It was impossible to hide my reaction, or the letter, which I still held in my hand, and so I was forced to share the burden with the one person I most wanted to spare. I found in those moments, in that secluded tower room, that the woman I loved was endowed with more strength than most men. She would keep the knowledge from her mother at all costs. She felt it im-

perative that the countess be shielded from humiliation and the knowledge that the painting she so prized was but forgery. We devised a plan to conceal the painting, to make it appear as if it had been stolen. Perhaps we were wrong. To this day I do not know if we did the right thing; but for your mother, there was no other way. And so, the deed was done.

Gaelle's plans to tell her mother of our marriage were soon forced into reality. She found, to our unending joy, that she carried our child, you, the fruit of our love that would grow to be the most important treasure of our lives. When she told her mother of our marriage and her pregnancy, the countess flew into a rage. It was her right to do, Serenity, and the animosity she felt for me was well deserved in her eyes. I had taken her daughter from her without her knowledge, and in doing so, I had placed a mark on her family's honor. In her anger, she disowned Gaelle, demanded that we leave the château and never enter again. I believe she would have rescinded her decision in time; she loved Gaelle above all things. But that same day she found the Raphael missing. Putting two and two together, she accused me of stealing both her daughter and her family treasure. How could I deny it? One crime was no worse than the other, and

the message in your mother's eyes begged me to keep si-
lent. So I took your mother away from the château, her
country, her family, her heritage, and brought her to
America.

We did not speak of her mother, for it brought only
pain, and we built our life fresh with you to strengthen
our bond. And now you have the story, and with
it, forgive me, the responsibility. Perhaps by the time
you read this, it will be possible to tell the entire truth.
If not, let it remain hidden, as the forgery was hid-
den, away from the world with something infinitely
more precious to conceal it. Do what your heart
tells you.

Your loving father.

Tears had fallen on the letter since its beginning,
and now as Serenity finished reading, she wiped
them away and took a long breath. Standing, she
moved over to the window and stared down at
the garden where her parents had first revealed
their love.

"What do I do?" she murmured aloud, still gripping the letter in her hand. *If I had read this a month*

ago, I would have gone straight to the countess with it, but now I don't know, she told herself silently.

To clear her father's name, she would have to reveal a secret kept hidden for twenty-five years. Would the telling accomplish anything, or would it undo whatever good the sacrifices made by both her parents had done? Her father had instructed her to listen to her heart, but it was so filled with the love and anguish of his letter that she could hear nothing, and her mind was clouded with indecision. There was a swift, fleeting impulse to go to Christophe, but she quickly pushed it aside. To confide in him would only make her more vulnerable, and the separation she must soon deal with more agonizing.

She had to think, she decided, taking several deep breaths. She had to clear away the fog and think clearly and carefully, and when she found an answer, she had to be sure it was the right one.

Pacing the room, she halted suddenly and began changing her clothes in a frantic rush. She remembered the freedom and openness that had come to her when she rode through the woods, and it was this sensation, she determined, slipping on jeans and shirt, that she required to ease her heart and clear her brain.

Chapter Ten

The groom greeted her request to saddle Babette doubtfully. He argued, albeit respectfully, that he had no orders from the count to go riding, and for once Serenity used her aristocratic heritage and haughtily informed him that as the countess's grand-daughter, she was not to be questioned. The groom submitted, with a faint muttering of Breton, and she was soon mounted on the now-familiar mare and setting off on the path Christophe had taken on her first lesson.

The woods were quiet and comforting, and she emptied her mind in the hopes that the answer would then find room to make an appearance. She walked the mare easily for a time, finding it simple now to retain command of the animal while still feeling a part of it. She found herself no closer to resolving her problem, however, and urged Babette into a canter.

They moved swiftly, the wind blowing her hair back from her face and engulfing her once more with the sense of freedom which she sought. Her father's letter was tucked into her back pocket, and she decided to ride to the hill overlooking the village and read it once more, hoping by then to find the wisdom to make the right decision.

A shout rang out behind her, and she turned in the saddle to see Christophe coming after her astride the black stallion. As she turned, her foot connected sharply with the mare's side, and Babette took this as a command and streaked forward in a swift gallop. Serenity was nearly unseated in surprise, and she struggled to right herself as the horse raced down the path with unaccustomed speed. At first all of her attention was given to the problem of remaining astride, not even contemplating the mechanics of halting the mare's headlong rush. Before her brain had the opportunity to communicate with her hands and give them the idea to rein in, Christophe came alongside her. Then, reaching over, he pulled back on her reins, uttering a stream of oaths in a variety of languages.

Babette came to a docile halt, and Serenity's eyes closed in relief. The next thing she knew, she was gripped around the waist and dragged from the saddle without ceremony, with Christophe's dark eyes burning into hers.

"What do you hope to accomplish by running away from me?" he demanded, shaking her like a rag doll.

"I was doing no such thing," she protested through teeth that chattered at the movement. "I must have startled the horse when I turned around." Her own anger began to replace relief. "It wouldn't have happened if you hadn't come chasing after me." She began to struggle away, but his grip increased with painful emphasis. "You're hurting me!" she stormed at him. "Why must you always hurt me?"

"You would find a broken neck more painful, *ma petite folle*," he stated, dragging her farther down the path and away from the horses. "That is what could have happened to you. What do you mean by riding off unescorted?"

"Unescorted?" she repeated with a laugh, jerking away from him. "How quaint. Aren't women allowed to ride unescorted in Brittany?"

"Not women who have no brains," he returned with dark fury, "and who have been on a horse only twice before in their lives."

"I was going very well before you came." She tossed her head at his logic. "Now just go away and leave me alone." She watched as his eyes narrowed, and he took a step toward her. "Go away!" she shouted, backing up. "I want my privacy. I have things to think about."

"I will give you something else to think about."

He moved swiftly, gripping her behind the neck and stealing her breath with his lips. She pushed against him without success, fighting both him and the whirling dizziness which flew to her brain. Gripping her shoulders, he drew her away, his fingers digging into her flesh.

"Enough! *C'est entendu!*" He shook her again, and she saw by his face that the aristocrat had fled and there was only the man. "I want you. I want what no man has had before—and, by God, I *will* have you."

He swept her up into his arms, and she struggled with a wild, primitive fear, beating against his chest like a trapped bird beating against the bars of its cage, but his stride remained steady and sure, as though he carried a complaisant child rather than a terrified woman.

Then she was on the ground, with his body crushing down on hers, his mouth savaging hers like a man possessed, her protests making no more of a ripple than a pebble tossed into the ocean. With a swift, violent motion, her blouse was opened, and he claimed her naked skin with bruising fingers, his lovemaking filled with a desperate urgency which conquered all thought of resistance, all will to struggle.

Struggle became demand, and her mouth became mobile and seeking under his; the hands which had previously pushed him away were now pulling him closer. Drowned in the deluge of passion, she reveled in the intimacy of his masculine hardness, her body moving with the ageless rhythm of instinct beneath him. Urgent and without restraint, his hands traced trails of heat along her naked flesh, his mouth following the blaze, returning again and again to drink from hers. Each time, his thirst grew, his demands taking her into a new and timeless world, the border between heaven and hell, where only one man and one woman can exist.

Deeper and deeper he led her, until pleasure and pain merged into one spiraling sensation, one all-consuming need. Helpless under the barrage of shimmering passion, the trembling began slowly, growing more intense as the journey took her further from the known and closer to the unexperienced. With a moan mixed with fear and desire, her fingers clutched at his shoulders, as if to keep from plummeting into an eternal void.

His mouth left hers suddenly, and with his breath uneven, his cheek rested against her brow for a moment before he lifted his head and looked down at her.

"I am hurting you again, *ma petite*." He sighed and rolled off her to lie on his back. "I tossed you on the ground and nearly ravished you like a barbarian. I seem to find it difficult to control my baser instincts with you."

She sat up quickly, fumbling with the buttons of her blouse with unsteady fingers. "It's all right." She attempted but failed to produce a careless-sounding voice. "No harm done. I've often been told how strong I am. You must learn to temper your technique a bit, though," she babbled on to hide the extent of her pain. "Geneviève is more fragile than I."

"Geneviève?" he repeated, lifting himself on his elbow to look at her directly. "What has Geneviève to do with this?"

"With this?" she answered. "Oh, nothing. I have no intention of saying anything to her of this. I'm quite fond of her."

"Perhaps we should speak in French, Serenity. I am having difficulty understanding you."

"She's in love with you, you big idiot!" she blurted out, ignoring his request for French. "She told me; she came asking for my advice." She controlled the short burst of hysterical laughter which escaped her. "She asked for my advice," she elaborated, "on how to make you see her as a woman instead of a child. I didn't tell her what your opinion was of me; she wouldn't have understood."

"She told you she was in love with me?" he demanded, his eyes narrowing.

"Not by name," she said shortly, wishing the conversation had never begun. "She said she had been in love with a man all of her life, and he regarded her as a child. I simply told her to set him straight, tell him that she was a woman, and… What are you laughing at?"

"You thought she spoke of me?" He was once more flat on his back and laughing more freely than she had ever seen. "Little Geneviève in love with me!"

"How dare you laugh at her! How can you be so callous as to make fun of someone who loves you?" He caught her fists before they made contact with his chest.

"Geneviève did not seek you out for advice about me, *chérie*." He continued to hold her off without effort. "She was speaking of Iann. But you have not met Iann, have you, *mon amour*?" He ignored her furious struggles and continued to speak with a wide grin. "We grew up together—Iann, Yves, and I—with Geneviève trailing along like a little puppy. Yves and I remained her 'brothers' after she grew into a woman, but it was Iann she truly loved. He has been in Paris on business for the last month, only returning home yesterday." A small jerk of his wrists brought her down on his chest. "Geneviève called this morning to tell me of their engagement. She also told me to thank you for her, and now I know why." His grin increased as amber eyes grew wide.

"She's engaged? It wasn't you?"

"Yes, she is; and no, it was not," he answered helpfully. "Tell me, *ma belle cousine,* were you jealous when you thought Geneviève to be in love with me?"

"Don't be ridiculous," she lied, attempting to remove her mouth from its proximity to his. "I would be no more jealous of Geneviève than you would be of Yves."

"Ah." In one swift movement he had reversed their positions and lay looking down at her. "Is that so? And should I tell you that I was nearly consumed with jealousy of my friend Yves, and that I very nearly murdered your American Tony? You would give them smiles that should be mine. From the moment I saw you step off the train, I was lost, bewitched, and I fought it as a man fights that which threatens to enslave him. Perhaps this slavery is freedom." His hand moved through the silk of her hair. "Ah, Serenity, *je t'aime.*"

She swallowed in the search for her voice. "Would you say that again?"

He smiled, and his mouth teased hers for a moment. "In English? I love you. I loved you from the moment I saw you, I love you infinitely more now, and I will love you for the rest of my life." His lips descended on hers, moving them with a tenderness he had never shown, lifting only when he felt the moistness of her tears. "Why do you weep?" he questioned, his brow creasing in exasperation. "What have I done?"

She shook her head. "It's only that I love you so much, and I thought…" She hesitated and let out a long breath. "Christophe, do you believe my father was innocent, or do you think me to be the daughter of a thief?"

His brow creased again with a frown, and he studied her silently. "I will tell you what I know, Serenity, and I will tell you what I believe. I know that I love you, not just the angel who stepped off the train at Lannion, but the woman I have come to know. It would make no difference if your father was a thief, a cheat, or a murderer. I have heard you speak of your father, and I have seen how you look when you tell of him. I cannot believe that a man who earned this love and devotion could have committed such a crime. This is what I believe, but it does not matter; nothing he did or did not do could change my love for you."

"Oh, Christophe," she whispered, pulling his cheek down to hers, "I've waited all my life for someone like you. There is something I must show you." She pushed him away gently, taking the letter from her pocket and handing it to him. "My father told me to listen to my heart, and now it belongs to you."

Serenity sat across from him, watching his face as he read, and she felt a deep peace, a contentment she had not known since her parents had been taken from her. Love for him filled her, along with a strong sense of security that he would help her to make the right decision. The woods were silent, tranquil, disturbed only by the whisper of wind through the leaves, and the birds that answered it.

For a moment, it was a place out of time, inhabited only by man and woman.

When he had finished reading the letter, Christophe lifted his eyes from the paper and met hers. "Your father loved your mother very much."

"Yes."

He folded the letter, replacing it in its envelope, his eyes never leaving hers. "I wish I had known him. I was only a child when he came to the château, and he did not stay long."

Her eyes clung to his. "What should we do?"

He moved nearer, taking her face in his hands. "We must take the letter and show it to Grand-mère."

"But they're dead, and she's alive. I love her; I don't want to hurt her."

He bent down and kissed shimmering lashes. "I love you, Serenity, for so many reasons, and you have just given me one more." He tilted her head so their eyes met again. "Listen to me now, *mon amour*, and trust me. Grandmère needs to see this letter, for her own peace of mind. She believes her daughter betrayed her, stole from her. She has lived with this for twenty-five years. This letter will set her free.

She will read in your father's words the love Gaelle had for her, and, equally important, she will see the love your father had for her daughter. He was an honorable man, but he lived with the fact that his wife's mother thought him to be a thief. The time has come to set them all free."

"All right," she agreed. "If you say this is what we must do, this is what we will do."

He smiled, and taking both her hands in his, he lifted them to his lips before helping her to her feet. "Tell me, *cousine*"—the familiar mocking smile was in place—"will you always do as I say?"

"No," she answered with a vigorous shake of her head. "Absolutely not."

"Ah, I thought not." He led her to the horses. "Life will not be dull." He took the reins of the buckskin in his hand, and she mounted without assistance. He frowned as he handed her the reins. "You are disturbingly independent, stubborn, and impulsive, but I love you."

"And you," she commented, as he moved to mount the stallion, "are arrogant, overbearing, and irritatingly confident, but I love you, as well."

They reached the stables. After relinquishing the

horses to a groom, they set off toward the château with linked hands. As they approached the garden entrance, Christophe stopped and turned to her.

"You must give this to Grandmère yourself, Serenity." He took the envelope from his pocket and handed it to her.

"Yes, I know." She looked down at it as he placed it in her hand. "But you will stay with me?"

"Oui, ma petite." He drew her into his arms. "I will stay with you." His mouth met hers, and she threw her arms around his neck until the kiss deepened, and they were only aware of each other.

"Alors, mes enfants." The countess's words broke the spell, and they both turned to see her watching them from the edge of the garden. "You have decided to stop fighting the inevitable."

"You are very clever, Grandmère," Christophe commented with a lift of his brow. "But I believe we would have managed even without your invaluable assistance."

Elegant shoulders moved expressively. "But you might have wasted too much time, and time is a precious commodity."

"Come inside, Grandmère. Serenity has something to show you."

They entered the drawing room, and the countess seated herself in her regular thronelike chair. "What is it you have to show me, *ma petite?*"

"Grandmère," Serenity said as she began moving in front of the countess, "Tony brought me some papers from my attorney. I didn't even bother to open them until he left, but I found when I did that they were much more important than I had anticipated." She held out the letter. "Before you read this, I want you to know I love you." The countess opened her mouth to speak, but Serenity hurried on. "I love Christophe, and before he read what I'm giving you, he told me he loved me, as well. I can't tell you how wonderful it was to know that before he saw this letter. We decided to share this with you because we love you." She handed the letter to her grandmother and then seated herself on the sofa. Christophe joined her, and he took her hand in his as they waited.

Serenity's eyes were drawn to her mother's portrait, the eyes that met hers full of joy and happiness, the expression of a woman in love. *I have found it, too, Maman,* she spoke silently, *the overwhelming joy of love, and I hold it here in my hand.*

She dropped her eyes to the joined hands, the strong bronzed fingers intertwined with the alabaster ones, the ruby ring which had been her mother's glowing against the contrasting colors. She stared at the ring on her own hand, then raised her eyes to the replica on her mother's, and she understood. The countess's movement as she rose from her chair interrupted Serenity's thoughts.

"For twenty-five years I have wronged this man, and the daughter whom I loved." The words were soft as she turned to gaze out the window. "My pride blinded me and hardened my heart."

"You were not to know, Grandmère," Serenity replied, watching the straight back. "They wanted only to protect you."

"To protect me from the knowledge that my husband had been a thief, and from the humiliation of public scandal, your father allowed himself to be branded, and my daughter gave up her heritage." Moving back to the chair, she sank down wearily. "I sense from your father's words a great feeling of love. Tell me, Serenity, was my daughter happy?"

"You see the eyes as my father painted them." She gestured to the portrait. "She looked always as she looked then."

"How can I forgive myself for what I did?"

"Oh, no, Grandmère." Serenity rose and knelt in front of her, taking the fragile hands in her own. "I didn't give you the letter to add to your grief, but to take it from you. You read the letter; you see that they blamed you for nothing; they purposely allowed you to believe that they betrayed you. Maybe they were wrong, but it's done, and there can be no going back." She gripped the narrow hands tighter. "I tell you now that I blame you for nothing, and I beg you, for my sake, to let the guilt die."

"Ah, Serenity, *ma chère enfant*." The countess's voice was as tender as her eyes. *"C'est bien,"* she said briskly, drawing her shoulders up straight once more. "We will remember only the happy times. You will tell me more of Gaelle's life with your father in this Georgetown, and you will bring them both close to me again, *n'est-ce pas?*"

"Oui, Grandmère."

"Perhaps one day you will take me to the house where you grew up."

"To America?" Serenity asked, deeply shocked. "Wouldn't you be afraid to travel to so uncivilized a country?"

"You are being impudent again," the countess stated regally as she rose from her chair. "I begin to believe I will come to know your father very well through you, *mignonne*." She shook her head. "When I think of what I allowed that painting to cost me! I am well pleased to be rid of it."

"You still have the copy, Grandmère," Serenity corrected. "I know where it is."

"How do you know this?" Christophe asked, speaking for the first time since they had entered the room.

She turned to him and smiled. "It was right there in the letter, but I didn't realize it at first. It was when we were sitting together just now, and you held my hand, that it came to me. Do you see this?" She held out her hand where the ruby gleamed. "It was my mother's, the same she wears in the portrait."

"I had noticed the ring in the painting," the countess said slowly, "but Gaelle had no such ring.

I thought your father merely painted it to match the earrings she wore."

"She had the ring, Grandmère; it was her engagement ring. She wore it always with her wedding band on her left hand."

"But what has this to do with the copy of the Raphael?" Christophe questioned with a frown.

"In the painting she wears the ring on her right hand. My father would never have made such a mistake in detail unless he did it intentionally."

"It is possible," the countess murmured.

"I know it's there; it says so in the letter. He says he concealed it, covered by something infinitely more precious. Nothing was more precious to him than Maman."

"*Oui,*" the countess agreed, studying the painting of her daughter. "There could be no safer hiding place."

"I have some solution," Serenity began. "I could uncover a corner; then you could be sure."

"*Non.*" She shook her head. "*Non,* there is no need. I would not have you mar one inch of your father's work if the true Raphael were under it." She turned to Serenity and lifted a hand to her cheek.

"This painting, Christophe, and you, *mon enfant,* are my treasures now. Let it rest. It is where it belongs." She turned back to her grandchildren with a smile. "I will leave you now. Lovers should have their privacy."

She left the room with the air of a queen, and Serenity watched her in admiration. "She's magnificent, isn't she?"

"Oui," Christophe agreed easily, taking Serenity into his arms. "And very wise. I have not kissed you for more than an hour."

After he had remedied the discrepancy to their mutual satisfaction, he looked down at her with his habitual air of confidence. "After we are married, *mon amour,* I will have your portrait painted, and we will add still another treasure to the château."

"Married?" Serenity repeated with a frown. "I never agreed to marry you." She pushed away as though reluctant. "You can't just order me to do so; a woman likes to be asked." He pulled her against him and kissed her thoroughly, his lips hard and insistent.

"You were saying, *cousine?*" he asked when he freed her.

She regarded him seriously, but allowed her arms to twine around his neck. "I shall never be an aristocrat."

"Heaven forbid," he agreed with sincerity.

"We shall fight often, and I will constantly infuriate you."

"I shall look forward to it."

"Very well," she said, managing to keep a smile from her lips. "I will marry you—on one condition."

"And that is?" His brow raised in question.

"That you walk in the garden with me tonight." She drew her arms around him tighter. "I'm so tired of walking in the moonlight with other men and wishing they were you."

★ ★ ★ ★ ★

*Don't miss the next enticing read from bestselling author
Nora Roberts*

Rebellion

Coming soon!

*Read on for a preview and fall under the spell
of Nora Roberts.*

Prologue

Glenroe Forest, Scotland, 1735

They came at dusk, when the villagers were at their evening meal, and the peat fires sent smoke curling from the chimneys into the chill November air. There had been snow the week before, and the sun had beaten down and then retreated until the frost had set hard as rock under the bare trees. The sound of approaching horses rang like thunder through the forest, sending small animals racing and scrambling for cover.

Serena MacGregor shifted her baby brother on her hip and went to the window. Her father and the men were returning early from their hunting trip, she thought, but there were no shouts of greeting from the outlying cottages, no bursts of laughter.

She waited, her nose all but pressed against the

window glazing, straining for the first signs of their return and fighting back her resentment that she, a girl, was not permitted to join hunting parties.

Coll had gone, though he was barely fourteen and not as skilled with a bow as she herself. And Coll had been allowed to go since he was seven. Serena's mouth became a pout as she gazed out through the lowering light. Her older brother would talk of nothing but the hunt for days, while she would have to be content to sit and spin.

Little Malcolm began to fuss and she jiggled him automatically as she stared down the rough path between the crofts and cottages. ''Hush now, Papa doesn't want to hear you squalling the minute he walks in the door.'' But something made her hold him closer and look nervously over her shoulder for her mother.

The lamps were lighted and there was the scent of good, rich stew simmering over the kitchen fire. The house was neat as a pin. She and her mother and her little sister Gwen had worked all day to make it so. The floors were scrubbed, the tables polished. There wasn't a cobweb to be found in any corner. Serena's arms ached just thinking of it. The wash had been done and the little lavender sachets her mother loved so much were tucked in the chests.

Because her father was laird, they had the best house for miles around, built of fine blue slate. Her mother wasn't one to let dust settle on it.

Everything looked normal, but something had set her heart to racing. Grabbing a shawl, Serena wrapped it around Malcolm and opened the door to look for her father.

There was no wind, no sound but the horses' hooves beating against the hard frost on the path. They would ride over the rise any moment, she thought, and for a reason she couldn't name, she shuddered. When she heard the first scream, she stumbled backward. She had already righted herself and started forward when her mother called out to her.

"Serena, come back in. Hurry."

Fiona MacGregor, her usually lovely face pinched and pale, rushed down the stairs. Her hair, the same red-gold shade as Serena's, was pinned back and caught in a snood. She didn't pat it into place, as was her habit before welcoming her husband home.

"But, Mama—"

"Hurry, girl, for God's sake." Fiona grabbed her daughter's arm and dragged her inside. "Take the bairn upstairs to your sister. Stay there."

"But Papa—"

"It's not your father."

Serena saw then, as the horses crested the hill, not the hunting plaid of the MacGregor but the red coats of English dragoons. She was only eight, but she had heard the tales of pillage and oppression. Eight was old enough to be outraged.

"What do they want? We've done nothing."

"It's not necessary to do, only to be." Fiona closed the door, then bolted it, more out of defiance than of any hope it would keep out intruders. "Serena—"

A small, slender woman, she gripped her daughter's shoulders. She had been the favored daughter of an indulgent father, then the adored wife of a loving husband, but Fiona was no weakling. Perhaps that was why the men in her life had given her their respect, as well as their affection.

"Go upstairs into the nursery. Keep Malcolm and Gwen with you. Don't come out until I tell you."

The valley echoed with another scream, and with wild weeping. Through the window they saw the thatched roof of a cottage rise in flames. Fiona could only thank God her husband and son hadn't returned.

"I want to stay with you." Serena's wide green eyes overwhelmed her face, damp now with the beginnings of tears. But her mouth, the one her father called stubborn, firmed. "Papa wouldn't want me to leave you alone."

"He would want you to do as you're told." Fiona heard the horses stop at the door. There was a jingle of spurs and the sound of men shouting. "Go now." She turned her daughter and pushed her toward the stairs. "Keep the babies safe."

As Malcolm began to wail, Serena fled up the steps. She was on the landing when she heard the door burst in. She stopped and turned to see her mother face a half-dozen dragoons. One stepped forward and bowed. Even from a distance, Serena could see that the gesture was an insult.

"Serena?" little Gwen called from the stairs above.

"Take the baby." Serena pushed Malcolm into Gwen's pudgy five-year-old arms. "Go into the nursery and shut the door." She lowered her voice to a whisper. "Hurry—keep him quiet if you can." From her apron pocket she dug a sugarplum she'd been saving. "Take this and go before they see us." Crouching at the top of the stairs, she watched.

"Fiona MacGregor?" said the dragoon with the fancy stripes.

"I am Lady MacGregor." Fiona kept her shoulders back and her eyes level. Her only thought now was to protect her children and her home. Since fighting was impossible, she used the only weapon at hand—her dignity. "By what right do you break into my home?"

''By the right of an officer of the king.''

''And your name?''

''Captain Standish, at your service.'' He drew off his gloves, waiting, hoping, to see fear. ''Where is your husband...Lady MacGregor?''

''The laird and his men are hunting.''

Standish signaled, sending three of his men on a search of the house. One overturned a table as he passed. Though her mouth was dry as dust, Fiona held her ground. She knew he could order her home torched, as easily as he had her tenants' cottages. There was little hope that her rank, or her husband's, would protect them. Her only choice was to meet insult with insult, and calmly.

''As you've seen, we are mostly women and children here. Your...visit is ill-timed if you wish to have words with the MacGregor or his men. Or perhaps that is why you and your soldiers come so bravely into Glenroe.''

He slapped her then, sending her staggering backward from the force of the blow.

''My father will kill you for that.'' Serena flew down the stairs like a bullet and launched herself at the officer. He swore as she dug her teeth into his hand, then swept her aside.

''Damn devil's brat drew blood.'' He lifted his fist, but Fiona flung herself between him and her daughter.

"Do King George's men beat small children? Is that how the English rule?"

Standish was breathing fast. It was a matter of pride now. He could hardly let his men see him bested by a woman and child, especially when they were Scottish scum. His orders were only to search and question. It was a pity the sniveling Argyll had convinced the queen, in her role as regent, not to enforce the Bill of Pains and Penalties. Scotland would indeed have been a hunting ground if she had. Still, Queen Caroline was furious with her Scottish subjects, and in any case she was hardly likely to hear of an isolated incident in the Highlands.

He signaled to one of the dragoons. "Take that brat upstairs and lock her up."

Without a word the soldier scooped Serena up, doing his best to avoid her feet and teeth and pummeling fists. As she fought, she screamed for her mother and cursed the soldiers.

"You raise wildcats in the Highlands, milady." The officer wrapped a fresh handkerchief around his hand.

"She is unused to seeing her mother, or any woman, struck by a man."

His hand was throbbing. He would not regain his men's esteem by thrashing a puny child. But the mother... He smiled as he let his gaze wander over her. The mother was a different matter.

"Your husband is suspected of involvement with the murder of Captain Porteous."

"The Captain Porteous who was sentenced to death by the courts for firing into a crowd?"

"He was reprieved, madam." Standish laid a hand lightly on the hilt of his sword. Even among his own kind he was considered cruel. Fear and intimidation kept his men in line; the same would work with one Scottish whore. "Captain Porteous fired on a group of rioters at a public execution. Then he was taken from prison and hanged by persons unknown."

"I find it difficult to sympathize with his fate, but neither I nor anyone in my family know of such matters."

"If it's found differently, your husband would be a murderer and a traitor. And you, Lady MacGregor, would have no protection."

"I have nothing to tell you."

"A pity." He smiled and moved a step closer. "Shall I show you what happens to unprotected women?"

Upstairs, Serena beat on the door until her hands were raw. Behind her, Gwen huddled with Malcolm and wept. There was no light in the nursery but for the moon and the flames from the fired cottages. Outside she could hear people shouting, women wailing, but her thoughts were all for her mother—left below, alone and unprotected, with the English.

When the door opened, Serena stumbled back. She saw the red coat, heard the jangle of spurs. Then she saw her mother, naked, bruised, her beautiful hair a wild mass around her face and shoulders. Fiona fell to her knees at Serena's feet.

"Mama." Serena knelt beside her, touched a tentative hand to her shoulder. She'd seen her mother weep before, but not like this, not these silent, hopeless tears. Because Fiona's skin was cold to the touch, Serena dragged a blanket from the chest and wrapped it around her.

While she listened to the dragoons ride off, Serena held her mother with one arm and cuddled Gwen and Malcolm with the other. She had only the vaguest understanding of what had happened, but it was enough to make her hate, and to make her vow revenge.